The Laura Black Scottsdale Mysteries

Books by
B A Trimmer

~~~~

The Laura Black
Scottsdale Mystery Series

Scottsdale Heat

Scottsdale Squeeze

Scottsdale Sizzle

Scottsdale Scorcher

Scottsdale Sting

Scottsdale Shuffle

Scottsdale Shadow

Scottsdale Secret

Scottsdale Silence

Scottsdale Scandal

Scottsdale Sleuth

~~~~

The Aloha Lagoon
Mystery Series

Hula Homicide

Homicide Honeymoon

Scottsdale Heat

Scottsdale Heat

B A TRIMMER

Editors: Leslie Galen, 'Andi' Anderson, and Kimberly Mathews

Composite cover art and cover design by Janet Holmes using images under license from Shutterstock.com and Depositphotos.com.

ISBN-13: 978-1-951052-32-4

Saguaro Sky Media Co.
060124-pb-lp

E-mail the author at
LauraBlackScottsdale@gmail.com
Follow at www.facebook.com/ScottsdaleSeries/

For Alison

*Remembering the fun of audiobooks on our
many long drives across the desert.*

Scottsdale Heat

Chapter One

As I've grown, I've gone through a lot of phases. I've also noticed that my phases don't always match everyone else's.

Like when I was eight, and every other girl in the neighborhood wanted to be Barbie, sailing with Ken on the Dreamboat, I wanted to be G.I. Joe. I thought it wasn't fair that Joe got to drive a tank and shoot a machine gun while all Barbie got was a kitchen and a pony.

Then there was the time when I was sixteen. I caused a minor family scandal by going to a Smack-Down wrestling match with my best friend Alison rather than the junior prom with Brian King. The way I looked at it, I could go to a dance anytime, but how many times could I see the Undertaker versus the Rock in a Texas cage match?

After college, I joined my friends by marrying the man of my dreams. Then, like my friends, I soon had a divorce.

Most of my friends from college were now on

their second marriages, complete with kids. But I decided a second marriage wasn't for me. Children are sticky, they smell bad, and they're constantly making noise. Who needs that kind of stress?

Of course, one of the good things about being married is that you can have sex whenever you want with a man who doesn't make you feel creepy when he sees you naked. Unfortunately, I didn't have anyone in my life. As a result, I thought about men all the time.

Take now, for instance. I was lying on a bed in a massive suite at the Scottsdale Princess Resort. Gazing out the balcony door, all of Arizona was spread before me.

My old boyfriend, Jackson Reno, lay next to me on the bed, wearing nothing but a pair of red silk boxers. He stared at me, breathing deeply with anticipation.

A wave of desire rolled down my body in a warm shiver. Having Reno back in my bed had been a fantasy of mine for months. Now, I was about to have him.

Anticipation built as I lay back on the pillows and held my arms out to him. As he leaned over me, I slipped my arms around his neck, drawing him close. Our lips came together for a slow, deep kiss.

He placed his hand on the bare flesh of my stomach but hesitated, as if unsure of what to do next. Just to be helpful, I gave his hand a gentle nudge. My heart pounded, and I stopped breathing, waiting to experience the moment.

The phone in the next room started ringing. Reno was still smiling, but his hand had stopped moving. I pushed his arm, trying to force it downward, but it wouldn't budge.

The phone rang again. This time it was the phone in our room.

No, no, no, I thought, *not now!*

Again, the phone rang. This time with Sophie's ringtone.

Damn!

I opened my eyes and glanced at the clock: eight twenty-three.

Damn!

I felt around on the nightstand, picked up my phone, dropped it, and then picked it up again.

"Wha'?" I mumbled into the phone, hoping she'd be quick so I could hang up and finish my dream with Reno.

"Hey, Laura, were you still asleep? You sound

terrible. How late were you up last night?"

"Sophie? Why are you calling me?"

"Lenny wants you to come in right away. Something new came in, and he's all hot to get on it."

I sighed. "What is it?"

"Don't know, but it's gotta be something pretty important. Lenny's been smoking and pacing in his office ever since the client left. You know how he acts when he gets a big retainer."

"Doesn't he remember I have three days off? Doesn't he recall what I've been through the past few weeks? Doesn't he know I have a life?"

"It must have slipped his mind."

"Okay, I don't have a life, but I'm still mostly asleep. It will take at least two hours to get in, maybe longer."

"Two hours? You seriously want me to tell him that?"

"Fine, tell him an hour and a half. I'll try to be there sooner."

"Alright, just don't take too long. You know who he'll bitch at the whole time."

That's okay. I told myself as I slowly sat up. *I can use the money.* Of course, since I'm usually broke, I can always use the money.

~~~~

As I was dressing, Marlowe, my gray and white tabby, got up from where he'd been lying next to me on the bed. He did a long slow cat stretch, dropped off the bed, and walked over to where I stood. As I checked myself out in the mirror, he fell against my leg and let out a pathetic squeak, his version of a meow.

I went into the kitchen and put on a pot of coffee. Marlowe strolled over to his empty bowl and stared pointedly into it.

He then sat down and glared at me. Knowing my job, I went to the pantry, opened a can of Super Supper, and plopped it into his dish. Marlowe stuck his head into the bowl and quickly sucked up the food.

I headed back into the bathroom to swipe on some mascara and eyeliner. Then, once the coffee was made, I poured the entire pot into *The Big Pig*, my oversized travel mug.

After grabbing a couple of chocolate chip granola bars, I headed out of my apartment. I skipped down the two flights of stairs and went out the back door into the parking lot.

I jumped into my cappuccino-colored Accord

and sped out of the lot in a blaze of glory. Well, more like a sedate cruise, but a girl can dream.

Damn, I thought, *this is a lousy way to start a Monday. The client had better be worth it.*

~~~~

I turned down the alley behind the law office and parked underneath the carport, between Sophie's yellow Volkswagen convertible and Lenny's red Porsche. Covered parking is a big benefit in Arizona, where summer temperatures can exceed one hundred twenty degrees.

Using my key, I opened the rear security door. I walked down the back hallway, past my cubicle, and through the polished wooden door into the front reception area. The contrast between the functional but plain back offices and the plush front offices is always startling.

When clients walk into the law office from the street, they first see Sophie's desk. It's beautiful and dominates the reception area.

On the wall behind her desk is a floor-to-ceiling bookshelf containing legal books of every description. Thick carpet and overstuffed red leather wing chairs fill the space. At the same time, Miles Davis, or some other Jazz legend, plays softly through overhead speakers.

Sophie saw me and smiled with relief. "I'm glad you made it. Lenny's got that pulsing vein thing going in the middle of his forehead again, and you know how nasty it is. Seeing it always makes me want to throw up in a trash can."

Sophie's parents came up from Mexico the year before her birth. She grew up in southern California and was a surfer chick for most of her youth. While working on getting her paralegal training, she'd been a singer for a punk rock band in L.A.

She then followed her husband from California to Scottsdale when he transferred about five years ago. The husband was soon gone, but Sophie became a permanent Arizona resident.

Sophie's tall and graceful, with long dark hair and expressive brown eyes. She knows most of my darkest secrets, and since we met, she's always been there for me.

I glanced at the door to Lenny's office and saw it was closed. This is his way of telling us he didn't want to be disturbed.

"So, what's up?" I asked.

"I haven't found out anything since I called you. Lenny was with the client when I got in. She wasn't in the appointment book, so she must have called him at home. I only got here in time to see her leave."

"Called him at home?" I asked, confused. "Lenny never gives out his home number. What's she like?"

"Well, she's old."

"And, what else?"

"Lots of wrinkles."

"And?"

"And she's rich."

"Really?" I asked. "How do you know she's rich?"

"When she left, I saw her get into a white Bentley. There was a driver with a uniform and stuff."

"Huh? I didn't think you knew that much about cars. How do you know it was a Bentley?"

"I saw a bunch of them last weekend on the Travel Channel. They had a show on European millionaires, and most of them had a Bentley. With that much money, I'd be surprised if she didn't have a Bentley or at least a Rolls Royce."

"Why didn't Lenny assign Gina?" I asked. "She always handles the big money cases."

"Lenny couldn't ask her," Sophie said. "She's been in Las Vegas the past two days, babysitting the son of Congressman Berry. She won't be back until later today."

"Why's Lenny having her do that? Daniel Berry's only in his first term. He doesn't have money or influence yet. Lenny usually goes after Senators. Besides, how old's the baby?"

"He's eighteen," Sophie said. "Representative Berry will chair a sub-committee to decide what to do with a big tract of land down by Casa Grande. Lenny's looking for inside information on the bidding so he can pick it up cheap. I think he wants to build Lenny Town or something like that."

The door to Lenny's office opened. He stuck his head out and waved me into his inner sanctum.

"Laura, great," he said with a touch of annoyance. "Get in here. It's time to save the world."

Lenny was generally a good boss, but his people skills were poor. Okay, to be honest, his people skills sucked. An anger management class would be a good idea for him too.

Physically, Lenny is short, no more than five foot five. His dark hair is receding and beginning to gray at the temples. He's also starting to get a little chubby. He sometimes reminds me of Louie from the old TV show *Taxi*.

I went in and sat in one of the wooden chairs in front of Lenny's desk. The chair's legs were short, so Lenny and his desk loomed over me.

"This morning, I met with Mrs. Margaret Sternwood," Lenny said. "I looked her up. She's old money, originally from southern California, mainly from oil and natural gas. Her grandfather was one of the original oil barons in the 1920s."

"Seriously? Sort of like a Rockefeller?"

"Yeah, after World War II, she married young and came out to Arizona with her husband. They were one of the groups who developed Scottsdale into what it is today. She thinks her grandson, Alexander, might be in trouble. She's asked us to look into it."

"What kind of trouble?"

"The kind where she can't go to the police. Right now, she doesn't know what he's gotten into, but she suspects it's something illegal, drugs, maybe."

"What makes her think that?" I asked.

"From what his grandmother says, he has a long history of petty crimes – shoplifting, breaking and entering, and various cons. According to Mrs. Sternwood, an internet auction scam caught up with him a few years ago."

Lenny flipped through a legal pad sitting on his desk.

"Alexander sold a 1967 Jaguar E-Type convertible over the internet six years ago for $48,200. Unfortunately, he didn't have a car to sell, only some pictures and forged documents."

"I'm surprised anyone would fall for that," I said, shaking my head.

"It was a while ago," Lenny admitted. "Alexander was arrested, convicted of fraud, and spent twenty-six months in the state prison at Florence. He was released a little over two years ago and has been clean since. Until last week, he had a sales position at an Audi dealership on McDowell Road and was doing well. Mrs. Sternwood thinks he even has a steady girlfriend."

"Sounds like things were going okay," I said. "What happened?"

"Last week, Alexander called his boss, William Martin and told him he was quitting. According to his grandmother, no one at the dealership knows why he quit or where he is now. Yesterday afternoon she went over to his apartment and was let in. There was no Alexander, but she did find some troubling things."

"Like what?" I asked.

"A new Rolex, or at least there was an empty Rolex box. There was also a new computer, a big-screen TV, and audio equipment, some of which were still in the boxes. The sort of things a guy in his mid-twenties would get if he suddenly came into money."

"Why doesn't she wait in his apartment for him to show up and ask him herself?"

"I asked her about that. Unfortunately, there's been a falling out between the two of them. She didn't say what it was, but I take it they no longer communicate."

Great, nothing I hate more than getting in the middle of a family squabble.

I kept my mouth shut as Lenny went on.

"If it turns out drugs or other illegal activities are involved, Alexander's grandmother wants to be informed of all the details."

"And if Alexander's picked up by the police in the meantime, we'll be representing him?" I asked.

"Most likely, so use your judgment on how closely you dig into any criminal activity. If something smells ugly, back off and let me know immediately. I'd rather the D.A. not call you to the stand to testify against Alexander. It's not the sort of thing a wealthy client appreciates."

Not that it would ever come to that. One of the reasons people come to Lenny is that his clients seldom go to trial. Using his extensive network of connections, things were usually settled out of court.

"Mrs. Sternwood's expecting you at noon," Lenny said. "Sophie has the address."

I looked down at my watch. It was eleven nineteen.

Damn.

I went out to Sophie's desk and asked for Mrs. Sternwood's address. She wrote it out and handed it to me. When I looked at it, I realized Sophie was right. Mrs. Sternwood *was* rich.

~~~~~

Leaving the office, I headed up Scottsdale Road to Lincoln. I shoved Fall Out Boy into the CD player and turned it up loud.

As I drove, I had time to reflect on my love life. So okay, maybe it was a mistake to think about that.

The last time I'd been intimate with a man was just over six months ago. He was a low-life golf pro named Dusty. But, several months before him, I'd dated a cop named Jackson Reno.

We'd gotten along great. He was warm, funny, and a terrific lover. I thought the relationship could take off. Unfortunately, the whole thing ended badly, which was mostly my fault.

By the time I tried to set things straight, Reno was with someone new. It's been almost a year since I've seen him, and maybe it's for the best. But it's sort of weird that I keep dreaming about him.

That has to mean something. Doesn't it?

~~~~

Margaret Sternwood lived in Paradise Valley, the mile-wide expanse between Camelback Mountain, Piestewa Peak, and Mummy Mountain. Paradise Valley is wealthy, even by Scottsdale standards.

From her address, I knew Mrs. Sternwood lived in a cluster of old money estates on the south side of Mummy Mountain. Heading along a narrow lane winding up the side of the hill, high hedges of pink and white flowering oleanders lined the sides of the road.

After half a mile, I passed through a large open gate and into a vast cobblestone courtyard in front of either a huge house or a small hotel. I checked the address against a plaque near the front door and confirmed I was at the right place.

I rang the bell, and after several moments, a butler answered. He was medium height and bone thin. I guessed his age at about a hundred and fifty.

"I'm Laura Black," I said. "I have an appointment with Mrs. Sternwood."

"Yes, Miss Black," he said with a shaky voice. "Mrs. Sternwood's expecting you. She's having cocktails by the pool and asks if you would join her." He then turned and led me down the hall.

~~~~

Mrs. Sternwood was reclining on a chaise lounge beside a sparkling tropical-lagoon-style pool. She had on a floppy straw hat and oversized white-rimmed sunglasses.

She stood up as I walked toward her. The butler announced me, and she motioned me to a poolside table. She held out her hand, and we shook.

"I'm Margaret Sternwood," she said in a bright and intelligent voice, "but all my friends call me Muffy. You're Laura Black. Leonard told me all about you. He says you're pretty good."

The butler asked me what I'd like to drink as we sat. Mrs. Sternwood was drinking white wine, her glass half full.

I hesitated. "Go ahead," Muffy said. "Have a belt. It's past noon, and I hate to drink alone."

"Okay," I said to the butler. "Scotch with one ice cube."

The butler bowed slightly and turned to shuffle back to the house. I usually don't start drinking until later in the day, but since Muffy had already started, I thought I should too. I tended to get better answers when the other person had a drink in their hands.

Muffy took off her sunglasses, and I got a good look at her. She was a small thin woman of about seventy-five years.

She wore about a hundred thousand dollars worth of gold and diamond jewelry on her fingers and wrists. Her dark blue eyes sparkled as she spoke to me.

"Thanks for coming over," Muffy said. "As I'm sure Leonard told you, I'm afraid my grandson's gotten mixed up in something again. I don't have any real evidence yet, but I know something's not right."

"What makes you think something's wrong?"

"Well, I wish I could only call it a grandmother's intuition. But, with Alexander quitting his job and spending money he couldn't have legitimately earned, I know he's somehow gotten himself in over his head."

The butler brought my scotch, and I had a sip. It was wonderful. Chivas, perhaps, but smoother. Maybe the eighteen-year-old stuff?

I guess there're advantages to being rich.

"Alexander's parents died while he was still quite young," Muffy said. "I've raised him since he was a pup. Even as a child, he was a hell-raiser."

"What happened?" I asked.

"He was arrested three times before he was eighteen. Twice for shoplifting and once for stealing a car. Finally, just after he turned twenty-one, was the business of the internet auction."

"That must have been quite a shock."

"When I heard about his arrest, I became so upset I almost threw a clot. I told myself it was high time my grandson learned to live with the consequences of his actions."

"What did you do?" I asked.

"Alexander had been scheduled to receive a considerable trust fund when he turned twenty-five. I told him he wouldn't receive a dime until he turned thirty, and that's only if he stopped being a crook. I told him if anything else happened, I was done with him. He'd be out, completely."

"But instead of understanding or appreciating what you were doing, he only became angry?"

"Oh, he was furious. Blames me for everything that's happened to him. Since his release from prison, he's refused to see me or speak with me on the phone."

"Do you know what he's been doing since his release?" I asked.

"He'd been working at an Audi dealership. From what I understand, he enjoyed it and was good at it. I spotted him having dinner with a young lady a few weeks ago. They seemed to be very fond of each other. His probation ended last month, and things seemed to have turned around for him."

Muffy saw my glass was almost empty and motioned the butler over.

"Do we still have any of the Balvenie Cask 191 scotch? The stuff we had when that actor, Stig Stevens, was here last month? Get her two fingers of that."

The butler again didn't respond. He gave his slight bow and turned back to the house.

"Alexander quit his job?" I prompted.

"I first heard about it when his parole officer, David Rasmussen, called me. David had called the Audi dealership last week to see how Alexander was doing. Alexander's supervisor at work, William Martin, said Alexander had quit without giving a reason. David called me to ask if I knew what had happened. You know the rest."

"Why do you think Alex quit?" I asked.

"I don't know, but I can't believe my grandson would return to crime after all the nonsense he's been through. Nevertheless, there's something wrong. I'd like you to find out what it is."

"Muffy," I said, "I'll do my best."

The butler walked back to the table. He set down the scotch and another glass of wine for Mrs. Sternwood.

I took a sip of the scotch. It took a second for my brain to realize what was happening in my mouth. The scotch seemed to melt on my tongue, dissolving down my throat in a wave of pure bliss.

Damn.

A slight shudder of pleasure traveled down my spine, and I felt a smooth warmth creep through me. I took another sip and glanced over at Muffy. She had a sly smile on her face.

"Do you like it?" she asked. "I'm not much of

a scotch drinker, but if I remember correctly, that scotch is older than you."

"Ooooh," I moaned. "It's like liquid sex."

"Sex in a bottle, huh?" Muffy laughed. "Now, that's something that would sell."

~~~~

We talked for almost two hours. Muffy gave me the names, phone numbers, and addresses of Alexander's friends.

She also gave me the places he had worked and the places she thought he hung out. By the time I left, I felt like Alexander and I were old friends.

~~~~

As I drove back to my side of town, I gave Sophie a call.

"Hey, it's me. It looks like it's going to be a couple of busy days, again. Do you want to do something before things get too crazy? I'm thinking dinner."

"Sure," she said. "Swing by about six. I'll be working on a deposition for Lenny until then."

"Do you have the file on Alexander Sternwood yet?"

"I'm pulling it together now. I'll have it for

you tonight."

Chapter Two

I drove east to Miller Road, then south to my apartment where I parked in the back lot. From there, I went through the rear door into the building.

My apartment house was initially constructed as a small hotel in the 1970s. They converted it into condominiums in the nineties and later into apartments.

The interior of the building is hollow, enclosing an enormous atrium. Standing on the ground floor, you can see the walkways circling each of the five floors.

A big TV surrounded by a cluster of chairs and couches is on the ground level, in the back corner. You can usually find six or seven residents watching TV, playing cards, or chatting.

The combination of time and spotty maintenance has caused the building to show its age, but it has a unique style. Besides, it's close to downtown and the rent is cheap. Cheap for

Scottsdale, that is.

Once in the elevator, I pushed the button for the third floor. The elevator is slow and makes a lot of noise, but it always makes it to my floor. I exited the elevator, walked down the hall, and unlocked the door to my apartment.

Marlowe heard me and came in from outside. I share a bedroom balcony with my next-door neighbor, Grandma Peckham. We've both installed cat doors, allowing Marlowe to come and go as he pleases.

Marlowe spends most of his day with Grandma and his nights with me. I think we both feed him. It could explain why he's gotten so fat.

I put on a fresh pot of coffee. The scotch had made me feel warm and tingly all over, but now I needed to perk back up. Sitting at the kitchen table, I organized what I had so far on Alex Sternwood. It wasn't much, but at least it was a start.

~~~~~

Traffic was heavy as I drove back to the office. I found Sophie at her desk, talking with Gina. The Black Eyed Peas played over the office audio system, so I knew Lenny must have already gone home for the night.

"Hey, Laura," Sophie said. "Look who came wandering back."

"Hi, Gina," I said. "How was Vegas?"

"Dull," Gina said. "It doesn't matter how old the baby is. I hate babysitting. He kept trying to get laid by picking up women at the Bellagio pool."

"How'd that work out?" I asked.

"He became so annoying the manager threatened to kick him out. Then, he had the great idea of going to the pool at the Mirage. For some reason, he thought the women would be easier there."

"How'd that go?" Sophie asked.

"About like you'd expect," Gina said with a laugh. "When he had no luck at the Mirage, he began hitting on *me*. I was afraid he'd start dry-humping my leg like a dog. I had to threaten to cut off his balls before he'd leave me alone."

"I don't know," I said, never missing a chance to tease Gina. "Maybe you missed out. An eighteen-year-old would have a lot of stamina. He could go all night."

"Yuck," said Sophie, puckering her lips.

"Eighteen?" Gina asked. "Seriously? That's so gross. I don't even want to think about having to deal with that."

"You ready for dinner?" I asked.

"Starving," Sophie answered.

"So am I," Gina said. "I haven't eaten anything today except for some packets of crunchy things they give you on the plane."

We walked across and down the street to Dos Gringos, a small Baja restaurant in the middle of the Old Town Arts District. The place has always had a charm to it.

The tables are mainly located outside on a patio. Each table has a large umbrella or is underneath one of several trees. Colorful strands of lights are hung everywhere. Alternative and popular music played out of speakers hung throughout the restaurant.

We found an open table near the front, next to a low brick wall that divides the seating area from the sidewalk. This location was perfect for us. We liked watching the guys as they strolled by on foot or cruised by in high-end convertibles.

After a minute, our waitress came by. We ordered dinners along with margaritas for Gina and me. Sophie ordered a drink called a Top Dropper.

"How'd it go with Mrs. Sternwood?" Sophie

asked. "What'd her house look like? Was it fabulous?"

"Her house is more than I could ever dream of," I said. "And that's even if I win the lottery."

Our waitress brought the drinks. Then we munched on chips and salsa while waiting for our dinners.

"Gina and I were talking about Alexander before you showed up," Sophie mumbled, her mouth half full. "What's the big deal?"

"What do you mean?" I asked as I grabbed a chip and stuffed it into my mouth.

"So, the guy has some money and quit his job. From what I understand, that family has piles of money lying around. Maybe he found a way to tap into some of it without his grandmother knowing. If I found a way to get my hands on a couple hundred thousand dollars, I'd quit my job too."

"It's not like that," I mumbled, my mouth half full of salsa. "All he has to do is keep his nose clean for a few years, and then he's mega-rich. He wouldn't blow that on something that dumb. If he goes to jail again, his grandmother will cut him off, like completely."

"Don't be too sure," Gina said. "Guys can be pretty stupid. Where are you going to start?"

"I'll begin with Alexander," I said. "I'll follow him around for a day or two. Get a sense of where he goes and who he sees. It shouldn't be too hard. It's not like he's in hiding. Muffy gave me a list of the places I'm likely to find him. Her information is outdated, but it's a start."

"Muffy?" Sophie laughed. "You're serious? Mrs. Sternwood? Her name is Muffy?"

"Are you starting tonight?" Gina asked, ignoring Sophie.

"Yeah, I imagine both Lenny and Muffy would appreciate hearing back sooner rather than later. Are either of you interested in coming along?"

Gina lowered her voice. "Are you looking for company or backup?"

"Company, for now."

"I'll pass then. I'm beat," Gina said, leaning back in her seat. "I'm going to stop by the gym for an hour. Then it's off to bed. That congressman's kid had me up until three o'clock this morning."

"Well, I'm in," Sophie said. "I was supposed to have a date tonight, but the jerk canceled. I'm sure Lenny won't mind paying my way, too. Besides, you and I always end up in the most bizarre places when we run surveillance."

"Sophie," I said. "That's the nicest news I've had all day."

My best friend took another sip of her Top Dropper. She seemed to think about something and looked up.

"Have you pissed anybody off yet?"

"Not yet," I said.

"So, there isn't going to be anyone shooting at us? You know how I hate it when they shoot at us."

"Not that I know of," I said. "I just started. It'll probably be pretty slow."

Our waitress appeared with three more margaritas. "From the guys at the table," she said, gesturing to a table against the back wall. Three college-aged boys, probably from Arizona State, were smiling and holding up their beers in the typical guy greeting. We waved back.

"Why do they always wait until we're ready to go?" Gina asked as she absentmindedly ran her fingers through her short, dark hair.

"Yeah, but it was sweet," Sophie said.

She got up and walked to their table. After talking to the guys for about a minute, she stood one of them up. She wrapped her arms around the guy and gave him a passionate kiss. She then turned and walked back to our table. The guy stood there with a happy, dazed look on his face.

"What was that about?" Gina asked.

"I asked them whose idea it was to send over the drinks. I told them we had to go, but I didn't want them to think we were ungrateful."

I looked down at the drinks. "What are we going to do with these?"

"Hey, no problem," Sophie said. "I have a couple of big insulated cups in the car. For dessert, we'll have a pitcher of margaritas, to go!"

~~~~

Sophie and I drove to Alex's apartment complex. It was in one of the new high-end communities that have popped up all over Scottsdale in the last few years. It had lots of palm trees, swimming pools, fountains, and water features.

Alex lived in a large one-bedroom on the second floor of a white stucco building that contained maybe eight apartments. We drove by his unit and saw lights in the living room.

We parked in a space overlooking Alex's doorway and kitchen window. His grandmother said he drove a black Jaguar, but there wasn't one in the lot. I checked my watch, and it was a little after eight-thirty.

We sat and talked while Sophie slowly worked her way through the margaritas. She stopped before she finished the last one, but by then, she'd gotten a case of the giggles. I still needed to focus, so I switched to Diet Pepsi.

Sophie had recently broken up with her latest boyfriend and was keeping her options open for the next one. I had no current options regarding men.

After Reno and I had broken up, I'd only gotten close to one other man, who turned out to be a complete jerk. That was a little over six months ago.

Dusty had worked as a golf instructor at the very upscale Excalibur Resort. At the time, I wasn't sure if the relationship would go anywhere. But he was reasonably cute and chewed with his mouth closed, both fine qualities in a man.

We'd dated for about a month and a half. Then Dusty stopped calling. Against Sophie's advice, I decided to look into it.

It only took me an afternoon to find out he'd been caught in the sauna with one of the resort's aerobics instructors. Both were immediately fired, which was why he hadn't called.

That did it for me. Men were all lying, cheating, worthless scum. It's only a shame they smell so good.

~~~~

After about an hour, the conversation dwindled. Sophie then went out to find some bushes to pee behind.

When she returned, she fiddled with the radio until she found a station she liked. We then sat, listening to music and looking up at the apartment, each of us lost in private thoughts.

~~~~

At about ten, the light in the kitchen went out. I thought Alex might be turning in for the night and was relieved.

Unfortunately, we saw movement through the curtains, and the front door opened. Sophie had started to nod off, so I gave her a nudge with my elbow. She perked up immediately.

Alex came out wearing a sports coat. We watched as he locked the door, then skipped down the stairs and into the parking lot. He pulled something out from his jacket pocket and pointed it at the row of cars under a long carport.

Underneath a white car cover, one of the

vehicles blinked its lights and gave a happy *chirp-chirp*, kind of like a cricket. Alex went to the car, removed the cover, folded it, and put it in the trunk.

"Damn," Sophie said, "That's a Jaguar. Looks like Alex isn't doing too badly for himself."

"It was a present for his twenty-first birthday, right before he got busted," I said.

Sophie just shook her head.

Alex got into the car and backed out. He took off down the length of the parking lot, and we followed at a safe distance.

At the entrance to the street, he paused and lowered the convertible's soft top. He then headed up toward North Scottsdale.

We kept several car lengths back, always keeping a vehicle between Alex and us. He was unlikely to spot us unless he was looking for a tail.

He drove north on Scottsdale Road, then took a right into an upscale subdivision just south of the Gainey Ranch Golf Resort. The houses here seemed to have been built around a similar Southwestern theme with white stucco walls and red tile roofs. Most of the lush tropical oasis yards had the look of professional landscaping.

Alex parked in front of one of the nicer ranch houses. Sophie and I parked on the side of the road, about fifty yards away.

Trotting to the front door, Alex pushed the doorbell. After a moment, the door opened, and he went in.

"Well," Sophie said. "What now?"

"I guess we sit."

~~~~

As it turned out, we didn't have long to wait. The door opened in less than five minutes, and Alex came out with a woman.

The lighting near the house was too dim to make out any of her features. All I could tell was that she was tall and had long blonde hair.

Alex walked her to his car, opened the door for her, and then let himself in. The car started and backed out of the driveway. Sophie and I ducked out of sight as the Jaguar returned up the street past our parked car.

We eased out of our space and followed, again staying well behind the Jaguar. They drove to Scottsdale Road, then south toward Old Town. They eventually turned into the nightclub district.

We were a block behind Alex when we saw him pull up in front of Nexxus. As his car stopped in front of the main entrance, valets jumped to either side and opened the car doors. Alex and the woman went inside while a valet parked the car.

~~~~

Although best known for golf, Scottsdale is also a city of unique clubs tailored to every taste. At the top end of the glamour club scene is Nexxus. On any given night, Scottsdale's rich and beautiful people gather here to spend vast sums of money and parade in front of each other.

I'd been here a few times over the years, usually if a new boyfriend wanted to impress me on a third or fourth date. Over the years, I'd come to realize my boyfriends regarded this as the *have sex with me tonight, or there won't be another* date.

~~~~

I parked at a public lot two blocks from the club. Sophie and I then walked to the entrance, where an enormous bouncer looked at us like we were a couple of kids out past our bedtime.

He pointed to a group of fifty well-dressed people behind a red velvet rope. We trudged back to the end of the line.

"Jeez," Sophie said. "This'll take forever. It looks like most of *Snobsdale* showed up tonight."

We didn't talk a lot as we inched toward the front of the line. I kept an eye out for Alex, hoping we'd get into the club before he left.

After almost thirty minutes, we were admitted. I paid the outrageous cover for both of us, then bolted for the bathroom.

~~~~

The two-story club was beautiful, decorated in purple, silver, and black. Sound pounded out from giant speakers as several dozen lights and lasers above the dance floor moved and flashed to the beat of the music.

Up in a DJ booth, a guy wearing about five pounds of gold chains was spinning disks. He was dancing in place along with the crowd on the vast dance floor.

Even though the club was packed, Alex wasn't hard to spot. We'd just walked upstairs when we saw him seated with the blonde in a semi-private recess.

The little nook had a thick purple carpet, a comfortable black leather loveseat, end tables, lamps, and an oversized coffee table. To tell the truth, the furniture looked better than the stuff in my living room.

The blonde's sizeable black shoulder bag and

two flute glasses, each half full, sat on the coffee table. A bottle of champagne in a silver wine cooler had been placed next to the end of the loveseat.

Sophie and I grabbed a table close enough to keep an eye on Alex but far enough away not to be too obvious. Up close, Alexander looked pretty much like he did in his pictures.

He was medium height, athletic, had short brown hair, and was clean-shaven. Overall, he had a handsome, boyish face. It looked like he was wearing the Rolex he'd bought for himself a few days before.

"Damn," Sophie said as she looked around. "This place is amazing."

"Haven't you ever been here before?" I asked.

"Nope, this is the first time. So far, I've seen two guys from the Arizona Cardinals and one of the Phoenix Suns here. They were both going into the VIP room. I wonder what it's like in there?"

"Somehow," I said, "I doubt we'll ever find out."

~~~~

We'd been sitting for about half an hour when a waitress, who could have been the poster girl for a plastic surgery clinic, brought Alex and his date another bottle of champagne.

Looking at the waitress, I'll admit she was impressive. Every inch of her body was perfect. Her nose, her mouth, and her boobs. All perfect.

Her makeup looked professionally applied, and not a hair was out of place. She was so perfect that I thought of her as *Plastic Surgery Barbie.*

While Alex was chatting with the waitress, I took the time to study his date. She seemed nice enough. She wore a mid-length sleeveless red dress with a plunging neckline that showed some deep cleavage.

She was tall, thin, and muscular, like a fitness instructor or someone who was into weightlifting. Her face was beautiful, with dark blue eyes, a delicate nose, and wide, full lips.

Her hair was a natural-looking honey blonde and hung halfway down her back. She parted it down the middle with big loose bangs that poofed out and hung down into her eyes.

The woman seemed to radiate sexuality. Several men had also noticed it and were casting glances her way.

Our waitress, similar in perfection to Barbie, approached our table. Instead of taking another drink order, she set two glasses of champagne on our table.

"From the gentlemen at the bar," she said, then turned and left.

We picked up the glasses and looked around. Two guys at the bar, in their early thirties, well-dressed and cute, were grinning at us and holding their glasses up in the universal guy salute. I looked at Sophie.

"Damn," I said. "They're cuter than the ones at the restaurant. It's too bad we can't hang out with them tonight. We've still got work to do."

Sophie narrowed her eyes and gave me a slight pout. For a second, I thought she was going to argue.

"Oh, alright," she said at last. "I'll get rid of them, but you owe me. Did you see their shoes? Those guys have money."

Sophie stood up and walked over to the two men. As with the guys at Dos Gringos, she found out who had sent the drinks. She wrapped her arms around his neck and gave him a passionate kiss.

They all talked for a minute, and then she kissed the other guy on the cheek. Both guys pulled out business cards and handed them to Sophie before she turned and walked back to our table.

"Well," I said, "that's one way to get rid of them."

"Hey," she said, "don't complain. They're both single, and I got their cards. Can you say double-date?"

~~~~

We sat for another hour, taking in the club and watching Alex and his date. The champagne had given way to Diet Pepsi for me and ginger ale for Sophie.

All of the energy had drained out of us, and I considered calling it a night. From the look on Sophie's face, I didn't think she would object.

Thankfully, about five minutes later, Alex placed the empty champagne bottle upside down in the cooler, and they got up to leave. We waited until they started down the stairs before hurrying after them.

They ended up in the valet line behind four other couples, giving Sophie and me time to leave through the patio entrance and rush back to my Honda.

We drove around the corner in front of the bar just in time to see the black Jaguar turn the far corner of the block. I followed closely for a few minutes until it was apparent Alex was taking the blonde back to her house.

I should have followed them to her house and ensured they were settled in before I called it a night. I should have, but I was dead tired and wanted to go home. Sophie was already asleep, her head bouncing like a dead woman's every time I hit a bump.

Besides, I reasoned, Alex's hand had been halfway up the blonde's dress for the last twenty minutes at the club. I doubted they were going anywhere other than the nearest available bed.

I drove us back to the office and woke Sophie up. She shook her head to clear it, gave me a sleepy, "See you tomorrow," and walked to her car.

She started it up, and I followed, trailing her for a mile or so. When we came to Miller Road, I made the turn and drove to my apartment building.

I was so tired that I leaned against the elevator's side as it slowly made its way to the third floor. Once in my apartment, I pulled off my clothes, put on an old ASU Sun Devils T-shirt, cleared off the bed, and then collapsed.

The last thing I can remember was setting the alarm for seven-thirty.

~~~~

I rose to consciousness while the alarm cheerfully chirped away. I hit the snooze bar and reasoned that the alarm must be some sort of mistake.

Maybe I'd set it for the wrong time? Perhaps it was some malfunction of the clock? It couldn't be seven-thirty yet. I was too tired to get up.

Nine minutes later, when the alarm did its chirpy thing again, I had enough energy to get up and crawl into the shower. After standing there for almost twenty minutes, the use of my limbs and mental functions slowly returned.

I toweled myself off and picked out a cute and comfortable outfit. I was now ready for a day of watching every move Alex made.

I went into the kitchen and started a pot of coffee before opening a can of Seafood Delight for Marlowe and plopping it into his dish. As always, Marlowe attacked it as if he was nearing death from starvation.

In the bathroom, I applied minimal makeup and brushed my hair just enough to put it into a ponytail. From the kitchen, I heard an all too familiar sound: *Aaaack! Aaaaaaaak!*

I didn't need to look. I knew the sound.

Marlowe was in the corner of the kitchen, throwing up his breakfast.

Every time I heard the sound, it reminded me of the movie *The Godfather*. Luca Brasi, the hitman, had made the same sound when they tightened the garrote around his throat.

I was thankful Marlowe only did it in the corner of the kitchen on the tile, but it was still kind of gross. Sometimes, I seriously think about trading him in on a hamster.

Going into the kitchen, I avoided looking in the corner and poured the pot of coffee into *The Big Pig*. I said goodbye to Marlowe and headed out the door.

~~~~

I jogged down the stairs. While staring at myself in the bathroom mirror, I'd decided I would start to sneak in a bit of exercise whenever I could.

Who needed a health club? I thought. I could get the same toned body and rock-hard abs with the equipment I already had at my disposal, like my stairs.

~~~~

I got in my Honda and headed north on Scottsdale Road to the blonde's house at Gainey

Ranch. When I got there, Alex's car was still in the driveway.

"Yes!" I said, pumping my fist up and down. I felt so smug. *Hah*, I thought, *I love getting it right*. It's these small victories that keep me going.

Driving to the end of the street, I didn't see an inconspicuous place to park. Even worse, there were people out.

Some were working in their gardens, and some were walking their dogs. What kind of place was this? Didn't these people have jobs?

I circled the neighborhood for twenty minutes, passing the blonde's house every few minutes. I knew I couldn't keep this up for long. Eventually, one of these nosy citizens would notice something amiss, and I didn't feel like explaining myself to the police.

Besides that, I now had to go to the bathroom. The pot of coffee had gone right through me.

I pulled out of the neighborhood and drove to a convenience store about two miles away on Hayden. Ten minutes later, feeling much better, I headed back to the blonde's house. Turning the corner, my heart sank. No black Jaguar.

"Damn it!"

Well, there was only one way he would have gone, probably. I hurried out and headed west.

When I was about a hundred yards away from the intersection with Scottsdale Road, I had to decide. I could go straight into a residential area, south toward Old Town, or north toward the golf resorts.

I mentally flipped a coin, pulled into the southbound turn lane, and then waited for the green arrow. I drummed my fingers on the steering wheel as I sat behind four other cars at the light.

"Come on, come on," I told the signal.

Finally, I got the turn arrow, and the line moved. I'd just cleared a truck in the middle lane when I saw the Jaguar turning north in the far right-hand lane.

"Damn it!" I shouted again.

Please don't let there be a cop nearby.

I got to the front of the left-turn lane and did a hard right, cutting across two lanes of waiting traffic, then headed north on Scottsdale Road. This clever maneuver was greeted with a chorus of blaring horns and rude gestures, but fortunately, no police.

~~~~

I followed Alex north on Scottsdale Road for about two miles. He turned west, and we drove until we entered Phoenix's city limits. He stopped at a small strip mall tucked behind a gas station.

The shopping plaza had seen better days. There was a take-out pizza joint, a beauty shop, a jewelry store, and a dollar store with a broken and taped window.

Alex pulled into an open space in front of the jeweler. He got out of his car and entered the store.

I parked at the gas station to get a clear viewing angle and took a closer look at the store. On the glass of the picture window, behind thick burglar bars, was stenciled *Meyer's Jewelry*.

From what I could see, Meyer's Jewelry handled mostly low-end watches, gold and silver rings, necklaces, and earrings.

I could only see one person behind the counter; a man about seventy years old with thick black-rimmed glasses. His black and gray hair was slicked straight back, giving him the look of a hoodlum from the 1950s. All he needed was a pack of cigarettes rolled up in his shirtsleeve, and the hoodlum look would have been complete.

Alex and the man talked for about two minutes. Alex then pulled what looked like a small black pouch out of his pocket and laid it on the counter.

The man looked into the bag, then walked to the front door and locked it. Hanging in the window was an *Open* sign that the man flipped over to *Closed*. Both men then disappeared into the back of the shop.

Ten minutes later, the old man unlocked the door and let Alex out. He got into his car, backed out, and pulled away.

I followed him back to Scottsdale Road, then south to the entrance of the Scottsdale Tropical Paradise Resort.

Built in the eighties, the Tropical Paradise was one of the first of Scottsdale's mega golf resorts. Back then, this part of Scottsdale had been nothing but cattle ranches, tall saguaros, and tumbleweeds.

Today, the Tropical Paradise boasts two of the finest golf courses in Arizona. Surrounding the resort was some of the most expensive and desired real estate in the city.

Alex entered the main entrance and drove past the resort's huge tropical fountain. He then wound up the hill to the ornate building containing the main lobby, shops, restaurants, and day spa.

He pulled into a no-parking space in front of the lobby's main entrance. He hopped out of his car and walked in.

I've noticed when you have a nice car, the resorts don't care where you leave it. Park in front of the lobby or next to the pool. They don't care.

If you have something flashy like a Ferrari, they practically insist the car be displayed near the front entrance. If I'd tried that with my Honda, it would've been towed, crushed, and melted.

Chapter Three

I parked on a side lot, a little down the hill from the main building, and walked up the steep sidewalk to the pool area. *Yet another chance to exercise*, I thought.

Ahead was a gate with a sign on it saying something about the pool only being for registered guests and that all visitors needed to sign in at the lobby.

Disregarding the sign, I opened the gate and went in. Still breathing hard from the climb, I thought it might be best if I limited my new exercise routine to once a day or maybe even every other day.

It was a beautiful Arizona winter day, warm without a cloud in the sky. Only the slightest breeze ruffled the fronds on the dozens of queen and date palms planted around the pool. The entire area was packed with tourists, all paying big money to sunbathe while their friends were at home, no doubt digging out from the latest blizzard.

Winding my way around bronze women in bikinis and packs of running children, I found a back entrance to the main lobby behind a high rock waterfall. I went in and started looking for Alex.

I searched a cocktail lounge called The Headhunter, a souvenir store, and a high-end jewelry shop. All without luck.

I was crossing the lobby to look into the Dreamland Cove Bistro when I spotted him. He was looking at some paintings and sculptures in an art gallery off the main hall.

The gallery was strictly high-end. I doubted there was a piece less than ten thousand dollars in the place.

From what I could tell, Scottsdale resorts never sell any art in these galleries. I think they only have them in the lobbies to give the resorts an air of sophistication. If they occasionally do sell a piece of overpriced art, it probably surprises them.

The wall between the gallery and the lobby was made entirely of glass. This allowed the people walking through the hall to admire the art without having to go in. I saw only one person in the gallery besides Alex, a woman.

She was perhaps forty-five years old. Her dark hair was pulled back in a tight bun, held in place with black chopsticks.

Her pinched face made it look like she was having a permanently lousy day. To make things worse, she was wearing black cat's-eye glasses. The whole effect combined to give her an evil librarian look, and not in a sexy way.

After fussing with a couple of paintings, she sat behind a large wooden desk and made a phone call. When she hung up, Alex went over to where she was seated, and they began to talk.

Alex and the woman talked for about fifteen minutes when another man entered the gallery. He was medium height and thin, maybe sixty years old.

The newcomer had a receding hairline and short blond-going-to-gray hair. He sported a trimmed gray beard and mustache.

Maybe it was a bad first impression, but he gave me the creeps. What bothered me most about him were his eyes. They were red-rimmed, watery, and looked a little insane.

The creepy man shook hands with Alex, then they both went into the gallery's back room, closing the door behind them. The woman walked to the gallery's front door, then closed and locked it.

She took out a small sign from her desk with a picture of a clock, along with the message: *Back in Ten Minutes*. She hung the sign on a hook next to the door so it was visible through the glass.

Instead of joining the men in the back, she went to the desk, picked up the phone, and punched in a number. She spoke into the phone for about half a minute, hung up, and then disappeared into the room in the back of the shop.

I parked myself on a couch in the lobby across from the gallery to wait. Fifteen minutes later, the woman unlocked the door and let Alex out. There was no sign of the older guy.

Walking with purpose, Alex went through the lobby toward the front entrance. I did an about-face when I saw he would make it to his car in less than a minute. I power-walked out to the pool area, through the sunbathers, past the screaming kids, down the sidewalk, and into the side parking lot.

Since I knew Alex couldn't see me from this angle, I sprinted the last thirty yards to my car. I hopped in and cranked the engine. It caught right away, and I took off after him.

When I caught sight of Alex, he was sitting at the light at the resort entrance, waiting to turn south on Scottsdale Road, about a hundred yards ahead. I was speeding up to catch him when a black Lincoln Town Car pulled out from a side lot.

I had to slam on my brakes to keep from hitting them. I expected a finger, but the driver ignored me.

Maybe it was only because my Honda had anti-lock brakes, and I hadn't made a lot of noise skidding the tires, but for some reason, the lack of a finger gave me a bad feeling about the black car. I drifted back and let it stay between Alex and me.

At first, the Lincoln pulled in tight behind Alex but then backed off a few car lengths. Two men were visible in the car, and after a few minutes, it was clear they were also following Alex.

I followed both cars in a weird kind of convoy. Both my curiosity and my confusion rose several notches.

Who were these men? What had Alex been doing in the art gallery? What had he been doing in the beat-up jewelry shop? He appeared to be fencing something small enough to fit in a little black bag. Was this the source of his money? Was any of this drug-related?

Help!

With these questions nipping at me, I continued tailing Alex and the Lincoln. We all drove south on Scottsdale Road, passing through Old Town. Alex was almost to the Loop 202 highway when he pulled into the parking lot of Jeannie's Cabaret.

Jeannie's is at the top end of the Scottsdale strip clubs. From the outside, the building appears to be a small casino. Fountains, landscaping, and lighting all mingled to give an affluent and elegant appearance.

Glancing around, I saw there were about forty cars in the lot. Not bad for a Tuesday lunch hour. Alex parked and went in. The Lincoln continued to the back of the lot, and the two men got out.

Now that I could look at them, I saw one was tall, one was short, and they both looked cranky. They followed Alex into the club.

I parked, waited two minutes, then walked to the entrance. Two doormen stood on either side of the doorway, like immovable stone towers.

Each was huge and formally attired in a black coat with a black bow tie. They both looked me up and down, then let me in.

~~~~

It took a minute for my eyes to adjust to the

low lighting after paying the cover and entering the cavernous room. Every time I go into one of these places, I'm amazed at what an industry is built around men watching naked women dance.

The first thing that caught my attention was the music. It was loud, hard, classic rock. What struck me was the pounding bass line seeming to accompany every song.

The room had several stages where the women could dance. The main stage was circular, maybe twelve feet across, connected by a runway to a backstage area.

A brass pole was bolted to the floor and ceiling in the center of the stage. Small tables and chairs, mostly occupied, crowded against the runway and stage.

Half a dozen cocktail waitresses were milling about, serving drinks, and chatting with the customers. There was also a bored-looking DJ in a booth in the corner, spinning out dance tunes.

A dozen men and four women were seated at the bar, which ran the entire length of one wall. Alex was near the end of the bar, drinking a beer, occasionally glancing up at the girl on stage.

The two big guys from the Lincoln were at a booth near the bar. Looking closer, they didn't act like the police or even trained professionals, more like hired thugs.

I settled into a booth against the far wall. Looking down at its surface in the dim light, I silently hoped it had been wiped down recently.

~~~~

In less than a minute, a waitress appeared. In her early twenties, she had olive skin, brown eyes, and loose black hair hanging well below her shoulders.

She was dressed in a string bikini top and red leather hot pants. I ordered a ginger ale and asked her if they served any food.

"There's a full menu starting at four o'clock," she said in a high-pitched Betty Boop voice. "This time of day, we have salads that come out of a bag. We also have what I like to call the *Heart Attack Special.*"

"What's that?" I asked.

"That's a platter of deep-fried onion rings, deep-fried zucchini, and deep-fried mushrooms – along with a bowl of ranch to dip them in. Or, we have a hot dog and chips for three dollars. We sell a lot of those. Can I get you one?"

"Um, sure," I said, not exactly wanting a hot dog, but I was getting hungry and needed something.

The girl on stage finished dancing, and another girl came on, a tall reedy redhead. The pulsing rock music started again, and she began to swing her lengthy hair, thrust her hips, and dance to the beat of the music. Men lined up against the stage for the chance to slip a dollar into her garter.

The waitress came back with my drink and the hot dog. I glanced over, checking that Alex was still at the bar. He was on his second beer but otherwise hadn't moved.

I took a bite of the hot dog and found it wasn't bad. I took a sip of the ginger ale, and my mouth puckered. It had a strong taste of plastic from whatever bucket they'd just dipped it out of.

The music from one song no sooner died down than another one started up. As soon as it began, there was a general yell of excitement from the crowd, and several men headed toward the stage. The music was apparently a cue for something unique that the regulars knew was about to happen.

I looked over at the stage and did a double-take. Seven or eight guys stood against the stage with their stiff Johnnies poking out of their pants. The guys were holding them proudly, and everyone was laughing and smiling.

As the music pounded, the girl on stage

beckoned for one man to come closer. As he went against the stage, she got down on her belly, hung her head over the side, and started to work on the man.

After she'd performed four or five long slow strokes, she bit off the tip and spit it into the crowd. This act of mutilation was greeted with cheers and applause.

What the hell?

The girl on stage called for another man. He approached, and she began to work on him too. I looked again and noticed a woman standing against the stage. Like the men, she was standing there with a stiffy in her hand.

Then the truth slowly dawned on me. They were all holding *hot dogs*. I looked down at my half-eaten lunch, and my stomach gave an involuntary twist.

Yuck.

~~~~

The hot dog girl finished her act and scampered behind the curtain. I looked over at Alex, now on his third beer, as the music started up again.

Alex's face brightened, and he began to clap. The next girl was apparently the headliner because the DJ got on the mike and introduced her.

"Ladies and gentlemen," he called out. "Jeannie's Cabaret is pleased to introduce *Gentlemen Player Magazine's* Miss November, Scottsdale's own – Miss Danica Taylor."

The announcement was met with scattered applause and whistles. I looked at the stage where the new girl had come out.

Realization hit me in an instant. She was the girl who had gone out with Alex the night before. The same girl he'd spent the night with.

I watched as she began her first dance. Last night she'd seemed merely beautiful and athletic. Today every move she made seemed to invite the men in the room to engage in their intimate fantasies. Several men went up to the stage to offer her money just so she'd spend a few seconds looking intently at them while she danced.

After ten minutes, the three songs comprising her act finished. The music faded, and the room seemed to come out of a trance. Men and women again began talking, laughing, and walking around.

The blonde gathered up the sizeable pile of bills that had accumulated in the center of the stage and disappeared behind the curtain.

Alex again sat down at the bar. I supposed he was waiting for her to come out again as a cocktail waitress.

My server came to the table carrying another ginger ale. "That's okay," I started to say. I hadn't drunk more than half of my foul-tasting drink and wasn't planning on ordering another.

"It's from the lady over there," she said, pointing to a table by the stage.

I looked over, and a woman was smiling and holding up her hand, wiggling her pinky at me. This was the same woman who had been standing next to the stage, wiggling her hot dog a few minutes earlier.

The woman got up and walked to my booth. She was a few years younger than me and a little shorter. She had short blonde hair cut in a style that fit her face nicely and just a splash of makeup.

"Hi. My name's Annie," she said. "I saw you when you came in."

Her soft voice was velvety, smooth, and soothing, almost like a cat purring.

"I'm Laura, Laura Black," I said as she slid into the booth across from me.

"It doesn't look like you're here with anybody,

so I was thinking if we're both here to pick up a guy, maybe we could do it together. You know, work as a team."

"I'm sorry," I said. "But I didn't come here to pick up a man. I'm working."

"Oh?" she asked in her soft voice. "It must be some job when you can do it in a room full of turned-on guys."

Danica, or whatever the blonde's name was, had come out of the back. She was now a cocktail waitress and talking to Alex at the bar. They chatted for several seconds before she gave out a squeal of joy and hugged him.

"I wish I could say my job was full of glamor and excitement," I said. "But most of the time, I follow guys around to places like this."

I looked at her and saw she was still glancing around at the men in the room.

"So, you came here to pick up a guy?" I asked. "How's it going?"

"Not so good," she said with an annoyed tone. "I'm trying to find a man for, well, you know. It doesn't need to be a long-term thing. I'd probably settle for a weekend. Even a one-night stand would be okay, but I'm sort of shy around men."

"If that's all you want a man for, it shouldn't

be hard to find one."

"That's what I thought," she said, clearly frustrated. "I've tried the clubs and some bars, but I can't work up the nerve to walk up to a man and ask him out. I never know how to start or what to say. The few times I've tried were disasters."

"Really?" I asked. "What happened?"

"Oh, I'd panic and stand there stammering while the guy looked at me like I was insane. I thought finding a guy would be easier in a strip club. All the guys here are already worked up, so it should be easier, right?"

"I'd think so," I said. "So, pick one you think is cute and walk over to him. You don't need to be clever. Introduce yourself and tell the guy you think he's handsome and you'd like to go out with him."

"Do you think that would work?" she asked.

"Sure, but don't take it personally if the first few guys turn you down. I suspect most of the guys here are married, ring or not. I bet by the fourth or fifth one, you'll have a date for tonight."

"Thanks," Annie said. "Maybe I'll try that. I can't do any worse."

Danica had begun her waitress rounds, and Alex was heading for the exit. The two big guys were also getting up, their eyes fixed on Alex. I threw eight dollars on the table, grabbed my purse, and got up.

"I'm sorry, Annie," I said, "but I have to leave. Good luck finding the right man, or at least one who'll go home with you."

She finger waved goodbye, and I followed the men out the door.

~~~~

After Alex left the club, he drove back to his apartment, the two guys following him. Half an hour later, he came out again, this time in a swimsuit, a towel in one hand, a beer in the other. He walked to the apartment's main pool, swam a dozen laps, and then laid out for over an hour.

The day had gotten warmer, still without a cloud from horizon to horizon. The two guys in the Lincoln sat in the lot about a dozen spaces from Alex's apartment, trying to look inconspicuous.

Somehow, they'd managed to find a covered parking spot. I wasn't so lucky and had to move my car every few minutes to take advantage of the shadow from a cluster of fan palms.

Strange as it sounds, I don't think they ever made me. I guess they never thought someone would be following them.

I called Sophie and asked her to run the license plate on the Lincoln. She called back ten minutes later and said the car was registered to Arizona Security Enterprises, whoever they were.

She did a quick check but couldn't find any more information on them. I knew she'd also run a full report on the company, but that always takes time.

~~~~~

At four o'clock, I called Lenny and downloaded him on Alex's activities. All I had at this point was that he was alive, had a stripper girlfriend named Danica Taylor, and was engaged in some suspicious activities, but nothing obviously illegal. I also told him about the tail from Arizona Security Enterprises.

Lenny's enthusiasm was restrained. He gave me a five-minute lecture about the importance of the assignment and not to screw it up. He then encouraged me to continue the surveillance to obtain something useful.

~~~~~

Alex walked back to his apartment at four forty-five, only to emerge fifteen minutes later wearing a Phoenix Suns jersey. I followed him, as did the Lincoln, to Duke's, a sports bar on the Scottsdale Greenbelt. A chartered bus was in front of the bar, and I suspected Alex was going to the basketball game.

Alex went into the bar, and I sat in my car. Ten minutes later, he came back out, leading a group of four men. They were all dressed in some type of basketball jersey.

They disappeared into the bus, along with thirty other people who'd also spilled out of the bar. I stayed until the bus pulled out of the parking lot. The Lincoln was on its tail.

Alex wouldn't be back to the bar until after eleven. I didn't think anything remarkable would happen at a basketball game, so I took off. I'd let the guys in the Lincoln follow Alex around the downtown Phoenix arena. I was relieved to have the evening off.

~~~~

I drove to Char's Thai restaurant, down the street from my apartment building. They've got the best green curry chicken in town. The spiciness level is somewhere between eye-watering and outright pain. I got an order to go, along with a couple of egg rolls.

Marlowe strolled in from the bedroom balcony when I walked into my apartment. I put the Thai food on the coffee table, opened a Diet Pepsi from the fridge, and flipped channels until I came across the Suns game.

Marlowe sniffed at the food, then went back out on the balcony. I knew he was going to Grandma Peckham's to see if she had anything better.

The Suns were playing the Lakers and were beating them badly. I looked for Alex in the crowd but didn't spot him.

After a half-hour of watching the hot, sweaty men run back and forth on the court, my mind drifted to passion and intimacy. Sadly, this made me reminisce about Reno and the two months we'd spent together.

Funny as it sounds, I'd met Jackson Reno at a Pimps 'n Ho's Halloween party Gina had a little over a year ago. When Gina first told me about the party, I told her I wasn't looking to meet anyone new. It was too soon after my divorce. She finally convinced me to go, for the fun of it.

When I got there, Gina introduced me to a guy she'd worked with in her former life as a detective with the Scottsdale police department. He was solidly built and movie-star handsome.

He got a drink for me, and we started talking. I found out his name was Jackson Reno, and he was a plainclothes cop for the city of Scottsdale.

I told him about doing investigations for Lenny's law firm, and he talked to me about being a cop. We discovered we both liked Thai food, Mexican beaches, and old Humphrey Bogart movies.

After a few drinks, I told him I was turned on by slow backrubs and firm butts. He told me he loved having his earlobes nibbled, and he liked firm butts as well. We started laughing, and before long, we were sitting close to each other on Gina's couch.

After what seemed like only a few minutes, it was after midnight, and the party was winding down. I apologized to Reno for keeping him to myself all night.

He leaned over and softly kissed me. He then wrote his phone number in the palm of my hand, like we were in high school.

We went out the next night, the next, and the next. Reno was sweet, patient, and a better cook than me.

Not only did he have a great body, but he was also a fantastic lover. He made me feel things I didn't think were possible.

Week after week flew by. Looking back, that

November was probably the happiest month of my life.

Starting in early December, life started creeping in on us. Reno had to start working on a series of night assignments.

Meanwhile, Gina and I were busy night and day trying to get evidence that an internet millionaire named Rocco Moro was unfaithful to his wife. Rocco had signed a prenuptial contract with a clause stating that the prenup would become invalid if he were ever unfaithful. If that happened, his wife, Lenny's client, would dump him and get half his millions.

Even with our scheduling conflicts, Reno and I still spent every moment we could together. I was so happy.

I had a real relationship with a normal guy who seemed stable. Since my divorce, it was the first time I felt things were going in the right direction.

But then, on Christmas Eve, it all fell apart. The night started well enough. After Reno and I had a beautiful dinner at Frankie Z's, our favorite Italian restaurant, we returned to his place and shared some incredible passion.

Afterward, as we lay in bed, we exchanged Christmas presents. I gave Reno a new watch. His had broken during a fight with a drug dealer a month before, and he needed a new one. I could tell he liked it, and it made me feel great to see him put it on.

When I opened my present, it was a pistol. The box said it was a nine-millimeter Glock, Model 26. I picked it up with my thumb and forefinger. It wasn't much bigger than my hand.

"Hey," I said. "What a cute little gun."

"Your twenty-five-caliber pistol wouldn't stop anybody," Reno said. "This one's small enough to fit in your purse, but it's scary enough to make the bad guys think twice. It's so small it's called the Baby Glock."

"Ahhh," I said. "Our first baby."

I was expecting him to come back with something sarcastic, but instead, he looked at me and asked, "Why don't you move in with me?"

I was stunned. My mind went blank. I even think I stopped breathing.

"You're over here most of the time anyway," he said. "It would save you a ton on rent. Marlowe would like it here too."

I sat there with my mouth open, making *ahhh, aahhh* noises. I didn't know what to say.

What, just give up my independence? Are you

nuts?

Reno was wonderful, but I'd just gotten out of a rotten marriage. Did I want to jump back into something serious again? After only two months of dating? Reno looked at me for a moment, reading my thoughts, and then his face fell.

"You don't want to?" he asked.

"Wow," I said. "It's not that I don't want to, but it's kind of sudden."

"Okay, do you have *any* interest in moving in with me?"

"Oh, I don't know, maybe, probably," I said. "I'm sorry. This is all happening sort of fast. Let me go home and sleep on it, and we can discuss it tomorrow morning. I'll come over first thing and make you a Christmas breakfast. Will that be okay?"

I could tell this wasn't okay as I hurried out of bed and got dressed, but he gave me a hug and a kiss anyway. I knew I should have stayed the night, but I felt trapped and wanted to go home and think. Even so, the front door to Reno's house made a sad and lonely sound as I closed it and stepped out into the warm Arizona night.

When I got to my apartment, it felt empty. Since I'd been gone so often, Marlowe had taken to sleeping next door at Grandma Peckham's.

I sat on the couch, flipping channels for an hour, trying to convince myself I wasn't in love with Reno. It wasn't working, and at last, I gave up.

Okay, I thought, *I'll go back over to Reno's and see about starting a new adventure with him.* Who knew? Maybe this was the way it was meant to happen.

As I was walking out the door, my phone rang. I figured it was Reno. Instead, it was Lenny.

"We've located Rocco Moro," he said. "He's with his mistress at a place in Valle d'Aosta, that's in Italy. The locals are keeping an eye on him. We've got to get solid evidence of his affair and a proper chain of custody before he disappears again. Gina will meet you at Sky Harbor Airport in forty minutes. It's time to save the world. Grab your camera, your passport, and move your tush."

In my rush to get out the door, I didn't take my toothbrush, makeup bag, or even a change of socks. I figured I could call Reno from the airport, but I had to run to get on the plane by the time I got there.

There was a blizzard in New York, and the flight was forced to circle JFK for an hour, which meant I also had to run to catch the Milan flight. Before I dashed onto the plane, I tried to call Reno, but he didn't answer.

Given the time, he was most likely still asleep or in the shower. I left a message telling him I had to miss breakfast but would call him back as soon as possible.

Before I knew it, it was eighteen hours later, and I was creeping along the snow-covered second-story bedroom balcony of a château in the Italian countryside. Gina was keeping a lookout on the ground below me. It was dark, the wind was blowing snow against my face, and I'd never been so cold in my life.

I ended up taking some great pictures of Rocco Moro doing some very naughty and inappropriate things with his teenage mistress. Now, I don't know about the laws in Italy, but I'm pretty sure some of the things they were doing would be illegal in Arizona.

I swung my leg over the balcony and started climbing down. The plan was for Gina and me to fade into the Italian countryside, find the car we'd stashed along the side of the road, then drive back to Milan.

Gina heard noises from the house and whispered for me to hurry. I'd lowered myself about five feet when my foot slipped on the ice. I tried to catch myself, but my numb fingers couldn't grip the snowy ledge.

I fell almost ten feet and landed badly on my leg. There was a loud snap and a hot bolt of pain. I knew it was broken.

Gina was able to get me to a rural clinic. Only the doctors spoke any English, my cell phone was dead, and there wasn't a telephone in sight of my bed.

Gina said she stayed with me for the first two days, but I was too doped up to remember much about her being there. She then flew back to Scottsdale to hand deliver the pictures.

Lenny was thrilled. Rocco's wife used the evidence to force a generous divorce settlement from her cheating husband. Lenny ended up making a pile of cash, as usual.

Sophie came to Italy two weeks later to help me return to the States. By then, I had a walking cast on my leg and could move around on crutches.

On the trip back, she asked if I had straightened things out with Reno. I told her, "No."

"Laura, you gotta call him," she said. "He's

going to think you've dumped him. Gina said he called her last week to see if she knew what was happening. She told him you were out of the country with a broken leg and would be back soon. She didn't think Reno believed her."

"I know," I said. "I was supposed to see him at Christmas, but that was two weeks ago. I can't just call him up now. I'd look like an idiot. He wanted me to move in, and I still don't know what I'll tell him. When I get back to Scottsdale, I'll go over and see him. With the cast, maybe I can use the sympathy ploy."

Only that didn't go as planned, either. I couldn't drive and didn't want to take a cab. After I got back, it was another three days before I got up the courage to have Sophie drive me over to Reno's house.

It was nine at night when we got there, and Reno wasn't home. Sophie and I parked across the street and waited.

Reno's car came down the street at nine-thirty, but we saw he wasn't alone. I didn't recognize who she was, but she had big blonde hair and wore a red dress.

We both ducked down while Reno pulled into his garage. Lights went on in the living room and five minutes later in the bedroom.

We stayed until it was obvious there were shadows of two people on the bedroom window shade. I started crying, and Sophie drove me home.

~~~~

The Suns beat the Lakers one hundred and fifteen to ninety-eight. At eleven o'clock, I drove back to Duke's.

Fifteen minutes later, the bus pulled into the lot. The people were in a rowdy mood as they spilled out. Alex got into his car and drove directly to his apartment, the Lincoln following almost on his bumper the whole way.

I was going to stay around for half an hour to make sure he wasn't going anywhere else, but in less than twenty minutes, the living room light went off. Five minutes later, the bedroom light went off as well.

Alex was in for the night. I drove home to Marlowe.

Chapter Four

The alarm started chirping, and I hit the snooze bar to shut it off. I remembered setting the alarm the night before, hoping to get to Alex's before eight o'clock.

When the happy chirping started again, I shut it off and looked at the bedroom window. It was still dark outside.

Damn.

The alarm went off, and I hit the snooze four more times. The fifth time, I realized my heart was pounding, and I was fully aroused.

That woke me right up. I vaguely remembered dreaming about Reno doing a slow striptease and then doing a naughty thing to me with his finger.

Damn.

I felt cheated. How unfair is it to have another great dream about Reno and not get to enjoy it?

I pulled myself out of bed and stumbled to the kitchen. I made a pot of coffee, got myself ready, and fed Marlowe.

Before he had time to throw up, I scratched him behind the ears and hurried out the door.

~~~~

When I pulled into the entrance to Alex's apartment complex, it was eight forty-five. It was later than I'd wanted to get there. I didn't expect Alex to be up so soon, but I didn't want to take the chance of losing him, especially now that he'd picked up some friends.

I drove around to the back of Alex's building and spotted the Lincoln in a space across from Alex's apartment. There were two men in the front seat.

I wasn't close enough to make out their faces, but they appeared to be the same two who'd followed Alex the day before.

Alex's Jaguar was under the car cover and parked in the same spot it had been the night before. I parked on the street outside the entrance to the apartment complex and waited.

~~~~

Alex pulled out of the lot at nine twenty, followed ten seconds later by the Lincoln. He then made his way to the Loop 101 freeway and headed south.

It appeared Alex was headed toward Mesa or maybe Chandler, two of the suburbs on the East Valley side of Phoenix. He had positioned himself in the middle lane of the freeway, about to pass the exit ramp for the Loop 202 freeway.

Without warning, Alex turned sharply to the right and shot across a traffic lane and onto the exit ramp. I saw smoke billow up from the tires as the car behind Alex hit the brakes. Alex almost hit the plastic crash barrier mounted at the end of the ramp, but he made it.

The Lincoln saw him exit but was blocked by a semi-truck in the right-hand lane. They tried to get around the truck by speeding up and diving in front of it.

Unfortunately, the semi clipped their back end with a tearing *thump,* sending the Lincoln into a spin and bringing the entire freeway to a screaming halt. I hit the brakes, as did everyone around me.

Tires screeched, and there were several loud *thuds* as cars behind me rear-ended each other. Blue smoke and burnt rubber filled the air.

For a moment, there was an eerie calm as every car on the highway came to a stop. When the smoke cleared, I was in the front of a rapidly-forming traffic jam.

The Lincoln had hit the same crash barrier Alex had managed to miss. It had come to rest in the middle of the freeway exit ramp. All four tires had blown, the right rear quarter panel was in tatters, and pieces of the car were scattered all over the road.

The semi had locked its wheels and jack-knifed but otherwise seemed okay. Unfortunately, the truck had an open bin in the back. It had carried a full load of oranges, several thousand of which were now scattered across the pavement.

After a minute, traffic began to filter around the accident, and I heard sirens in the distance. The tattered Lincoln completely blocked the off-ramp Alex had taken.

There was no way I could get around them, but it didn't matter. Alex was already lost for the day.

I followed the trickle of cars going around the jack-knifed semi. I felt the soft squish under my tires as I ran over several oranges. The smell of citrus mingled with the burned rubber.

As I passed the Lincoln, I saw the two men were out of the car, both looking a little shaken. Apparently, neither had been wearing a seatbelt.

The tall guy was holding a towel to his bleeding nose. The short guy was holding his right arm close to his side as if he'd cracked a rib or two. His good arm was holding a phone.

Although I couldn't make out the words, the sound of his shouting into the phone carried to my car. As usual, neither man looked happy.

~~~~

I drove back home to decide what to do next. Since my day of surveillance was turning out to be a bust, I decided maybe this would be a good time to get some background on Meyer's Jewelers and the creepy people at the Tropical Paradise.

I also thought this might be an excellent excuse to talk to Jackson Reno. *Who knows,* I thought, *maybe my erotic dreams about him were a sign.*

I took a deep breath, pulled out my phone, and called him at his old number. He answered on the third ring.

"Hey," I said. "Remember me? It's been a while. What are you doing for dinner tonight?"

The phone was silent. The kind of silence where you know the person is still on the other end, but they aren't talking. I was about to ask again when he spoke.

"Laura Black," he said with a sigh. "I always

knew you'd show up again someday."

"And, that's a good thing, isn't it?" I asked.

"No."

"We always had a good time together."

"Good time?" Reno asked, his voice starting to rise. "As I recall, you dumped me. I also remember that while we were dating, you had people trying to kill you. I mean, seriously trying to kill you. How's that a good time? Do you know how it feels to have people actively trying to kill your girlfriend?"

"It was only a couple of times and never while we were actually on a date," I said, trying to sound reasonable.

"There was that guy who rammed into your car and made you crash through the side of a car wash. Remember that?"

"Well, yeah. But that was before we'd even started to date, and nobody got hurt. Besides, it was only a rental."

"And there was the crazy woman who put all those scorpions in your purse. Remember that?"

"Well, yeah. But wait a minute," I said, my voice starting to rise. "You're a cop. People try to kill you all the time too."

"No, they don't, and besides, that's

completely different."

"No, it's not."

"Yes, it is," he said. "You said we always had a good time together? I don't remember it that way. What'd we ever do together that was so good?"

"The sex was pretty good."

There was another pause on the other end of the phone. Then he sighed, again. "Okay, the sex was great. But that doesn't mean I had a lot of fun the rest of the time."

"Yes, you did. You're only upset because we stopped seeing each other."

"Stopped seeing each other? As I recall, you dumped me. No goodbye, no kiss my ass, nothing."

"I didn't dump you. I was tied up and couldn't see you."

"For over a year?"

"Well, it was only for a couple of weeks. But when I became available, you'd already started seeing someone else."

"I won't even begin to tell you I understand a word you're saying. Besides, I haven't had a serious girlfriend since you dumped me."

Oh, really? Humm?

"I didn't dump you. And what about Cynthia Redburn? Tall with long blonde hair? You were seeing her. She spent the weekend over at your house less than a month after we stopped seeing each other."

"So, you dumped me and then stalked me?"

"I didn't stalk you. Sophie did. And you're avoiding my question about Cynthia."

"Cynthia was my rebound after I hadn't heard from you for like three or four weeks. And yes, I spent the weekend with her but never saw her again after that."

"Why not?"

"It's really none of your business, but she spent the entire weekend trying to get me to suck her toes. I mean all of them, all at once. I'd wake up, and she'd have her foot shoved in my mouth."

"Eeeyuuww, gross."

"Exactly."

"Okay, so let me buy you dinner," I said. "To sort of make up for it. And actually, I wanted to talk to you about business."

"I don't think so. Besides, dinner wouldn't make up for it. What kind of business?"

"Cop business," I said.

"What kind of cop business?"

"Like, where would I go if I wanted to fence some expensive merchandise?" I asked.

"You're trying to fence something? Your old engagement ring, perhaps?"

"Maybe. Where would I fence it if I wanted cash and no questions asked?"

"You could go to a lot of places," he said. "Did you have anywhere particular in mind?"

"Maybe at Meyer's Jewelry or maybe at the art gallery in the lobby of the Tropical Paradise?"

The phone went silent again. I waited it out.

"So," he said. There was an edge to his voice. "You want to tell me what this is about?"

"Sure, over dinner?"

"No, not over dinner. Dinner would make it seem like a date."

"Okay, how about lunch? Frankie Z's today at one o'clock?"

Again, with the sigh. "Okay, sure. But I'm going to regret this. Don't say I won't because we both know I will."

"You won't."

~~~~

Frankie Z's is a small, family-run Italian restaurant off Hayden and Via Linda. Reno and I had been there several times before. If anywhere could be considered *our* restaurant, Frankie Z's was it.

As I drove closer to the restaurant and thought about seeing Reno again, some long-forgotten feelings of excitement began to wake up in the pit of my stomach. I pulled into Frankie's parking lot five minutes after one. Hey, almost on time.

Walking in the door, the aroma of oregano, baked garlic, and olive oil wrapped around me. I hadn't been to Frankie's since I was last here with Reno over a year ago. Walking in the door felt good, sort of like coming home.

Frankie Zappitelli greeted me with a warm smile as I walked in. Frankie is the owner, full-time hostess, and part-time chef.

She's a small, ageless Italian woman. As always, her black and gray hair was pulled back into a tight bun. She stopped and gave me the once-over. Her dark eyes sparkled as she spoke.

"Where you been?" she asked. "It's been too long. You used to come here all the time, then you disappear. Look how skinny you are. Hey, that's okay. I fix you up good now. Both you and your cute boyfriend."

I followed close behind as she went through a maze of tightly packed tables. She led me out to the patio where Reno was waiting. He looked up and saw me. He then stood and took me in with his eyes as I walked over and sat.

Even though I hadn't seen him for almost a year, he was exactly as I remembered. His body was the kind you see on the covers of fitness magazines – strong and tight.

He wore a faded Hawaiian Aloha shirt, blue jeans, and cross-trainers. This was his typical uniform for surveillance and undercover work.

I took a moment to look him over. Yup, those feelings were awake all over now. My stomach was full of butterflies, and I started having very naughty thoughts.

I've never been able to explain why I've always felt this way about Reno. It isn't just because he's good-looking. I know lots of handsome guys. It isn't his great sense of humor or his firm body.

Reno's a natural leader who knows where he wants to go. He has a real direction in his life. He also knows the difference between right and wrong, which draws me to him.

"Well, Laura Black," he said. "You look great. I hear you're still working for Lenny. I suppose he's doing well, even though he's probably still a jerk."

"Sure," I said. "Lenny's doing great. He has more money than he could ever spend. And yeah, he's still a jerk."

"I ran into Gina a few months after you dumped me," Reno said. "She said you were dating a golf pro?"

"Yeah, him. His name was Dusty, and it didn't last more than a few weeks. Since then, I haven't had time to get involved with anyone else."

Okay, so that was a big fat fib. After I found out about Dusty boinking the aerobics instructor, I swore off men for a couple of months.

Jeez, I remember thinking at the time, *an aerobics instructor? How retro can you get? She probably wore pink leg warmers while he was doing her.*

Since then, I hadn't found anybody I wanted to be with, at least anybody who also wanted to be with me.

Dominic, the waiter, came by with a basket of warm bread. The menu hadn't changed since we were last here, so we each ordered our favorite lunch.

His was still the grilled chicken breast and a side of steamed vegetables. I had the sausage sandwich, an extra side of marinara, fries, and garlic bread.

"You wanted to talk cop business?" Reno asked.

"I'm looking into a guy named Alexander Sternwood," I said, lowering my voice. "He's from a wealthy Paradise Valley family, although he hasn't inherited his share yet. All of a sudden, he's come into a lot of money."

"Okay."

"He may get his money by selling things that don't belong to him. Do you know about a fence at Meyer's Jewelers store on 32nd Street in Phoenix?"

Reno thought about it for a moment. "The guy who runs the jewelry store is Jimmy Meyer. He's been around for years. He used to be the muscle for a crime family out of New York. If our information is right, Jimmy maintains a loose connection with organized crime through the DiCenzo family. He's semi-retired and is only involved in the small stuff, at least as far as we know."

He leaned closer to me. "The part that interests me is how you know about the art gallery at the Tropical Paradise. We only found out about it last month. Since the Tropical Paradise is controlled by the DiCenzo family, we think there's a connection between the family and the fencing operation there."

"I've been hearing about the DiCenzos for years," I said. "But I really don't know a lot about them."

"Well," Reno said, "the DiCenzos are Arizona's largest organized crime family. They control about a quarter of the high-end Scottsdale golf resorts, including the Blue Palms and the Tropical Paradise. They also handle illegal aliens entering the U.S., private gambling, high-end prostitution, and illicit arms traffic in Mexico and Central America. Rumor also has it they're trying to broaden their influence into narcotics, heroin, and the like.

"Seriously?" I asked.

"The head of the family is Anthony 'Tough Tony' DiCenzo. He relocated to Scottsdale from New York about thirty years ago. Some in the precinct say the move was voluntary. Some say otherwise. In either case, since he's taken over, things have remained relatively quiet in

Scottsdale, at least as far as turf wars are concerned."

"I've always heard Tough Tony came out here to retire, not to head up a crime family."

"I wish that were the case, but no. Let's go back to yesterday. I take it you saw Sternwood make a sale at the Tropical Paradise," Reno said. "When was this?"

"About noon, maybe a few minutes after."

Reno pulled his cop notebook from his back pocket. He flipped a few pages, then looked up at me. His face had an odd expression.

"When your guy was at the Tropical Paradise, who'd he make the sale to?"

"At first, there was just a woman there. Then a man showed up. He got there maybe ten or fifteen minutes after Alex arrived."

"The man?" Reno asked. "What'd he look like?"

"Um, medium height and thin. Somewhere in the neighborhood of sixty. He had short blonde hair, a gray beard, and a mustache. He was businesslike, but the guy gave me the creeps. He had these small watery eyes, and the lids were red. Like he had allergies or something."

Dominic brought the lunches to the table. The

beautiful aromas wafting up from the plates reminded me how hungry I was. Neither of us spoke for several minutes while we attended to business.

"The woman who works there is named Ingrid Shanker," Reno eventually said between bites. "She isn't so much involved with the fencing. She's more of a bookkeeper."

"That makes sense. She looked like an evil librarian."

"The man you saw is most likely Albert Reinhardt. He's better known as 'the Iceman'. He spends most of his time in Europe but comes to the U.S. two or three times a year. Usually to Palm Springs or Scottsdale."

"Okay, what's so special about him?"

"His specialty is jewelry and fine art. He acts as a middleman. He has a reputation for being an honest broker for his clients. He can spot a fake within seconds and apparently won't let a client pay money for something that's not genuine."

"So, how do you know so much about this guy?" I asked.

"It's funny you ran into him," Reno said, ignoring me. "We knew he came into town last week for what was supposed to be a major buy.

Word had it he was going to be a middleman on something special. I was on a team monitoring him when the deal seemed to fall apart."

"What happened?"

"We don't know. Reinhardt's usual MO is to come into town in the morning, conduct business, and then leave that same night. Instead, he just checked into the Scottsdale Princess Resort and has spent a week golfing and lying by the pool. He may have come here for a vacation, but I doubt it. I think something went wrong."

"But what about my guy?" I asked. "Is it possible Reinhardt came into Scottsdale for a buy with Alex?"

"We've had people shadowing Reinhardt since he came into town last week. Our guys saw him meeting with an unknown man at the art gallery at the Tropical Paradise yesterday, possibly even making a minor buy. They're in the process of tracking him down. I'll let them know it was your guy, Alexander."

"Why didn't they stop the buy?"

"The detective judged it wasn't important enough to interfere or call for backup. You can usually tell when something big is going down, and our guys didn't think this was it."

"I guess that's good to know," I said.

"It's doubtful the Iceman flew here for Alexander," Reno said with a shake of his head. "He only deals in amounts above a million dollars. We're usually talking about a suitcase full of merchandise."

"And he hasn't done his deal yet?"

"We know Reinhardt always leaves the country immediately after his buy goes down. Since he's still here, we assume it hasn't happened yet. Perhaps he took on Alex as a spur-of-the-moment thing, or maybe his main deal fell through, and he was looking for something to make the trip worthwhile. Who knows?"

"Do you know anything about Arizona Security Enterprises?" I asked. "They've been following Alex around since yesterday. They look pretty serious but more like thugs than anything else."

"No, but they're not one of ours. I can ask around."

As he talked, I looked at his wrist and saw he was wearing the watch I'd given him the year before.

"You're still wearing the watch?" I asked.

He looked down at it and shrugged. "It's a

good watch."

"Do you think of me when you put it on?"

"I try not to."

There was a moment of uncomfortable silence as Dominic brought over coffee. Reno picked up the small pitcher of cream and poured it into his cup. He stared at it, watching as the cream swirled around.

"So, why'd you really call me?" he asked. "Don't you know any other cops you can pump for information?"

"Let's just say I've had some positive thoughts about you over the last few days."

He arched his eyebrow but, to his credit, didn't say anything.

~~~~

After lunch, I drove up Hayden to Gainey Ranch. I doubted Alex was with Danica, but I had to start looking somewhere.

I cruised into Danica's neighborhood and then did a slow drive-by past her house. Most of the interior shutters were closed, and there wasn't a sign of life in the other windows.

I parked a block away and strolled over to her house. Walking past, it didn't yield any more information than the drive-by. I continued to the end of the block and turned the corner.

Danica lived in a newer subdivision where the backyards butted up to each other and had no alleys. I continued around the block until I was directly behind Danica's house. Unfortunately, the view from this angle didn't show anything new.

I debated the merits of hopping the wall and seeing if she had left a door or window open when my phone rang with Sophie's ringtone.

"Hey, Laura," Sophie said. "Lenny wants you here for a meeting right away. Haul your tush back over here."

"Alright, I'll be over as soon as I can. What's the meeting about?"

"I don't know, but he asked for Gina too. She'll be here in about ten minutes."

"Didn't Lenny even give a hint?"

"No, but he's in with a client now. Somebody called Maximilian. Probably has something to do with him. Speaking of butts, you should see the client. This guy's got an ass as good as Jon Bon Jovi."

"Bon Jovi? Have you been watching his old videos again?"

"They had a Bon Jovi special on VH1 Classic

last night. The man might be getting older, but I'd still have his baby."

"I'll be there in about twenty minutes, but save Butt Man for me. My hormones are running in the red zone right now."

"So, you're interested in men again? It's about time."

"I've always been interested in men, but more so today."

"Really? How bad is it?" Sophie asked.

"Do me a favor. If I proposition Lenny, throw some cold water on me. Or better yet, shoot me."

"Sex with Lenny? *Eeeeyuuww* gross!"

"I was kidding!"

~~~~

When I got to the office, Sophie and Gina were having an animated conversation about Shawn Phillips, a guy Sophie had met at a Christmas party a few weeks before. They'd been having this same conversation since Sophie found out Shawn was married. Of course, she'd found this out on their second date and dated him several times since.

"Hey, Sophie," I said. "I thought you said you'd broken up with that loser?"

"Well, I have now, for good this time. I was telling Gina we had a date set up for tonight. He was going to take me to that rotating restaurant at the top of the downtown Hyatt, the Compass Room."

"What happened?" I asked.

"He called ten minutes ago to tell me he couldn't make it. His wife got tickets to an opera at the Herberger Theater for tonight. She'd supposedly forgotten to tell him about it until today. He's leaving me to sit home alone just so he won't cause a scene at his house."

"But you knew he was married," Gina said in her motherly tone. "I would imagine this sort of thing will happen from time to time."

"Well," Sophie said, waving her finger at Gina. "That does it for me, epic fail. That man is a good-for-nothing lying piece of dog shi..." Sophie's words trailed off, and I looked at her.

She was staring at the door to Lenny's office. Her lips puckered, and I heard her utter a soft *"Ooooohh."*

I saw Gina glance over, then she let out a little moan of pleasure. *"Yummy."*

I turned to see what was causing the commotion.

There, in the doorway to Lenny's office, stood a man. He was looking directly at me through an expensive pair of tinted glasses.

I saw his eyes moving down to my feet and then slowly back up, stopping to linger over my chest before traveling up to my face.

That's just great, I thought to myself. *He's staring at me like I'm a piece of meat. Who is this guy?*

I turned, staring at him like he'd looked at me. He was somewhere in his mid-thirties and tall, well over six feet. He looked lean, solid, and strong.

His hair was short and dark. His face was angular, his lips were full and sensual, and his expression was serious.

His skin was the color of mocha, and he was gorgeous. He reminded me of the former pro-wrestler, now actor, Dwayne "The Rock" Johnson.

He wore a closely-tailored gray suit, black shirt, and metallic silver tie. His black shoes looked Italian and soft as butter. My eyes started back up from the shoes, and I couldn't help noticing his sizeable package.

Wow.

I felt my face flush with heat.

Get a hold of yourself.

I felt my heart start to pound, and my stomach did a flip-flop. I looked back up into the tinted glasses, wanting to see his eyes. I searched his face and then felt his gaze locking onto mine.

The air between us seemed electric as he sized me up. He stared for a second longer and cracked a slight smile. He then slowly walked toward me.

I seemed to enter into a dream world. The music faded into the distance, and the lights seemed to dim. The only thing I could see was this man walking towards me. My libido, awakened by my meeting with Reno, now kicked into high gear.

Who was this guy?

He stopped in front of me and looked down into my eyes. His face was calm, betraying no emotion. In contrast, my face was hot, and my breathing was fast. He paused momentarily, then bent down and pressed his lips against mine.

You bastard! I inwardly shouted. But then my outrage was slowly replaced by a wave of pleasure starting from his lips and washing over my entire body.

My breathing stopped. The whole of my being

was taken over by mounting excitement. My lips took on a will of their own as I kissed him back.

He curled his arm around my waist and gently pulled me closer. All thoughts of who might be watching faded away as I pressed myself against him.

Even through the layers of clothing, I felt his body responding to mine. His tongue worked to seduce me, and I felt helpless. The heat from his body was intense, making me feel something I hadn't experienced with a man in way too long.

I was floating on a cloud of passion. I didn't even try to stop it. I let the sensations take me closer and closer until I knew the moment was at hand.

How could this happen with just a kiss?

Then, as I felt myself starting to let go, he withdrew his lips and loosened his grip around my waist. A feeling close to panic set in.

No, no, please, not yet!

But his lips were already gone. He gently released me, holding my waist without pressing against me. My face contorted, and my body shook with desperation. Tears of frustration came to my eyes.

Oh, damn it!

I looked up into his eyes but was unable to speak. He regarded me for a moment, then reached out and touched my cheek with his fingertips.

"Who are you?" I managed to croak out.

"My name's Max," he said in a voice that was soft but deep and powerful. He again cracked a small smile. "Later, gorgeous."

He then turned and walked out of the office.

I turned to see Gina and Sophie staring at me, mouths open, stunned. Sophie was the first to come out of it.

"Damn, girlfriend, did you just do what I think you did?"

"No," I gasped. "But I was so…damn…close." The truth was, I was still close. My body was still shuddering with the unmet need.

Damn all men!

"Who was that guy?" Gina asked.

"Well, whoever he was, why didn't he come over and do the same thing to me?" Sophie asked. "I'm pretty sure I could also use a Standing-O."

"So why did he *do* that?" I wondered aloud.

Gina started laughing. "Laura, you were

giving him bedroom eyes and staring at him like he was a piece of meat. A guy like that? You didn't give him a choice. He had to do it."

Lenny heard the laughing and stuck his head out of his office.

"Hey, Lenny," Gina called. "Who was that guy?"

"Forget it," Lenny called out. "He's out of your league."

"What do you mean, out of our league?" Sophie asked. "Three fine ladies in their prime like us? He only wishes he was in our league."

"His name's Maximilian," Lenny said, walking up to us. "He runs with the big money out of the DiCenzo resorts."

"What would a DiCenzo goon want with us?" Gina asked.

"He's hardly a goon," Lenny said. "He seems to be more on the finance side of the family rather than the leg-breaking side."

That didn't exactly boost my opinion of him. But to be honest, all I was thinking about was the kiss and how soon I could get another one.

Chapter Five

Gina and I followed Lenny into his office. He waited for us to come in, then closed the door behind us. Gina took one of the seats in front of his desk. I took the other.

"There was a theft last week at the Blue Palms resort," Lenny said. "A wealthy Russian businessman had a piece of luggage stolen. More correctly, it appears his bag was switched with a look-alike in a scam. The original bag contained a substantial amount of cash, several sensitive papers, and some computer disks. They're anxious to retrieve everything and asked us to look into it."

"Computer disks?" Gina asked. "I haven't seen a computer that uses disks in a while. Are we talking floppy or optical?"

"I didn't ask. I'm assuming optical, like a CD, but I suppose it could be either."

"How do they know it was a switch?" Gina asked.

"They didn't know until a few days ago," Lenny said. "The bag was reported stolen to hotel security last Tuesday afternoon. The hotel first thought someone had merely stolen the contents of the bag, but the Russian was insistent the bag itself was switched. It took hotel security several days of reviewing the surveillance videos for them to guess how it was done."

"Now, for some reason, the DiCenzo goon wanted you to take this assignment," Lenny said, pointing at me. "I told him Gina has more experience in this sort of thing, but he still wanted you. I finally told him you were on assignment already and couldn't be the primary, but you could act as a backup investigator to Gina. After that, he seemed satisfied with the overall arrangement."

"Way to go!" Gina said, turning to give me a high five. "Looks like you're getting a reputation out there as a bad-ass."

A big-screen TV with a DVD player was in the corner of Lenny's office. When Lenny hit the button on the remote, the TV flickered on, and a video began to play. I saw the main lobby of the posh Scottsdale Blue Palms resort.

As resorts go, the Blue Palms is one of the best. The year before, *International Resort*

Traveler had listed it as one of the fifty greatest golf resorts in the world. The ownership of the resort by Arizona's most prominent crime family apparently didn't enter into the voting one way or the other.

The black-and-white image on the screen was grainy and jumpy. The DVD was probably a copy of a hotel security tape that had been recorded over too many times.

The camera showed about half of the cavernous main lobby of the resort. Groups of people came and went. Knots of people stood talking, and bellboys walked by with luggage piled high on carts.

"Look at this group here," Lenny said as he pointed to three people standing near a grand piano.

From the angle and distance of the camera, I could only make out three men dressed in dark suits. I couldn't see a lot of detail. I could see a short, slender man standing between two enormous men, apparently bodyguards.

The large man on the right was carrying a suitcase in each hand. The massive man on the left held a bag with one hand while another hung on a strap from his shoulder. The short man in the middle was holding a small black bag.

As we watched, there was some sort of commotion off-camera to the right. The big man on the left pointed, and I could just make out all three heads turning to look, but it was sort of hard to tell with the poor quality of the video.

The man in the middle and the man on the right set down their bags. Everyone seemed to be looking at the disturbance off-camera for ten or fifteen seconds, then the men picked up their bags and walked off to the left, out of camera range. The scene lasted for maybe ten seconds longer, and then it ended.

"Did you see anything unusual?" Lenny asked.

"No," I said. Lenny looked at Gina, but she only shook her head.

"I didn't see it the first time either. The DiCenzo goon had to show me," Lenny said. "I'll slow it down. Look closely at the black gym bag the little guy in the middle is holding."

Lenny went frame by frame. As the big man on the left pointed to the commotion, the other two put down their bags. I noticed a new man walk behind the group of three men.

He didn't seem connected to the group, and I'd ignored him until now. He was medium height and had a medium build, meaning he could have been anybody. He was also carrying a small black bag.

As he passed behind the group of three men, the new man ducked down slightly and then went on. I looked at the position of the small black bag the man in the middle had set on the ground. It moved as the new man walked by. It wasn't much, but it was a definite move.

"It looks like the new guy switched his bag with the bag on the floor," I said.

"That's what security at the Blue Palms thinks as well," Lenny said. "They think the bag was switched as part of a scam last Tuesday, and they want it back."

"Why don't they go to the police or look for it themselves?" I asked. "They have plenty of people at their disposal."

"The DiCenzos won't go to the police on general principle," Lenny said. "And from what Maximilian said, they've been looking for it with their people with no luck. They need outside help."

"Okay," Gina said, "I'll get on it."

"Call me if you need help," I said.

~~~~

I left the office around four-thirty. Before leaving, I downloaded everything I had on Alex to

Sophie. I love how she can turn my rambling story into a crisp report for Lenny.

I went home to feed Marlowe. As he ate, I told him everything that had happened during the day.

I told him I was worried about Alex and whatever he'd gotten mixed up in. But I don't think Marlowe heard much of what I said over the noise of his chewing.

Next, it was back out to my Honda to try and pick up Alexander's trail again. The closest and first on the list was Jeannie's Cabaret. Alex's car wasn't in the lot, and the bartender said Danica Taylor wasn't working tonight.

Next was Alex's apartment. Same story, no lights, no black Jaguar, and no Alex. I cruised the valet lots of the downtown clubs without success. I drove back up to Danica's neighborhood at Gainey Ranch at about ten o'clock.

Bingo.

The Jaguar was sitting in Danica's driveway. The lights were on, and I saw movement inside the house.

I parked on the street, two doors down from her house. I walked up the driveway and rang the doorbell. After maybe a minute, I heard footsteps approach. The peephole went dark as someone looked through it.

A moment later, the door opened to the length of a thick security chain. Danica was visible in the shadows, dressed in a red silk robe belted at the waist.

"I'm Laura Black," I said through the opening. "I'm an investigator looking into Alexander's activities at his grandmother's request. I hadn't planned on talking to him, but something's come up, and I need to speak to him."

She stared at me for a moment with a puzzled look. Without a word, she turned and closed the door.

I wasn't sure what to make of that. I stood there, not knowing if I should ring again or not. I heard voices at the back of the house, but I couldn't understand what they were saying.

The voices grew louder as they came closer to the front. The door opened again, but this time it was Alex behind the chain, dressed only in navy-blue silk pajama pants.

"My grandmother sent you to spy on me?" Alex asked. The tone of his voice was half anger, half disbelief.

"She's worried about you," I said. "And to be honest, I'm starting to get worried too. I have some information you may be interested in. I'd like to come in so we can talk about it."

From the look on his face, I didn't know if he was going to open the door or slam it in my face. Finally, he slid off the chain and opened the door.

The inside of Danica's house was as beautiful as the outside. In the typical Scottsdale southwestern style, the ceilings were high, and the rooms were open with wide archways.

The walls were off-white, and the windows were fitted with white plantation shutters. Bright original oil paintings and tropical plants provided splashes of color.

A shorthaired black cat was lying on a white leather loveseat. He looked at me with bright gold eyes while his tail flicked from side to side. An old Joni Mitchell song was playing quietly in the background.

Alex led me out to the backyard. The landscaping here was as lovely as the front, done up with queen palms, orange trees, and flowering lantana, all surrounding a lagoon-style swimming pool. There was a noisy little waterfall and a fiber optic lighting system that changed the color of the water every few seconds.

Alex motioned me poolside to a white picnic table. He sat on one side while I sat on the other.

Next to the table was a brass fire pit with a crackling fire.

Danica paced back and forth on the far corner of the patio, a half-empty drink in her hand. As we sat down, she took a few steps closer. She hovered and paced near the fire, not sitting down but still within easy listening distance.

There was a moment of uncomfortable silence as we each waited for the other to speak.

"We haven't been introduced," I said. "I'm Laura Black. Yes, I've been following you at the request of your grandmother. After you quit your job, she became worried. It's also been noticed you've been spending some serious money. I've been asked to look into things to make sure everything is okay."

"Well," Alex snapped. "Now that you've spent your time spying on me, what's your assessment? Is everything okay? Do my activities measure up?"

"Look, I usually don't talk to the people I'm investigating. It's not very professional. It's none of my business what you do with your life. But I know you no longer have a visible source of income. I know you're spending a lot of money. I also know you've been fencing things all over town with some pretty nasty people."

Alex cringed when I mentioned the fencing. Danica stopped pacing. Her intense gaze shifted between Alex and me.

"So, I have money," Alex said, now more boisterous than angry. "What's the big deal? Hell, my family has more money than most developing countries. Okay, so I've spent some of it recently, and sure I quit my job. Who cares? I'm no longer required by the state to be employed. You do know I just got off parole, don't you?"

"Yes," I said. "And to be honest, I could care less about your money or how you got it."

Alex stopped and looked at me. I could tell my remark puzzled him. "So, why are you here?"

"Do you know you're being followed? Not only by me but by a couple of seriously mean guys."

"Followed?" Alex asked. A wave of shock and fear passed over his face, quickly replaced by a forced look of casual unconcern.

"Yes, they picked you up outside the Tropical Paradise yesterday afternoon after you fenced whatever it was at the art gallery there. The only reason they aren't parked across the street right now is because of that move you pulled on the highway today. It put them out of commission, temporarily. That makes me think you knew you were being followed. And I say 'temporarily' because I saw how pissed they were after they crashed. They'll be back. I only knew you'd be here because I've been following you since Monday."

While we were talking, Danica had been inching closer to the table. When she heard about the tail, she came over and slid into the seat next to Alex. She was staring at me, her eyes wide.

"There're men following Alex?" she asked. Genuine worry and panic crept into her voice. She then turned to him. "What's she talking about?"

I expected some sort of reply from him, but instead, something weird happened. After I told Alex about the tail, a change seemed to come over him. His head cocked slightly to the side, and a knowing little smirk appeared.

"Well, I'll tell you what, Laura Black, if that's even your real name," he said smoothly. "I'm not worried about anybody following me. I'm sure you're either mistaken, or more likely, my grandmother has hired two, or maybe even three, firms to check up on me independently. It really wouldn't surprise me."

As soon as he spoke, it hit me -- he had just gone into car-salesman mode. Maybe that was his way of handling stress. All he needed was a lime-green plaid jacket, and the transformation would have been complete.

"I don't think you understand the situation," I said. "These guys could have picked you up at any time. They're following you to see where you go and what you're doing. They've also seen the two of you together. It's only a matter of time before they'll come over here. They might want more than a friendly chat when they find you."

"No," he said. "I think you're the one who doesn't understand the situation. You don't know my grandmother. Her style would be to have more than one group looking in on me. She's done it before, mainly out of guilt over what she's done to me over the past few years. So sure, keep following me if you need to, if it's your job. But I can assure you, I can look after myself and my girlfriend."

As he was assuring me, he was patting Danica on her leg. She was giving him a look of frank disbelief, maybe mixed in with a bit of anger.

I wanted to ask about the guys tailing him. Did he know who they were? What did he have that someone else would want? Instead, Alex stood, came around the table, and firmly took me by the arm.

"I think you should leave now," he said.

Danica started to protest. She obviously wanted to know more about what was happening, but Alex ushered me through the house and out to the front door.

As a rule, I don't let anybody manhandle me. I was tempted to give him a quick kick to the kneecap.

Unfortunately, I didn't think it would be a good idea to get into a fight with the guy I was supposed to be secretly watching from a distance. Lenny tended to be fussy on that point.

When we reached the front door, he released my arm. I turned and faced him.

"Look," I said. "You could be in real trouble here. These guys look professional, plus you've pissed them off. I'd seriously consider going to the police. They could pick them up and at least find out what they're up to."

"No," he said, his salesman's voice was back. "That won't be necessary. You can tell my grandmother you've done your duty. Your conscience is now clear. I trust you won't feel the need to bother either myself or my girlfriend ever again." He said it more as a statement rather than as a question.

He opened the door, and I again found myself on the front porch. The door slammed shut behind me.

Well, damn.

~~~~

I woke up early and drove over to Alex's apartment the following day. Lenny expected me to follow the guy around, which I intended to do.

At least Alex would know he was being tailed. I hoped it would prevent him from doing anything stupid.

Hope is a beautiful thing. It doesn't cost anything and makes you feel good all over.

Problem number one – Alex wasn't there. Problem number two – the men who'd been following him weren't there either.

I'd expected the same two guys in another car. Of course, if the men were still hurt from the crash, then maybe two new guys would be tailing Alex today.

There wasn't anybody in the parking lot or outside on the street. Well, I reasoned with myself, Alex was probably still over at Danica's, and the men were driving around looking for him.

Hope sprang back to life as I drove to Gainey Ranch and Danica's house. But then hope was again dashed when Alex's Jaguar was again a no-show.

~~~~

I drove by Meyer's Jewelry without seeing anything interesting. I then headed to South Scottsdale and Jeannie's Cabaret. The bouncer didn't know Danica's schedule, but he let me in without paying with the promise that I wouldn't stay more than a few minutes.

Talking to the bartender, I found out Danica was scheduled to work from five to midnight. If I couldn't find Alex before five, there was a good chance he'd come here to watch Danica dance or meet with her after she got off.

Looks like I'd be back.

~~~~

I went out to my car and gave Sophie a call at the office. I was surprised when Lenny answered.

"Hey, boss. It's me. Is Sophie in?"

"If Sophie was here, would I be answering the phone? She went over to Apache Junction to pick up some exhibits. She'll be back in an hour or two, assuming she doesn't get distracted along the way."

Next, I called Sophie on her mobile.

"Hey, Sophie, have you had lunch yet?"

"No," she said. "And I'm about to starve to death. You know, I was looking at myself in the mirror last night. My ass looked so big I felt like throwing up. I decided I was going to start a fasting diet."

"Really? How's that working out?"

"Well, I'd been thinking about fasting until my ass went down to about a size four. But since I've been fasting since last night, I'm starting to get one of those hungry headaches. So now I'm thinking, screw the fasting. I'll start the diet again tomorrow. I'm thinking about lunch at the lake. Do you want to come along? I'd love the company."

"Great idea," I said. "I could use a lunch at the lake. When'll you be there?"

"I'm about to leave A.J., so I'll arrive in about twenty-five minutes. If you leave now, we'll get there about the same time."

"I'll see you there!"

~~~~

Saguaro Lake is located in the Superstition Mountains, southeast of Scottsdale. It's the closest of four huge reservoirs along the Salt River that hold irrigation and drinking water for the Phoenix area.

On a hill on the west end is Lakeside Restaurant, overlooking the marina and the high cliffs on the eastern shore. During the afternoon, it's a good place to day-drink and watch the boats on the lake. In the evening, it's a great place to drink and watch the sun go down.

~~~~

I drove to the lake and parked in the main marina lot. I walked up the hill to the restaurant, where the hostess led me out to the patio. I saw Sophie had beaten me there and was already working on a margarita. She looked up and waved me over.

It was a beautiful day, and several boats and jet skis were on the lake. Since this was January and the temperature might drop below seventy degrees, the management had thoughtfully scattered several industrial-sized heaters throughout the seating area.

"Hey, Laura," Sophie said as I sat. She looked at me for a moment. "Why so glum today?"

"Does it show? I lost Alex."

"Where'd you lose him?"

"Actually, I never had him today."

"So, when was the last time you did have him?"

"Last night. I found him at Danica's house. I talked to him and warned him about the guys who were following him."

The waiter came over. He was a quiet guy in his mid-twenties. He had a pouting lower lip, small square glasses, and brown hair that hung into his eyes. He sort of looked like a young Johnny Depp.

I ordered a French dip with fries and a margarita. Sophie ordered the lobster bisque, the fried mushroom appetizers, the Malibu chicken sandwich, and another margarita. The waiter turned and walked back to the kitchen.

As he walked away from us, I noticed that even though he seemed a bit sulky, he did have a nice butt. From the way Sophie's eyes were following him, she'd seen it too.

"You talked to Alex?" she asked, raising her eyebrows. "Isn't that breaking the official private investigator rules?"

"Well, yeah, sorta, but I think the guy's in trouble. I can't stand by and see somebody getting hurt. Somebody needed to convince him he could be in real danger."

"Did he listen?"

"No, I didn't get through to him at all."

"What about his blonde girlfriend, Danica? At the club the other night, she looked like a bimbo.

What's she really like? Dumb as a box of hammers?"

"At first, I thought she'd probably be some sort of airhead. I didn't get much of a chance to know her, but she seemed alright. Honestly, she seems more in touch with what's going on than Alex. Oh, you should see her house. I'd love to get a chance to go through her closets. I think strippers make way more than we do."

"What time did you leave her house?" Sophie asked.

"It was before eleven. I would have liked to stay longer, but Alex wasn't in a talkative mood. I figured he'd either spend the night at her house or do her and go home. I was back over at Alex's apartment by seven-thirty this morning, but he was already gone."

~~~~

The waiter with the nice tush brought out our lunches. Sophie and I ate and chatted for another half-hour. It was a beautiful day, and I could have easily spent the afternoon there.

The waiter brought the bill and then took an order at another table. As he walked away, Sophie followed him with her eyes. We both put down some money, and I started gathering my things, but Sophie just sat there.

"Um, you go ahead," she said. "I'll be along in a few minutes."

I knew the tone in her voice. I also saw the light pink blush that had started on her face. The one she gets when she mixes alcohol and men.

"The waiter? You want the waiter?" I asked. "You're serious? He's not even your type."

"Well, maybe, but did you see his butt? After seeing Jon Bon Jovi on TV and that guy who kissed you yesterday, all I've been thinking about are butts and how much I love them. It'll be worth buying him a dinner to get a peek at it."

"Seriously?"

"I wonder what his butt feels like. It looks firm. I bet he works out a lot. I wonder if he's into having his naked butt spanked. I hope it's not hairy. You know I like a smooth ass, like a baby's."

"Don't you think you should know more about him before you start spanking him?"

"Like what?"

"Like, is he a nice person? Does he have any ambition? Does he even like women?"

"Hey, I'm not going to marry the guy. Besides, I know everything I need to know about him just by watching him walk back and forth in front of our table."

"You know, Sophie, most women get more conservative as they get older. You're getting looser."

"I know, and it's killing me. I'm horny all the time. What's it going to be like when I reach my sexual peak? According to Cosmo, I've still got about ten years to go. How many men a week will I need when I'm at my sexual peak?"

~~~~

I left Sophie, who'd already started a conversation with the waiter and went down to my car. I got in and took off down the two-lane highway that winds its way through the mountains and eventually heads back to Scottsdale.

I'd gone about half a mile when a black Mercedes sedan pulled in tight behind me. The car stayed on my bumper for a quarter of a mile before pulling up beside me.

Rather than pass me, the passenger side window lowered. There were two men in the car. Both were big middle-aged white guys in dark suits. Both had military haircuts and full mustaches. The passenger had a semi-automatic pistol and pointed it at me while waving for me to pull over.

Like that's going to happen.

I hit the gas and started to pull forward. The Mercedes easily stayed with me.

A car suddenly crested a hill in the oncoming lane. The Mercedes stomped on its brakes and darted behind me to avoid a head-on collision. I pushed the Honda up to seventy, but after a moment, the Mercedes smoothly pulled next to me again.

The passenger pointed his gun out the window and shouted something at me while waving his hand. The driver eased his car against mine and started to force me off the road.

I had the steering wheel in a death grip, trying to keep control. Metal ground against metal as the Mercedes shoved my car onto the dirt shoulder.

I'd just started to slow down when we came to a dirt road that branched off the highway and wound down into a narrow gully. The Mercedes pushed me hard, forcing me onto the side road.

I managed to keep the Honda straight for a couple of seconds, but I was going too fast to maintain control. The road turned to the right, and the Honda skidded sideways. I hit the brakes, and the world spun in circles.

When it stopped, I was facing back toward the

main highway, and the Mercedes was coming to a stop thirty yards ahead of me. Through the cloud of dust, I saw I'd gone about sixty or seventy yards down the dirt road and was completely out of view of the highway.

Crap.

I locked my doors and pulled out my Baby Glock. My heart pounded as I peered over the dashboard in the direction of the Mercedes.

The two men were now standing behind their open doors, guns drawn. They started shouting at each other in what sounded like Russian.

The driver motioned to the passenger, who came out from behind his door. He walked toward my car, the gun held tightly in his hand.

I lowered the window enough to stick my Glock out. I aimed as best as I could and fired off a shot. The front windshield of the Mercedes exploded.

Both men hit the deck. There was more shouting and then an argument as the men slithered back to their car. I guess the idea of an uppity American woman with a gun didn't fit into their plans.

As I watched them arguing, I became convinced these were the two Russian bodyguards

I'd seen on the hotel security video earlier in Lenny's office. They were the same size, and who else would be shouting in Russian? My only question was, what did they want with me?

They seemed to come up with a new plan because after a moment, the shouting stopped. The driver reached into the car and released the parking brake.

The Mercedes began slowly rolling down the hill, the men using the open doors as shields. They had gone about twenty yards and were almost to my car when the driver set the brake to stop their sedan.

"Miss Black," the driver shouted. "Please do not shoot us until you hear what we have to say."

He spoke in a thick Russian accent. He sounded like Boris Badenov from the old *Rocky and Bullwinkle* show. "We will not harm you. We only wish to discuss certain matters that are of interest to both of us."

"Sure, what do you want to talk about?" I shouted back.

"Please, Miss Black. We are standing in the middle of the American Sonoran Desert. Why don't we go to our hotel suite back in Scottsdale? We can be much more comfortable there."

"I like the desert," I said. "It's a great place for a discussion."

The Russians quietly talked for a moment amongst themselves.

"As you wish," Boris said. "We merely wish to know the location of a small black bag. We have reason to believe you know where it is."

"I don't know what you're talking about," I shouted back.

"Please, Miss Black, we can resolve this matter without the use of violence. All we ask is you come with us now and show us the location of the bag."

"I don't know where it is. It seems like you're the ones who lost it. Why don't you find it?"

"You may know certain friends of ours who are helping us to recover our property," Boris said. "We know they have hired the lawyer, Leonard Shapiro, to help them locate it."

"Okay, what about it?" I asked.

"It seems strange that our friends would need to hire a lawyer to find what was stolen from us, no? We also have information they asked that you lead the investigation into the recovery of our bag. We know the methods of our friends. They would not have asked for you specifically unless you already had some association with our property, even if you did not recognize the importance of what you knew."

"If you're talking about the DiCenzos, you can forget it. I'm not even on that assignment. Lenny gave it to someone else. You got your facts wrong on this one."

"I think not. You will now return to Scottsdale with us, and we will question you further."

The passenger aimed his gun at me. He was very tall and very broad. If the driver was a Boris, this guy was an Ivan.

"I will inform you that we are under strictest orders not to kill you," Boris said. "But we have been granted permission to freely torture and abuse you if you do not voluntarily cooperate. If you attempt to shoot us or do not immediately come into our vehicle, we will repeatedly shoot you in non-fatal areas of your body. We will then take you with us and question you at our leisure until you tell us what we wish to know. You will decide, *now!*"

Boris joined Ivan in sighting his gun on me as I ducked behind the dash. I then heard the slam of car doors and the sound of shoes walking on gravel.

I stuck my head up enough to see both of them

slowly walking toward my car, their guns still trained on me. I pulled my head back down and held my breath as the Russian's footsteps grew louder.

Crap. I hate it when this happens.

The footsteps approached the front of my car, then there was a pause. Boris and Ivan mumbled to each other in Russian.

The low talking continued for some time as they worked out their strategy. Then the footsteps started up again.

The crunching of shoes on gravel moved closer until I could tell both men were on either side of my car. I could feel them looking at me through the car windows. I tightened the grip on my gun and got ready to shoot the first one who tried to get at me.

Suddenly, there was the loud and rapid *thump-thump-thump* sound of gunfire and bullets hitting metal. I expected to feel my car buckle as the bullets tore through it.

But, to my surprise, my car didn't move. Instead, it sounded like the Mercedes was taking the hits. As the gunfire continued, I stuck my head up in time to see a line of holes appear in the side of the Mercedes.

Boris and Ivan ran to the far side of their car, firing up the hill as they ran. Their rear window shattered, then the side windows. The Russians reached their vehicle, and each fired two or three more shots in the general direction of where the bullets had come from.

There was a pause, then another *thump-thump-thump* as a new line of holes streaked from the trunk of the Mercedes to the front fender, then to the dirt between our cars, and then to my car! I felt my vehicle shudder as a bullet slammed through what I imagined was the side of my trunk.

"Damn it," I shouted to whoever was shooting. "That's *my* car!"

Screaming at each other, both Russians fired in the direction where the shots came from. They scrambled back into their car and slammed the doors.

Gravel flew as they whipped the big Mercedes around and sped back to the highway. The dust cleared, and it became eerily quiet.

Damn, that was freaky.

I stayed low for about five minutes until I was pretty sure nobody else wanted to shoot me. I stuck my head up and looked around to make sure no one else was in sight. I then got out of my car and looked at the damage.

The paint on the driver's side door and the front fender was scraped. Streaks of black color were now smashed in with the original brown.

Part of the front fender was crumpled, but it still looked drivable. My side mirror had broken off. It dangled against the door, held on only by a cable. And now, I had a bullet hole in my trunk.

Great, how will I explain a bullet hole to my insurance agent?

~~~~

I drove back to the office. It was no surprise that Sophie had beaten me there and was filing a stack of papers. She took one look at me, and her eyes opened wide.

"Yikes! What happened to you?"

"I'm having a shitty day," I said.

"Again? What happened this time?"

"Two Russians forced my car off the road. They were going to kidnap me or shoot me first, then kidnap me."

"You're serious? Real Russians? I've never seen a real Russian. So, what happened? How'd you get away?"

"Somebody started shooting at them. They got scared and left."

"Do you know who the Russians were?"

"I think they're the ones from the Blue Palms that Gina's looking for."

"No shit? Do you know who shot at them?"

"No, but I definitely owe someone dinner."

"Sounds like you owe someone sloppy doggy sex. Are you going to call the police this time?"

"Maybe, but not until I find out more about what's going on. Every time I bring the police in, things get muddled."

"How bad's your car?"

I shrugged my shoulders. "Some scraped paint, a crumpled fender, a broken mirror, and a bullet hole."

"Damn. I'm glad we drove separately."

Chapter Six

I still didn't know where Alex was or where else to look, so I decided to spend the afternoon getting some more background information on him. I was hoping I could pick up some clues about what was going on.

I left the office and headed south to the Scottsdale Motor Mile, a group of a dozen car dealerships, mostly high-end. Scottsdale Desert Audi was nestled between the Ferrari and the Lexus dealerships.

I pulled into a visitor's space and was met by a smiling man in a light blue sports coat. "Hi," he said, holding out his hand. "My name's Bob. Let me know if I can answer any questions."

He bent down and looked at my car, grimacing as he ran his finger along the scraped paint. He then examined the crumpled fender.

He wiggled the broken mirror, which was still only hanging on by the cable. He walked to the trunk, stuck his finger in the bullet hole, then turned to me with a big, friendly grin.

"Good thing you live in Arizona, and it's so dry. Bullet holes can rust out pretty quickly. If you lived back east, the rust would rot out the entire side of your fender in a year or two. Maybe you'd like to test drive an Audi A6? They're the greatest."

"Not today," I said. "I'm just looking for William Martin."

"Okay, sure," Bob said, not missing a beat. "He's probably in his office. There's a hallway in the back of the showroom. His office is the big one, second door to the right."

~~~~

I found William Martin's office and knocked on his open door. William was sitting behind an enormous desk. When he saw me, he stood and held out a giant hand.

He must have been six two or three and about three hundred pounds. He had a round face, a full mustache, and a thin comb-over of reddish hair, which only partially covered a large bald patch on the top of his round head.

"I'm William Martin," he said. "What can I do for you today?"

"I'm Laura Black," I said while shaking his

hand. "I called yesterday."

"Sure," he said. "You're interested in Alex Sternwood. You're working for his grandmother, if I recall."

"She hasn't heard from him since he quit. She's really worried about him."

"Well, I'd like to help, but I don't have a firm grasp on why Alex left. He was one of our best sales associates."

"He didn't give you any indication he was unhappy or was thinking about leaving?"

"None at all. I was as surprised as anyone when he quit."

"Is there anyone here who was close to him? Maybe they'd know more about this?"

He thought for a moment. "As far as I know, the only person he was close to was Joan. She's working today. Perhaps you'd like to talk to her?"

"Sounds great," I said. "Where can I find her?"

"She's working the pre-owned lot. She has on a bright yellow coat; you can't miss her."

"Thanks," I said. I appreciate your help." I handed him a card. "Would you mind giving me a call if you think of anything else?"

He took the card, then made a "gun" with his

thumb and first finger. His thumb let loose with a couple of rounds; the *gunman's salute*. I took this as his way of telling me he would.

~~~~

I walked through the showroom and out to the lot. I spotted the woman I took to be Joan, her yellow coat shouting her location like a neon billboard.

She was medium height and a little older than me, with short blonde hair that pleasantly framed her face. She had a clipboard in her hand and was writing down numbers from a sticker in the window of a small red sports car.

As I got closer, she broke into a smile and walked toward me, her hand extended.

"Hi," she said, "I'm Joan. I hope you're in the mood to buy a car. We just got this little red Miata in today, and I'm itching to test drive it with somebody."

She seemed likable enough and had a great smile. "Sorry," I said, "I love Miatas, but I'm not buying today. I'd like to talk to you about Alexander Sternwood."

"Sure," she said, her smile fading. "But I'm afraid Alex doesn't work here anymore. He quit last week. Didn't even tell anybody goodbye. He just called in and said he quit."

"Do you have any idea why he'd resign like that?"

"None at all," she said. "But, I've been thinking, since his family has money, perhaps he got his inheritance?"

"This may seem like a strange question," I said, "but do you know if he had something else going on the side? Another job or business? Something that would give him a better income than he could get here?"

"Like what?" Joan asked.

"Could be anything," I said, slowly shaking my head. "I'm an investigator at a law firm here in Scottsdale. Alex's grandmother asked us to look into what was going on. It's not reasonable for somebody to quit a good job unless they have another source of income."

She paused for a moment, thinking. "I don't think Alex is involved in anything outside the dealership. Well, other than his girlfriend, Danica. He talked about her all the time."

"Do you know how they got together?"

"Sure, they met right over there," she said, pointing to the far side of the lot.

"Danica came in last year looking for a car. I

think she felt an attraction to him from the start. Alex ended up selling her a low-mileage Porsche 911 convertible. They started going out right after that, and they've been together ever since. They never fight, and he seems completely loyal to her."

"Do you know if he ever dated anyone who worked here? Maybe he had another close friend he would have confided in?"

"No," she said. "He never went out with any of us after work for drinks or anything like that. He pretty much kept to himself."

"Alex's parole ended a month ago. Perhaps that had something to do with his quitting?"

"Sorry," she said, "I wish I could help, but Alex and I aren't as close as we were."

"Thanks, I appreciate your help," I said, handing her a card. "If you can think of anything else, feel free to give me a call."

"Sure," she said. "When you catch up with Alex, tell him to give me a call sometime."

"Will do," I said. With that, I walked back to my car and took off.

~~~~

I drove to my apartment building and took the elevator to my floor. Unlocking my door, I went in and looked for Marlowe. I searched the apartment without any luck, then went out into the hall and knocked on Grandma Peckham's door.

She answered, wearing a purple jogging suit with white running shoes. Her silver-gray hair was tightly curled, and today her cheeks were bright pink. In her hand was a Diet Pepsi.

"Why, Laura," Grandma said. "I haven't gotten a chance to talk to you for days." She rested her fingertips against my arm. "Come in. We need to catch up."

I walked in and saw Marlowe sprawled across the afghan on his chair. Two years before, Grandma had crocheted the cat-sized afghan and designated a chair for him to sleep on. As I came in, Marlowe turned his head toward me and yawned.

I was sort of expecting he'd jump down and rub against my leg or sit at my feet and meow to be picked up. After all, he was my roommate and my friend.

Instead, he closed his eyes and laid his head on the afghan. Within seconds, he was asleep.

Some friend.

Grandma went to the refrigerator. She came back holding a fresh Diet Pepsi and handed it to me.

As far as I know, it's the only thing Grandma Peckham drinks. Before I met her, I'd never had a Diet Pepsi, but now it's about the only soda I drink.

Grandma Peckham adds a little Appleton Rum to her Diet Pepsi when she's feeling frisky. She calls her drinks Jamaican Jerks.

Grandma starts talking with one Jerk in her, and you can't get a word in. After two Jerks, Grandma stops talking coherently and mumbles while staring glassy-eyed into space. But after three Jerks, Grandma leans over in her chair and falls asleep.

We sat on the sofa next to Marlowe and his cat chair. "So, what did I miss?" Grandma asked. "Has everything been alright the past week?"

"I got shot at and almost kidnapped this morning by Russians. It sort of trashed my car, but I ended up being okay."

"You seem to get shot at a lot. Have you thought about getting a different job?"

"All the time."

"I'm sorry to hear about your car. It seems like after you pay off a vehicle, the first thing that happens is you get into an accident, or someone shoots at it."

"It's always something," I agreed.

"I'm glad to hear you're okay. To tell the truth, I've been a little worried about you. I'm somewhat psychic, as you know, and I've been having some troubling visions about you."

"What kind of visions?" I asked.

"So far, there hasn't been anything specific, mostly visions of you surrounded by a threatening masculine aura."

"Being surrounded by anything masculine doesn't sound so bad right now," I said, winking at Grandma.

"Oh, I know you think I'm nuts, but you also know my visions usually come true. Tell me you'll stay away from strange men for a few days. You haven't started seeing anyone new, have you?"

"I keep trying, but no luck so far."

"Well, maybe it's just as well," Grandma said. "It's been nice and quiet over at your place the past year, not like when you were dating that policeman. Land sakes alive, when you were with him, you made *a lot* of noise."

"Really? I did?"

"Oh, yes," Grandma said with a nod. "The first

night you had him over, I thought he was slapping you around and hurting you. I almost called the cops on him. But when I saw the two of you in the hall the next morning, you both seemed happy."

"I remember that day," I said. "And I *was* happy."

"That's what I thought as well. So, I figured maybe he was slapping you around, but you liked it. I try not to judge."

"No, he was very gentle."

"Yes, I eventually figured out the truth. After the first few nights, I learned you were simply a moaner and a screamer, so I let it go."

I felt my face flush with heat.

God, how embarrassing.

"I haven't been close with anyone lately," I said. "But, I did have some scotch the other day that was almost as good as sex."

"Really? What was it called?"

"I'd never heard of it before. It was called Balvenie Cask Number something, I don't exactly remember."

"Hmm, as good as sex?" Grandma asked. "Maybe I ought to learn to drink the stuff. It's been years since I've been with a man. The last time I tried was two years ago with Walter

Dobson from the drugstore. He worked in the pharmacy, and I'd known him for years."

"Really? What happened?"

"We went over to his house one afternoon and tried to do it, but he couldn't get his penis to work. Figure that, and Walter wasn't even seventy then."

I was starting to get disturbing visions of Grandma and Walter.

"I tried every trick I knew to make it work. I even did the *Velvet Hummingbird* thing I'd read about in Cosmopolitan magazine. That one was listed as one of the top-five sex moves that men crave. It had been guaranteed to drive any man to ecstasy or, at the very least, give him a good stiffy, but it was nothing doing. You'd think working in a pharmacy, he could take something to fix that."

Grandma sighed and looked a little melancholy.

"My granddaughter Meghan says I should get a vibrator, then I wouldn't ever want a man again. She said after her divorce, she got a vibrator, and now she doesn't even think about dating men anymore."

"Really?"

"Oh yes. She said she wished she'd found out about vibrators before she got married. She said if she had a chance to do it all again, she'd get a vibrator and adopt children from Africa rather than get married and have children the normal way."

As Grandma was talking, I got up and made my way over to the cat chair. I'd also read about the *Velvet Hummingbird,* and the thought of Grandma Peckham doing that to Walter Dobson from the drugstore was giving me the heebie-jeebies.

I picked Marlowe up and set him against my shoulder. He yawned but otherwise didn't protest. I thanked Grandma Peckham for the Diet Pepsi and returned next door to my apartment.

~~~~

I arrived back at Jeannie's Cabaret at about eight o'clock that night. I drove around the parking lot looking for Alex's car without success. The parking lot was packed, and I was forced to park in one of the few remaining spots near the back.

As I walked to the front, I noticed a red velvet rope had been stretched across the entrance. A small line of men stood behind the rope, all waiting to be let in.

I walked to the back of the line when the doorman called me over. He was the same one who I'd talked to earlier in the day.

"After six o'clock and on weekends, ladies don't pay a cover. They go right in," he said, opening the rope and waving me in.

As I entered the cabaret, I could see why they encouraged women patrons at night. The room was filled with men, mostly in small groups, but there were also many singles.

Most of the singles had a look of quiet desperation and confusion. It was as though they couldn't understand why giving a naked woman ten or twenty dollars didn't make her hop off the stage and follow them home for a night of passion.

I'm so glad I'm not a man.

I scanned the room, looking for Alex or Danica. Instead, I saw Annie, the girl I'd met the last time I was here. She was seated with another woman at a table near the main stage.

I started winding my way toward them. About halfway to their table, I caught Annie's eye. She smiled and waved me over to their table.

The other woman was several years older than Annie, somewhere in her late forties. She looked very stylish in a low-cut blue cocktail dress.

Her long auburn hair hung down her back, while subtle makeup emphasized her flawless complexion. She had the appearance of a woman who has both a personal trainer and a favorite plastic surgeon.

The drink in front of her appeared to be the remains of a gin and tonic. Annie's glass of white wine was still half full.

"Hi, Annie," I said, talking loudly to be heard over the pounding music. "Has Danica Taylor been out yet?"

"You just missed her," Annie said as she waved me to a chair next to the woman. "She got off the stage about five minutes ago. But don't worry, I'm sure she'll be back on stage again tonight. She seems to be very popular."

"I need to talk to her," I said. "Do you know how long it takes for the women to come out after dancing?"

"It seems like they come out almost right away. It looks like they get good tips from the guys who weren't able to make it over to the stage."

Annie then seemed to remember the other woman at the table. "Oh, sorry," she said. "I'm being so rude. Jackie, this is Laura; Laura, this is Jackie."

I reached over to shake Jackie's hand. "You must be helping Annie find a man," I said.

"Oh, you know about her problems around men?" Jackie asked, her face brightening.

"I met Jackie the same day I met you," Annie said. "We were both over at the Casablanca Lounge, and I told her about my problem around guys. She said picking up a guy isn't a big deal. She does it all the time. She said she'd even come back over here where the guys are already horny and help me pick one out."

"I'm not sure why Annie can't talk to men," Jackie said. "For some reason, she gets tongue-tied. I've been dating a lot since my divorce, mostly younger guys. I think we can find her a man, especially in a place like this."

"I hope so," Annie said, smiling. "I have a lot of needs, if you know what I mean. And for some things, you need to have a man. It's driving me crazy."

"Why date younger guys?" I asked Jackie. "Why not guys closer to your age?"

"I was married for a long time to a man who treated me like shit. He thought because he made a lot of money, he could treat me like a slave. A few years ago, he started having these mood swings that would last for weeks at a time."

"That sounds terrible," I said.

"Oh, it was a nightmare. I divorced him a year ago, and I'll be damned if I ever marry anybody else. I started out dating guys my age, but lately, I've been dating younger guys, and it's been great."

"Okay," I said. "I get they're young and have nice bodies. But then, isn't it just sex?"

"Yes, and that's the beauty of it." She saw my puzzled look and went on.

"There're few things clingier than a fifty-year-old divorced guy. It's impossible to be with a guy like that for more than about three dates before he wants to introduce you to his kids."

"Did that happen a lot?"

"Almost every time," she laughed. "But I have all the money I'll ever need, so I don't need a man to provide anything for me. I simply want to find a guy, use him a few times, then toss him away. I get what I want, and they always seem to enjoy themselves."

"Seems reasonable to me," I said.

"Annie told me about this place, and I thought,

why not," Jackie said. "I usually hit the nightclubs, along with some friends of mine, but I thought it might be easier for Annie to go into a room full of extremely aroused men. This way, there won't be a lot of talking involved."

"That seems like a plan," I said.

"We'll pick up a couple of men and use them tonight. If they're good, maybe we'll see them again. If not, we'll grab a couple of new ones for tomorrow. I know there's a man for Annie in here somewhere."

Jackie looked out over the crowd and nodded in the direction of two guys at a table. They were both in their late twenties and were dressed well.

"Those two, for instance," she said. "I've been watching them, and they seem like they'll be respectful and compliant."

"I'm a little jealous," I said, laughing. "Good luck."

Jackie looked over at Annie. "Are you ready?"

Annie looked a little nervous but nodded. Jackie got up and led Annie to the table, where the two men were watching the girls on stage. Jackie did the talking.

In less than a minute, the girls were sitting at the table, and one of the guys had called a waitress over. I noticed Jackie's fingers casually resting on the guy's arm.

As I got up, Annie looked over at me and flashed me a nervous smile. She then gave me a finger wave goodbye.

The guy at the table started talking to her, and she turned to focus her attention on him. I went over to an empty seat at the end of the bar.

~~~~

Danica came out from backstage less than five minutes later. With her long blonde hair, she was easy to spot. As I'd hoped, she headed toward the waitress station next to my barstool.

"Hi, Danica," I said as she stood beside me, organizing her waitress tray.

She looked over but didn't seem to know who I was. After looking at me for about three beats, recognition flooded her face. What followed was a wave of something I took for fright or worry.

She bent down, and I caught a whiff of an expensive perfume. She put her lips next to my ear, her soft voice barely audible over the pounding music.

"Have you seen Alex today?" she asked.

"No," I said. "And I've tried his apartment, your house, and every other place I could think of.

I haven't seen him anywhere."

"I think he's missing. He left my place at about two this morning. He was supposed to meet me for lunch today but never showed up. He never breaks a date without calling. I'm really worried about him."

"Do you have any idea where he could've gone?"

"That's just it. He wasn't supposed to go *anywhere*. He said he was beat and was going home to sleep all morning. When he didn't show up for lunch, I called his phone several times, but he didn't answer. I drove to his place, but his car wasn't in the lot. I even called the emergency room at Scottsdale General in case he'd gotten into an accident."

"Do you have a key to his apartment?" I asked.

"Yes, but I don't know if I should just walk into his place. What if he's there and only wanted to be left alone for the day?"

"Do you believe that?"

"Well, no. Maybe you're right, but I don't want to go there alone. I get off tonight at midnight. Meet me outside the stage door at about twelve twenty. We can go over and look together. Okay? Maybe he'll be back by then."

Great, another late night.

"I'll be there," I said, hoping my lack of enthusiasm didn't show.

Chapter Seven

I walked out to my car and called Sophie. I didn't know if she already had a date tonight, but I figured it was worth a shot. If she was busy, I'd try Gina. I really didn't want to go home and flip channels until midnight.

Sophie's phone rang several times. It was about to go to voicemail when she answered. I heard music and voices in the background.

"Hey, Sophie," I said. "Did I catch you at a bad time?"

"No, you caught us at a great time. Gina and I are at the Beach Club. Come on over. Drinks are half-price tonight. The guys are young, but some of them are totally adorable."

In the background, I heard Gina yelling, "Hey, Laura, get your skinny butt down here!"

"Okay," I said, "I'll be there in ten minutes."

~~~~

The Arizona Beach Club overlooks Tempe

Town Lake, just north of Arizona State University. It's a notch down from the clubs of Scottsdale, but the drinks are cheaper, and you can park without using a valet. Of course, being so close to the university, the crowd is inevitably several years younger than the clubs in Scottsdale.

I walked in and looked around for Sophie and Gina. They weren't in the main room, so I walked out back to the large outdoor patio.

I always prefer the patio whenever I come here. There are two bars, a small stage, several flickering Tiki torches, and a big fountain that splashes in a friendly way. It's a little quieter than inside and a lot more pleasant.

I found Sophie and Gina sitting at a table against a white wall, next to the trunk of an enormous date palm. There were three full drinks in front of each of them. I slid into an empty chair, and they each handed me a glass.

I turned and looked around the patio. "Is it me, or do the guys here look younger than the last time we were here?"

"Sorry, girlfriend," Sophie said. "They stay the same. You're maturing."

"I hear you met the two Russians I've been looking for," Gina said.

"I wouldn't exactly say 'met.' They sort of ran into me and invited me up to their place."

"Any ideas on who shot up their car?" Gina asked.

"Not a clue, but I owe somebody big time. The Russians are still looking for the missing bag. They think I know where it is."

"Wow! Do you?" Sophie asked, concern on her face.

"Not as far as I know. How close are you to finding it?"

"Not very," Gina said. "The bag was switched a week ago, and all I have to go on is a piece of grainy video. What I've found out so far is the two guys who threatened you were Russian Mafia bodyguards for 'the Courier'."

"Who's that?" I asked.

"That's what everybody's calling the little guy in the middle on the surveillance video. The bodyguards are still looking for whoever switched the bag, so they're accounted for. The Courier's a no-show."

"As in, he's disappeared?" Sophie asked.

"Yeah," Gina said. "I've been chasing my tail all day. Everyone I talk to gives me a different answer about where to find him. I get the feeling

I'm getting the run-around at the resort."

"On the video, there was some big commotion right before the switch. Did you find out what it was?" I asked.

"I talked to a bellman who was working at the time. A woman wearing a red string bikini had come in from the pool. She was walking through the lobby when she apparently tripped over a chair and somehow lost her top. She had a hard time getting it back on, so naturally, every guy in the lobby came over to help her or at least get an eyeful."

"That sounds like a diversion," Sophie said. "Did you find out who the woman was?"

"Nope. The bellman only remembers her as a tall brunette with huge boobs and great tan lines."

"Well, jeez, that's not very helpful," I said. "That describes half the women in Scottsdale."

"Yeah," Sophie laughed. "The other half are blonde."

"Did the bellman see the guy who did the bag switch?" I asked.

"No," Gina said. "Nobody remembers anything other than the brunette and her boobs."

"Were there any other camera angles of the lobby?"

"Don't know yet. That's next on my list tomorrow. Someone named Milo is delivering copies of all the security videos made that day. He should have them to the office by ten."

"Milo?" Sophie asked. "Is he hot?"

"How should I know?" Gina asked. "He's probably just another goon."

"I don't know," Sophie said. "That goon who kissed Laura was damn fine. Maybe they'll send over a hottie for me too."

"Everything's revolving around the bag," I said. "Did you ever find out what's actually supposed to be in it?"

"No, and I don't even have a good idea what it looks like, other than a black gym bag. The official story is still money, documents, and computer disks," Gina said. "I get the feeling there's more to it, but so far, everybody's being very close-lipped. The higher up the chain I go, the less they seem to know about it. It must be something pretty big."

~~~~

We talked until almost midnight. I had my keys out of my bag and got ready to go when the waitress brought over three more drinks. "From the table over there," she said and pointed.

The table was behind me, so I let Sophie and Gina look.

"Well, anything worthwhile?" I asked.

"*Yummy*!" Gina proclaimed. She began biting her lower lip.

"*Ooooohh,*" Sophie breathed. "They're cute."

I turned to look. The drinks came from two boys wearing ASU T-shirts who looked barely old enough to shave. They were smiling and holding up their beers.

I turned back to look at Gina and Sophie. They were both holding up the drinks and waving back.

"You can't be serious," I said. "They look like they're still in high school. They probably snuck in here. You should go for older guys, you know, the ones with *money*."

"Nah," Sophie said. "Look at their T-shirts. We're talking college men here."

"Don't think of them as young," Gina said, still waving to the boys. "Think of them as vigorous."

"Yeah," Sophie said, "young, vigorous, plenty of stamina."

"Hey," I said. "The other day, we talked about that eighteen-year-old trying to seduce you. Didn't we agree that was way too young? Didn't you say it was gross?"

"Oh, sure," Gina said. "Eighteen is way too young, but if they're in here, they're at least twenty-one. Twenty-one is *completely* different."

"Oh yes, completely different," Sophie said, her face taking on a light pink glow. "It's like you said the other day. These boys could pleasure us all night long."

"Well, I can't fight against your liquored-up libidos," I said. "Do me a favor and make sure they're legal. Check their IDs before anything happens."

"Hey, Laura, that's good advice," Gina said, staring at the boys, slowly running her tongue over her lips.

"Yeah, um, I'll keep it in mind, too," Sophie said, absent-mindedly fluffing her hair.

I stood up and waved the two guys over to our table. They came bounding over like two puppies.

"Boys," I said. "This is Gina and Sophie. They've been drinking, and they're not as young as they used to be, so please be gentle with them tonight."

The boys sat down. Gina waved goodbye, and Sophie blew me a kiss. Smiling, I shook my head and headed out to my car.

~~~~

Danica exited the stage door twenty minutes after midnight and spotted me in my Honda. She smiled and gave me a little wave.

As she walked over, I got out and stood next to my car. During the night, the temperature had dropped into the lower fifties. Being a seasoned Scottsdale girl, I'd put on a thick jacket.

"Alex's place isn't far," Danica said. "Do you want to go in one car?"

I was about to say no when she pointed towards a blue Porsche 911 parked four spaces over from my Honda.

"Is that your car?" I asked.

"Yeah, I got it a couple of years ago. It's a lot of fun to drive."

Jeez, how much money do you make by taking off your clothes?

Okay, so I'll admit it. I didn't want to pass up a chance to ride in the Porsche. I locked the Honda and walked around to the side of her car. Danica beeped the remote and unlocked the doors.

There's something extraordinary about climbing into a Porsche. The black leather seats seemed to wrap around me. It felt like sitting in a big soft hand.

Danica started the motor, and the car trembled with energy.

"You'd better put on your seatbelt," Danica said. "I drive sorta fast."

"Don't you get tickets?" I asked. "A car like this practically calls out for the police to stop it."

"Well, I often get stopped, but they never give me tickets. I guess I'm good at talking my way out of them."

You don't get tickets?

I mentally chalked up one more reason to be a beautiful sexy woman.

With the engine giving out a low powerful growl, we pulled out of the parking lot and headed up Scottsdale Road to Alex's apartment.

"I love your car," I said. "Now, you don't have to tell me, but I'm curious. How much do you make dancing?"

"Well, after taxes, I cleared about a hundred and forty thousand last year."

Damn, I'm in the wrong business.

Danica looked over and saw what I was thinking.

"Yes, the money's good, but it's not easy. I'm always on a diet. I have to work out five days a week. I also go to the dermatologist twice a month. Getting a zit is a disaster when you dance for a living."

I guess there are pluses and minuses to everything.

"Alex seems to have come into a lot of money recently," I said. "Did he tell you where it came from?"

"He said his grandmother had released some of his trust funds. But I'm not sure if I believe that. From what he told me, his grandmother was holding off giving him anything until he turned thirty. Then you came and said he was selling things and being followed. It seems like the money and the sales must somehow be related to Alex being missing."

After that, we drove through the empty streets in nervous silence. We were passing through a retail district, about three miles from Alex's apartment, when I saw something out of the corner of my eye.

"Stop the car!" I yelled. Danica obliged by slamming on the brakes, throwing us both forward. I turned my head to look down the street we'd just passed. Danica saw it at the same time.

"Alex's car!" Danica yelled. "I know it's his."

She pulled over to the curb and started to take off her seatbelt.

"Stay here," I said. "Let me see what we're dealing with."

I looked over to see if Danica understood. Her eyes were wide, and she was breathing hard, but she nodded. I opened the car door and climbed out.

The wind had started to pick up, and I zipped up my jacket. I already had my penlight out of my purse.

"Oh God, please don't let Alex be dead. Please don't let Alex be dead." I walked up to the car, repeating the words. It was as if just saying the words would keep anything horrible from happening.

I got to the Jaguar and shone my light through the window and onto the driver's seat. No Alex, which was bad, but there were no dead bodies visible, which was good. With my heart pounding, I angled the light around to look in the passenger seat.

"Is he in there?" shrieked a voice directly behind me.

I was so startled I almost wet myself. I turned and snapped at Danica, who was standing less than three feet from me.

"Don't sneak up on me like that!" My heart was pumping so hard that I felt my head pulse with each rapid beat.

"Sorry," Danica said in a small and shaky voice. "I couldn't wait. Is Alex in there?"

"Not that I've seen so far. As long as you're here, let's look on the inside. Do you have keys to his car?"

With a trembling hand, Danica pulled out a set of keys. She used the remote to unlock the doors.

I opened the driver's side door and looked in. The car was spotless. I then walked over to the passenger's side, opened the door, and sat down.

The glove compartment was empty except for the registration and the owner's manual. I used the button in the glove compartment to unlock the trunk. With a click, the hood popped up an inch. Danica went to the back of the car but didn't seem in a hurry to open the lid.

I was climbing out of the car when I saw a yellow CD case on the floor between the passenger seat and the door. I opened the case and took the disk out.

I turned it over, but there were no labels or writing anywhere on it. It appeared to be a homemade recording, but I couldn't tell if it was a CD, a DVD, or even a Blu-Ray.

"Danica," I asked. "Does Alex have a DVD burner?"

"No, but I know he's planning on getting one sometime. I think he wants to copy some of my old CDs and movies. He loves music, but he doesn't like paying for it."

I shoved the disk into my coat pocket before joining Danica at the back of the car. She was looking down at the trunk lid.

I knew what she was thinking because I was thinking the same thing. Alex could be in there. And if he was, he was probably dead.

I took a deep breath and opened the trunk. No dead body, no suspicious clues, nothing. Clean as a whistle.

~~~~

We poked around the car for another five minutes but didn't find anything useful. When we were done with the search, I turned to walk back to the Porsche.

"We can't leave his car here," Danica said. "Wherever Alex is, he'll be upset if somebody steals his car. This isn't the best neighborhood."

My first instinct was to leave the car where it

was and call the police. Moving the car would destroy any evidence that hadn't already been compromised by our nosing around the interior.

But Danica was probably right. The car wouldn't be here for long if we took off now. I was amazed it hadn't been stolen already. As Danica said, even considering this was Scottsdale, it wasn't the best neighborhood.

"One of us will need to drive it back to his apartment," I said.

"I'll do it," Danica said. "I've driven it before, and he doesn't mind. Besides, if anything happens, he won't get as mad if I'm the one who did it."

She took the Porsche key off the ring and handed it to me.

"Be careful. The brakes are sensitive." She then turned, climbed into the Jaguar, and closed the door.

Smiling just a bit, I climbed into the Porsche and started it up, cursing the bad luck that Alex's apartment was only three miles away.

Two and a half minutes later, we pulled into the parking lot of Alex's complex.

~~~~

We walked up the stairs to Alex's apartment.

Danica rang the doorbell while I tried to look through the kitchen window.

The lights were off, and I couldn't make out any interior details. Danica opened the door with her key, and we went in. I found the light switch and flipped it on.

Crazy as it sounds, it took two or three seconds for us to see that something was wrong. Then it hit us both like we'd been slapped. Danica made a sound, sort of like a dog whimpering. I might have done the same.

The entire apartment had been trashed. The couch had been flipped and gutted. Shredded books littered the floor in front of an overturned bookshelf. Chairs were knocked over and torn open. Even the stereo speakers had been knocked over and ripped apart.

In stunned silence, we walked into the kitchen. Every drawer had been pulled out of the cabinets. The refrigerator and the cupboard doors all stood wide open. Food from the freezer and boxes of cereal had been dumped out in a pile in the center of the floor.

We heard a noise – a soft scraping sound that seemed to come from the back of the apartment. It wasn't loud, but we both jumped. I pulled the Baby Glock out of my bag and loaded a round into the chamber.

I looked over at Danica. Her eyes were bugging out, staring at the gun.

"Stay here," I whispered. "I mean it. Don't move."

~~~~

I inched my way through the living room and then down the hall toward the bedroom. I mentally thumped my head for not checking the apartment when we first arrived.

Whoever trashed the apartment could be hiding, waiting to ambush us. Gina wouldn't make a mistake like that. I guess the sight of the destruction threw me off my game.

The first door in the hallway was open. I peered in, seeing the bathroom. There didn't appear to be anyone in there, but the door to the shower was closed.

I didn't see a dark shape hiding behind it, but you never know. Crouching low, I pulled open the shower door. Nothing.

I crept further down the hall to the bedroom. Here the door was closed. I listened, but the sound had stopped. I again crouched low and turned the handle.

I gave a light push, and the door opened

smoothly without a squeak. I looked inside, the Glock following the movement of my eyes.

Sitting on the bed was a man with his back resting against the wall. I noticed two important things about him.

First, it wasn't Alex, thank God. Second, a large bullet hole was in the middle of the man's forehead. His mouth was gaping open in a silent scream. His milky eyes stared into nothingness.

As I slowly stood up, I realized both of his hands were gone, hacked off at the wrists. So okay, make that three important things about him.

"Oh my God!" a hysterical voice behind me cried out.

I jumped, and there was a loud *Boom!* I looked down to see smoke coming from the end of my gun.

"Don't do that!" I yelled, turning to Danica, my voice rising almost to panic level as well.

"There's a dead guy on Alex's bed," Danica said, her voice coming out more like a high squeak than anything else. "Oh, my God, he doesn't have any hands. That is *so gross*."

The world started to spin, and nausea knotted in my stomach. Black and white dots danced in front of my eyes, and I went down to one knee to keep from passing out.

After a minute of breathing deeply, the spinning more or less stopped. I was able to stand and scan the rest of the room.

A set of mini-blinds were hanging in front of an open window. As I watched, a small gust of wind blew into the room, causing the mini-blinds to softly bang against the window frame. This was the noise we'd heard.

Looking around to find where my bullet had gone, I saw no obvious holes in the wall. The ceiling was unmarked, and the floor looked okay too. I looked over at the bed and saw a hole in the dead guy's shirt. I didn't remember it being there before.

Jeez, the paperwork on this is going to take all night.

"Don't touch anything," I said. "I'm going to have to call this in."

I pulled my phone out of my back pocket and called 911. Danica and I then went into the living room to wait. From previous experience, I knew it would take at least five minutes for the first of the cops to arrive.

I looked around the apartment until I heard a car pull into the parking lot below. I didn't find anything useful, but one thing was obvious, the destruction in the apartment hadn't been random.

Whoever had trashed the place was likely searching for something specific. I wondered what they were looking for and whether or not they'd found it.

I went back into the living room to wait for the police to come up the stairs. I looked over and saw that Danica was staring into space and shaking. She looked like she was about to lose it.

"Are you doing okay?" I asked.

"Who could have done this?" she asked, her voice shaky and distant. "What did they do with Alex? He has no enemies. Do you think it was the same men who were following him?"

"I don't know. But I promise I'll get to the bottom of it."

Outside, just below the apartment, the sounds of a police scanner could be heard.

"Listen to me for a minute," I said, taking both of her hands in mine. "There's going to be a ton of police here soon. They'll ask a bunch of questions, most of them pointless and repetitive. Try not to get angry with them. We still don't know if this has anything to do with Alex's disappearance. He may be partying in Vegas for all we know."

Danica nodded that she understood. We then went outside and stood on the small porch.

Although I was trying to be brave for both of us, the truth was I had a bad feeling about what had happened to Alex. I didn't know how I was going to tell Lenny, or Muffy, about this.

~~~~

Two officers came up the stairs, and I recognized them both. The senior officer was Chugger McIntyre. I'd gone to school with Chugger, both of us having grown up in the Granite Reef section of South Scottsdale.

Chugger was six foot four and easily weighed two hundred and fifty pounds. His short, cropped red hair and freckles showed his Irish heritage. Living in Scottsdale had given him a year-round sunburn.

His partner was Arnulfo Montoya, better known as Arny. Arny was originally from Mexico but gained American citizenship a few years back.

Although not nearly as tall as Chugger, Arny was solid. He had short, curly black hair and a full mustache. When Chugger saw me, he began to laugh.

"Hey, Arny," Chugger said, a happy grin on

his beefy face. "Didn't I tell you last week that Laura Black was due for another dead body soon? Laura, how long has it been since the last one? Two, three months?"

"Hey, Chugger," I said. "He's in the bedroom. He was dead when we got here, but I sort of, um, accidentally shot him."

Chugger's grin broadened.

"You shot a dead guy? No shit? Oh man, they'll never believe this down at the station."

Arny stayed to keep an eye on us while Chugger went to the back of the apartment. He didn't stay long. When he returned, his face was pale, and his smile was gone.

"Whoa," Chugger said. "That guy's hands were chopped off. Not a lot of blood, though. He was probably killed elsewhere and brought up here. What kind of sick fuck does that?"

Chugger called in the report on his walkie-talkie and then walked over to me.

"Let's clear the apartment," he said. "The M.E. and forensics team will be here in about half an hour, same with the homicide detectives. Expect everybody to be in a bad mood. Nobody likes getting up this time of night."

We went down to the parking lot, and Arny

pulled two clipboards out of the cruiser. He gave one to both Danica and me so we could write our initial statements.

Chugger was right about the bad moods. Fortunately, they kept it relatively short. The part where I shot the dead guy caused a stir with one of the detectives, but since the victim had already been dead when I shot him, it eventually worked out in my favor.

By four-thirty, I was back at my apartment, and Marlowe was asleep on the bed. When I turned on the light, he opened an eye, stretched, and yawned.

He rolled over, poking all four feet in the air. I rubbed his tummy for a few seconds, then pulled off my clothes and collapsed next to him on the bed.

~~~~

It was a beautiful warm day. I was driving Danica's Porsche in the vast Arizona desert between Gila Bend and Yuma. The road was flat, clear, and there wasn't another car in sight.

My hands gripped the leather-wrapped steering wheel as I jammed the Porsche into high gear and floored it. The car shot forward like a bullet from a gun.

Faster and faster, I drove until the dashed lane-dividing stripe blurred into a solid yellow line. My foot was pegged to the floor, and the car went faster. The roar of the motor sounded like a jet engine running full out, and it felt like the car was flying.

I felt the warm sensation of a hand touching the inside of my leg. Looking over, I saw Maximilian, the gangster from the office who'd nearly brought me to a climax with only a kiss.

The car motor briefly sputtered but then caught again. He smiled a beautiful smile and blew me a kiss. A wave of desire washed over me as his hand gently stroked my bare thigh.

The motor sputtered again, sounding almost like my cell phone. *That's weird*, I thought. *Porsches don't usually sound like cell phones, especially phones with Sophie's ringtone.*

The engine smoothed out briefly, but the ringtone sound happened again.

What?

By the fourth time it happened, I knew what the sound was. Both the Porsche and Maximilian faded as I fumbled around blindly on the nightstand. I found my phone and managed to pick it up without dropping it.

"Wha," I muttered into the phone, as always, hoping it was a prank call so I could go back to sleep.

"Hey, Laura. Wow, you sound terrible. How late did they keep you up last night?"

"Sophie? I'm sorry, but I'm not awake right now, and this phone call isn't likely to wake me up any time soon. Maybe you should call me back around lunchtime?"

"Did you really shoot a dead guy? They're saying you found a dead guy in Alexander Sternwood's apartment, and then you shot him."

"Well, yeah, I sort of did."

"Didn't you know he was already dead, and you didn't need to shoot him? Or was he coming after you, even though you knew he was already dead, like a zombie? You know, if he was a zombie, you'd have to shoot 'em in the brain. The brain's the only place you can kill a zombie, well, unless he was a vampire. But you know, lead bullets wouldn't have stopped him if he was a vampire, even if you shot 'em in the brain. You'd need a silver bullet for that."

"Sophie, I think that's werewolves, and why are you calling me?"

"I'm pretty sure silver bullets work for both

vampires and werewolves. I remember I once saw a movie where they killed a bunch of vampires with silver bullets."

"Sophie?"

"Sorry, Lenny's in a panic. He says he wants you down here right away. He got your voicemail from last night. You know, you sounded terrible then too. He's been on the phone with the police for the last twenty minutes. He has an appointment set up with Mrs. Sternwood at one o'clock. I think he wants to hear what happened from you first. Lenny's really stressing over this."

"Great. How bad is he?"

"I'm wearing my loose red top today, and he hasn't tried to look down it. Not even once. When that happens, you know he's distracted."

"Down to the office? It figures," I said. "What time is it now?"

"It's almost eight-thirty. You're burning daylight."

Great.

Chapter Eight

I took a quick shower and threw on some clothes. By nine-fifteen, I was out the door. The drive over to the office was pleasant, but I wasn't looking forward to talking with my boss.

In court, Lenny's always calm and in control, but that's because he's had weeks to prepare. When confronted with the unexpected, Lenny tends toward the hysterical.

~~~~

I walked into the front office and saw Sophie hunched over her keyboard, typing furiously. She looked like she was trying to keep low and away from any flying shrapnel. From previous experience, I knew she only did this when Lenny was on the warpath.

"Hey, Sophie," I said quietly, not ready to announce my presence to Lenny yet.

"Hey, Laura," she mumbled without looking up. "That dead guy you found last night really stirred up the shit around here. The mayor's office has called twice, and Mrs. Sternwood's called three times. The last time she called, she told Lenny he was completely useless and didn't know why she was paying him."

"How'd you know she told Lenny he was useless? Were you listening in again?"

Sophie stopped typing and looked around the office to see if anyone was listening. She motioned for me to bend down so she could whisper to me.

"Well, yeah, sorta. She also said if Lenny was half the lawyer everyone said he was, he would've been able to see that something like this was likely to happen to her grandson."

"That sounds like Muffy," I said, my voice lowered to a whisper to match Sophie's.

"Yeah," my best friend said, still whispering. "But that's not the worst of it. After Mrs. Sternwood hung up, Tony DiCenzo called. The actual *Tough Tony,* the mobster."

"Wow, seriously? What'd he talk to Lenny about?"

"Are you crazy? I'm not going to take any chances. I might overhear something Tough Tony DiCenzo says. What if he found out I knew something? It would be goodbye Sophia and hello shallow grave in the desert."

"Well, you answered the phone. What did he sound like?"

"He sounded like the devil."

I looked at Sophie to see if she was kidding, but she'd grown pale, and her eyes were big.

"How do you know he sounds like the devil? Have you ever heard the devil before?"

"I'm Catholic," she said in a slightly offended tone. "All Catholics know what the devil sounds like, and DiCenzo was it."

"But you're only Catholic when something bad happens," I said.

"If you think the devil calling isn't something bad, then I don't know what is."

"Did Gina stop by the office yet? I'd like to compare notes with her. It's weird that Tony DiCenzo keeps popping up for both of us."

"Sorry, Gina's come and gone. Lenny scolded her for not finding the missing bag. She got so mad I thought she was going to smack him. I almost wish she would have. He can get so irritating when he's like this. Well, you'd better talk to Lenny before the governor of Arizona, or maybe even the president, calls him."

~~~~

I walked into Lenny's office and found him pacing in front of his window. He had a lit cigarette in one hand and a half-full glass of Jim Beam in the other. I looked at his desk and saw there were already half a dozen cigarette butts in the ashtray.

He saw me and raised both arms in a gesture of frustration.

"I thought both of these cases were going to be easy money," he said. "Watch a guy for a few days. Find a missing bag. How hard could it be, I asked myself. Really, how hard could it be?"

He stopped and took a noisy sip of his Beam. "Now, on the one hand, you're back to finding dead bodies, but you lose the guy you're supposed to be watching. Both the mayor and the millionaire client have become unglued. On the other hand, Gina's come up with Jack squat on the missing bag, and I've got the Godfather breathing down my neck."

"Sophie said he called. What did he say?"

"DiCenzo's telling me he's all in a rush to get the bag back. No surprise there. But he also said that maybe he should send over a couple of guys to help me out. What's that supposed to mean? If I say yes, then I'm admitting I'm incompetent. If I say no, and we don't find the bag, I'm dead meat."

He stubbed out his cigarette, then ran his fingers through his hair. "I don't know," he said. "Sometimes, I think I should move back to New Jersey with my cousin and drive a cab."

I gave Lenny everything new I had on Alex, which wasn't much. I then told him all I knew about the dead guy, which was even less.

"I need that Alexander guy found," Lenny said. He was facing the window, almost mumbling the words to himself. He then started pacing again.

"I might need some help," I said. "If something comes up, do you mind if I borrow Sophie?"

He turned to me and almost shouted: "Borrow whomever you want. Sleep with whomever you need to. Go ahead and shoot somebody else if you think it'll help, but find Alexander Sternwood. *The sooner, the better!*"

~~~~

I went back to my desk and tried to organize my thoughts. My assignment had morphed from simply watching Alex to going out and finding him. The problem was I was out of leads.

As I thought about Alex, the mental picture of the dead guy kept swimming in front of me. I needed to talk to somebody who would understand what I was going through. Gina was out, but I knew of someone else.

I called Reno, but he didn't pick up. I got his voicemail and waited for the beep. "Call me," was all I said. I figured he'd still remember the voice.

Okay, so I wanted to talk to Reno about the murder, but I also wanted to see him again. The lunch at Frankie Z's had sort of been an experiment. After my erotic dreams starring Reno, I wanted to see how it felt to be with him again.

It turns out he was still as hot as ever, and seeing him brought back some beautiful memories. Every time I thought of Reno, I got a warm and fuzzy tingle that made me feel good all over.

I went back up to the reception lobby. Sophie was still hunched over her computer, typing away. I walked over to her and touched her shoulder. She jumped, letting out a loud squeak.

"Don't do that!" she said, breathing hard and holding her hand to her chest. "You almost made me diarrhea my pants."

"Sorry. I might need some help on this Alexander thing. Lenny said we could partner up if it's okay with you."

"Anything to get me out of the office would be great. When do you need me?"

"I don't know yet. I'm waiting for a phone call from Jackson Reno. I'll need to see him again before I figure out where to go next. Maybe tomorrow or the next day?"

"Reno? You're seeing Reno again? That man is truly fine. But after what you did to him the last time, I'm surprised he'd let you get within twenty feet of him."

"What do you mean *what I did to him*? Besides, we're not exactly dating again, at least not yet. So far, we've only seen each other once."

"Uh-huh? I see the look on your face. When are you going to tell him he's back to dating you?"

"I'm thinking we should probably see each other another two or three times and see how it goes before there's any talk about dating again."

"I remember how it worked out the last time. You were in a crappy mood for months after you broke up with him. I hope you know what you're doing."

Me too.

My cell phone rang, and I saw it was Reno.

My heart skipped a little, and I walked into the back offices before answering.

"Hey," I said, trying to keep my voice steady. "I need to talk to you."

"Can it wait?"

"No."

"I heard you shot a dead guy last night."

"Oh, um, you heard about that?"

"Christ, Laura, the entire department's heard about that."

"The dead guy I found in Alexander's apartment is seriously bugging me," I said. "You find dead bodies all the time. I thought maybe I could talk to you about it."

"I don't find dead bodies all the time. You find more than I do. I think you find more than anyone else in the entire department. You're like a dead body magnet."

"Okay, maybe, but this one's different."

"Look, I can't meet with you now. I start work in about an hour and a half."

"It won't take long, really."

I heard his famous sigh. "Okay, I'm working across from the Phoenician today. I can meet you for a few minutes there at the Oasis. Do you remember where it is?"

"You mean the cute tropical bar in the middle of the resort's pools? The one where you felt me up under the table on our third date, about a year ago?"

There was a pause on the phone, and I heard a *thump*. I could visualize Reno hitting his palm against his forehead.

"Yup, that's the one," he said.

"I'm at the office," I said. "I'll be there in twenty minutes."

~~~~

The Phoenician is one of the nicest resorts in Arizona. It sits on the southeast side of Camelback Mountain, about three miles west of Lenny's office.

It has exceptional views of both Phoenix and Scottsdale. I drove west until I came to the enormous fountain and tropical display marking the main entrance.

About seventy-five yards inside the resort was a security booth. As I stopped my car, a guard stepped out.

He gave both me and my car the once over. I grimaced a little as his eyes lingered on the side mirror, still hanging by the cable, before moving over to the bullet hole in the trunk.

He bent over and politely asked how he could help me. I told him I was going to the Oasis for drinks. He paused, as if he was having an internal debate, then he directed me to the visitor's garage.

~~~~

The Oasis is a cozy bar and grill that sits in the middle of three levels of Arizona-sized swimming pools. To get there, you need to walk through a maze of sunbathers and then down a narrow path between two of the larger pools.

I managed to make it to the restaurant and remain dry. Reno wasn't there yet, so I went to the bar.

My nerves were doing flip-flops, and I thought a drink might help calm them down. Glancing over the menu, I debated between the eight-dollar, the twelve-dollar, and the twenty-dollar scotch options. I thought about my rent and settled on the eight-dollar version.

I found an empty table and sat in a chair facing the hotel. As I waited, I swirled the ice cube around the glass with my finger.

~~~~

After about five minutes, Reno exited a door on the hotel's lower level and walked down to the pools. As he trotted down the steps leading to the uppermost pool, I could see the muscles ripple underneath his Aloha shirt. I also noticed more than one bikini-clad woman follow him with her eyes as he walked through the upper pools and then into the restaurant.

Reno stood at the entrance and scanned the crowd. I waved and caught his eye. As he made his way through the lounge, I had a brief memory of the first time Reno and I had been here, over a year before. The thought of that gave me a pleasant smile.

"Well, Laura," Reno said as he sat. "Fancy meeting you here at the Oasis. Haven't we been here before?"

I looked at him and saw the sparkle in his eyes. It was the same look Reno had given me so many times before when we were dating.

Seeing that look turned up the tingles that were spreading all through my body. It also gave me a feeling of relief that was hard to explain. Somehow, I knew he wanted me as much as I wanted him, even if he didn't know it yet.

The waitress came over, and Reno ordered a Coke.

"I can't stay more than fifteen minutes," he said. "I'm relieving a team working across

Camelback Road in a half-hour."

"What happened to your Iceman, Albert Reinhardt?" I asked. "Has he made his buy yet?"

"Not that I should be telling you any of this, but no. There's a team on him twenty-four hours a day. So far, all we know is he sunburns easily and shoots scratch golf. Have you heard from Sternwood yet? The detectives want to question him about the murder."

"Nobody knows where he is," I said. "He disappeared the night before last. Lenny gave me the lead in finding him. I don't think he had anything to do with the murder. I think it's more likely whoever did the killing is also after Alex."

"I get that feeling too. If you hear from him, have him get in touch with the homicide detectives at the Foothills District Station right away. There're a lot of people looking for Alexander, and everybody's getting rather anxious. Margaret Sternwood has connections and has already been to see the mayor. There's a lot of pressure to wrap this up quickly."

The waitress came over with the Coke, and Reno handed her a five. He picked up the Coke and took a long drink, draining half the glass.

"Did you shoot the dead guy with the Glock I gave you?" Reno asked, a slight smile forming at the corners of his lips.

"I didn't mean to. Alex's girlfriend, Danica, came up behind me, and it went off."

"Well, I'm glad you found a good use for the Glock," he chuckled. "Although you probably shouldn't make a habit of walking around with your finger on the trigger of a gun. I'm surprised Gina didn't mention that."

"That's not funny," I said. "I'm never going to live this down, plus it's giving me the creeps. When I walked into the bedroom, he was staring at me. Did you hear his hands had been hacked off? Why would anybody do that to somebody?"

"Cutting off the hands is usually associated with an organized crime ritual," Reno said. "It could signify he was killed because he took something that didn't belong to him. Of course, the hands could also have been used as proof the job was done. Or, maybe the killer likes to collect trophies. Who knows?"

"Did you get anything on Arizona Security Enterprises?" I asked.

"Turns out ASE is a private security company affiliated with the Tropical Paradise, so maybe they just decided to have Alex followed after he made the sale to Reinhardt. Of course, Tony DiCenzo ultimately controls the Paradise. It may mean nothing, or it may mean he's involved too."

I took a sip of my scotch, and Reno sipped his Coke. We both sat there for a moment in silence.

"So, why did you dump me?" he asked, looking up. "I know all of that happened a long time ago, but it still bothers me. We were getting close, and I thought things were going great, but then you disappeared. You were going to come over to my house on Christmas morning for breakfast. You were also going to let me know if you wanted to move in with me or not. You left me that lame phone message, but I assumed you not showing up was your way of saying no."

"It wasn't like that," I said. My mind raced. I wanted to say more, to tell him I'd planned to move in with him, I'd wanted to be with him, but I couldn't form the words.

"I spent days wondering what I'd done wrong," Reno continued, ignoring me. "I asked around and started looking for you. I thought we could work things out if I could talk to you. But nobody knew where you were. I called Gina, and she said you were out of the country, but I wasn't sure I believed her."

Reno paused for a moment as he took a sip of his Coke. "After a couple of weeks, I figured I'd scared you away, and you'd gone off to greener pastures. I ended up with Cynthia for a weekend. That was my way of trying to forget about you. But I told you she had this weird foot fetish thing going on."

"You slept with another woman to forget about me?" I asked.

"Then, a week after Cynthia, you called me up to yell at me and tell me I was a jerk," Reno said, still ignoring me. "That wasn't easy."

"No," I said, trying not to get pissed off. "You've still got it all wrong. After we were together on Christmas Eve, Lenny sent me to Italy with Gina – very hush-hush. I ended up busting a leg and had to spend a couple of weeks in a clinic in the middle of nowhere. At first, I was too doped up to even remember my name, then I was going to call you, but I didn't know what to say. I wasn't even sure you'd believe me."

"Huh," he said. "So you really did break your leg? I'd heard that rumor but didn't know if it was true or not."

"Yes. I got back to Arizona in the middle of January, but by the time I got the nerve to see you again, I found out you were sleeping with Cynthia. Do you blame me for being upset? Okay, so maybe I didn't call you when I was supposed to, and maybe I was a little late in coming over, but it didn't take you long to forget about me and find somebody else."

I stopped to take a breath and see Reno's reaction. As usual, he only showed his stony detective face.

"Anyway," I continued, "after I thought I was over being upset about Cynthia, I called you. I'd planned to ask you if we could start over again. Then I started thinking about you sleeping with her and got upset again. So, yeah, I ended up yelling at you, and I called you a jerk."

"But it wasn't serious with Cynthia," Reno said. "I went on a total of two dates with her."

"A weekend only counts as one date?"

"It was a long date, but yeah. Only two dates."

"Let me get this straight. You slept with her after only one date?"

"I was trying to get over you."

"We didn't sleep together until we first had three dates."

"I respected you."

"So," I said. "Sounds like we had a little bit of a misunderstanding."

Reno gave a little shrug. "Sounds like it."

"What do you want to do about it?" I asked.

"What do you mean, do about it?" Reno asked. "Like, do you want us to start dating again?"

I smiled my sexiest smile at him. The one that always softened him up when he was annoyed with me.

He paused, then a horrible look appeared on his face. It was like he had tasted something awful.

"Are you insane?" he asked, almost yelling at me.

Oops, wrong reaction.

"Do you know how many sleepless nights I've had because of you?"

People at nearby tables stopped talking and turned to look at us.

"I would lay there at night, worrying about you and blaming myself for whatever I did to make you go away. I lost almost fifteen pounds because I didn't feel like eating for a month. Now I find out you put me through that hell because you had some kind of weird 'misunderstanding,' and now you want to do it to me all over again? Are you nuts?"

This definitely wasn't going well.

"Look," he said, standing up. "Don't get me wrong. This has been a lot of fun, but I have to relieve the team in a few minutes. I'll see you around." He got up, made his way through the tables, and then disappeared into the hotel.

Maybe I should have been disappointed, but somehow, I wasn't. Sure, he was pissed, but I saw how he looked at me when he first saw me. I could tell he still wanted me. He wanted me bad. He just didn't want to admit it yet.

~~~~

I finished my scotch, returned to my car, and then drove back to my apartment. The only lead I hadn't followed up on yet was the CD in the yellow case I'd found in Alex's car.

I had no idea what was on it; most likely just music or maybe a movie. But all of my other leads had dead-ended, and I was running out of options.

~~~~

I was up for another burst of exercise, so I power-walked up the two flights of stairs to my floor. By the time I got to the top, my heart was pounding, and my breath was coming in short gasps. I unlocked the door to my apartment and went inside.

Marlowe was asleep on the floor in front of the window. He had positioned himself so his body was lying in a shaft of sunlight while his head was in the shade. He's not so dumb.

I went to the closet and found the disk from Alex's Jaguar still in my coat pocket. I put it in my DVD player, but nothing happened when I pressed the play button, so I took the disk from the player and slipped it into my aging computer.

After a few seconds of whirring sounds and flashing lights, a window displayed a computer file. I clicked on the file to open it. After a few more seconds of whirring and flashing, a message popped up indicating the file was locked and password protected.

Okay, so what would Alex use as a password? I typed in *Alex*. Nothing. I tried *Danica*. Still nothing. On a whim, I tried *Sit-on-my-face*. Nope. None of these was the correct password.

Okay, I thought, *who knows about these things?*

I had a sudden inspiration. A woman on the second floor, Suzie Lu, taught Computer Science at ASU in Tempe. I didn't know her well, but we'd talked a few times at parties and were on a friendly *hello* basis on the elevator. If anybody could figure out how to read the computer file, it was probably Suzie Lu.

Continuing my exercise routine, I walked down the stairs and knocked on her door. No one answered, so I walked back up the stairs to my apartment.

I looked up her office number at Arizona State and tried calling, but I only got her voicemail. I was going to leave a message, but she gave her cell phone number at the end of her greeting.

I wrote down the number and opted to give her a call. She answered on the third ring and said she was downstairs in the atrium, watching TV with a friend, and she'd be glad to meet with me. I took the elevator down and went over to the TV area.

I found Suzie perched in the middle of the oversized couch facing the big-screen TV. A slender woman several years older than me, Suzie has dark, intense eyes and long black hair. Her boobs were likely granted to her by a generous plastic surgeon rather than genetics.

Today, her boobs were shown to their best advantage. Instead of a shirt, she wore a snug red-leather vest unbuttoned to her navel. To complement the vest, she wore skin-tight black leather pants.

Her friend turned out to be a middle-aged man with a round pleasant-looking face. His navy-blue suit paired with a white shirt and a red tie that screamed "business", while the expensive gold rings he sported on his fingers shouted "money". I also took note of the wedding band.

The black leather dog collar around his neck somewhat clashed with the whole business vibe he had going. It had long silver spikes and a leash attached to it. Suzie held the other end of the leash.

What made me pause was the sight of the man on his hands and knees in front of Suzie. Her shiny black boots with the five-inch stiletto heels were resting casually on his back as if he were just some random ottoman.

The only other person in the TV area was Mrs. Nottingham. Mrs. Nottingham is a tiny woman with short curly silver hair and thick glasses who lives on the fourth floor. She's about two hundred years old and spends most of her afternoons watching TV in the atrium.

On the TV, an episode of some reality show blared away. Glancing at the caption, I saw the show was about a teenage boy who was having a secret affair with his girlfriend's mother.

I couldn't help myself. I watched as the mother and daughter got into a catfight while the boyfriend looked on, a big smile on his face.

For some reason, this didn't strike me as being especially weird. Maybe it had something to do with the man on the floor redefining weirdness for me today.

I walked around to the front of the couch. "Hi, Laura," Suzie said in her soft, velvety smooth voice. She saw me eyeing the dog-collar man. "Oh, don't worry about him. He's in training."

"Training? For what?"

"Training to be in my stable. He thinks he's worthy, but he's wretched and quite pathetic. I doubt he'll even last the afternoon."

The man shifted his position. I'm not sure how long he'd been there, but his knees were probably getting sore.

"I didn't give you permission to move, bitch," Suzie said to the man, now with a menacing undertone to her voice.

"So, this is sort of like an audition?" I asked.

"You could look at it that way. I'll see if he has the ability to obey and serve me without question. If so, then perhaps he'll become one of my boys."

"What happens then?"

"Then I'll let him come to my apartment and perform menial tasks. He'd be allowed to clean my bathroom, do my laundry, or maybe clean my kitchen. If he's especially obedient during our session, I might even let him paint my toenails."

As soon as Suzie mentioned a chance for him to paint her toes, the potential slave let out a nervous giggle. Suzie looked sternly at him and picked up a long wooden paddle with her left hand. She swung it down hard.

With a *whoosh,* it landed with a loud *slap* across the man's ass. He let out a surprised yelp, like a frightened small dog.

"Listen, cretin," Suzie said to the man. "You're on thin ice here. I won't tolerate any further disobedience from a worthless little turd like you. Today, you're nothing but a piece of furniture. Shut your hole and don't move a muscle while I have a quiet conversation with my friend. Got it?"

Dog-collar man hung his head down. "Forgive me, Mistress McNasty. I'm not worthy."

A small smile spread across Suzie's lips. I was stunned by this.

"*Mistress McNasty?*" I asked. "Do you pay them to act like this?"

Suzie's kohl-lined eyes opened wide, and she laughed deeply, making her whole face light up. Using the spiked heel of her boot, she gave the man a firm poke in the ribs.

"Slug, tell this woman how much you pay for

the privilege of serving me."

"I gladly pay one hundred dollars an hour, Mistress McNasty. I am grateful you have allowed this lowly one to serve you."

"Damn," I said. "You're kidding, right? Why would anyone pay you to abuse them?"

Suzie again prodded the man with her heel. "Slave, explain your sick perversions to this woman, and be quick about it."

"My deviancies include submissive behavior, masochistic behavior, and I also enjoy public humiliation."

"Eeeeyuuuw, yuck, " I exclaimed.

"Disgusting, isn't he?" Suzie said with a giggle. "Have a seat, and we can talk. If you'd like, you can use him as a footstool too. It's quite relaxing."

I sat, but my stomach twisted at the thought of putting my feet on the man. He looked clean enough, but I didn't know where he'd been.

Mrs. Nottingham looked up from the TV. "Dear, would you mind if I used your young man? When you get to be my age, your feet hurt all the time. I always thought they should put an ottoman down here."

Suzie nodded and waved her over. Mrs.

Nottingham got up and tottered over to the couch. As she sat, she slipped off her loafers and lowered her feet onto the man's back. She made herself comfortable on the sofa and smiled.

"Actually," I said to Suzie. "I wanted to know if you could help me with a project I'm working on." I pulled out the disk and handed it to her.

"This disk has a computer file on it. But when I try to open the file, a message says I need a password. Is that something you can get around?"

"It depends on the software they used to encrypt the file. Some are simple, and some are tough. But sure, I'll have one of my grad students work on it."

Suzie then looked at the yellow CD case. "This is old school. It's rare to see a file on a CD anymore, but we have an optical reader in the lab. I'll give you a call when I find something out."

With the extra weight of Mrs. Nottingham's feet on his back, the man had begun to fidget again. Suzie gave him a warning prod in the ribs. This produced another giggling fit from the man. Suzie shook her head and picked up the paddle.

"Dear," Mrs. Nottingham said to Suzie. "He's getting a little out of hand. Would you mind if I punished your slave?"

"Please, be my guest," Suzie said.

Mrs. Nottingham slowly got back to her feet, and Suzie handed her the paddle. Mrs. N shuffled into position next to the man and clasped the paddle in a two-handed grip. Drawing the paddle back like a golf club, she swung it down with surprising force on the man's ass.

Slap!

The man cried out in pain. He also flew forward a good five feet, smashed his head against a chair leg, then skidded to a stop on the carpet. He let out a soft moan as his body went limp.

Suzie and I got up and walked to where the man lay. There was a moment of shocked silence as the three of us bent over his unmoving body.

"I wonder if I killed him?" Mrs. Nottingham asked as she turned to look up at us.

Suzie used the toe of her boot to roll the man over. As she did, he let out another low moan.

"Wow," said Suzie, her face had broken out in a big smile. She turned to Mrs. Nottingham. "That was great! You know, sometimes my clients want some two-on-one action. I might give you a call sometime."

"Any time, dear. If you'd like, I'll be glad to show you how to properly train your bitches. I've watched you, and to be honest, you're a little soft on them."

With that, I'd seen and heard enough and got up to go.

"Um, thanks, Suzie," I said, handing her one of my cards. "My cell number's on the card. I appreciate your help."

"Glad to be of service," she said. "I'll call you as soon as I have something."

As I walked away, I heard a feeble voice moan: "Oh, Mistress McNasty, I'm so unworthy."

~~~~

I went back up to my apartment and opened a Diet Pepsi. I then sat at my kitchen table and spread out all the notes and information I had on Alex.

The police had been looking for him all day in the obvious places. My only hope of finding him was to search somewhere that wasn't so obvious. I'd just started sorting through the piles when Sophie called.

"Mrs. Sternwood wants to see you as soon as possible. She's at the Barrett-Jackson auto auction over at WestWorld. She'll be there until about eleven o'clock tonight. She said she'd leave a ticket for you at the will-call window."

"Why does she want to see me? I thought Lenny already told her everything we knew?"

"Well, he did," Sophie's voice dropped to a whisper. "But I don't think Mrs. Sternwood was very impressed with Lenny's explanations. She called him a useless little twerp."

"So, she wants me to go over and tell her exactly the same thing as Lenny did?"

"That's about the size of it. Although I imagine you'll do it in a nicer way. You know how Lenny is when he gets worked up."

"I know. He tends to spit when he talks. It always grosses me out too. Is Lenny okay with me talking to her?"

"He *told* me to call you. Mrs. Sternwood just about chewed him a new butthole today. I think he wants to spread the pain around."

Chapter Nine

I went to my closet and found a fresh outfit. I then touched up my make-up before taking the elevator down to the atrium floor and walking out to my car.

The Barrett-Jackson auto auction is held yearly at WestWorld, a giant indoor arena in north Scottsdale. Each year, sixteen hundred of the rarest and most collectible cars in the world are sold at auction during the week-long event.

After finding a space to park, it was a five-minute walk to get to the arena. I then searched around to find the line for the will-call ticket window. After showing the woman my driver's license, she gave me a VIP pass for a seat on the bidding floor.

Once in the vast arena, I walked down to the auction floor. There were eight thousand seats, all full of people talking loudly to each other.

Telephones rang as phone bids came in, and the sound of motors filled the arena as cars drove on and off the stage. Over this noise, the amplified voice of the auctioneer shouted out the bids.

I showed my pass to an usher, and he escorted me to the front row. Muffy Sternwood was there, and beside her was an empty seat. She saw me and invited me to sit.

"I'm glad you could make it. This business with Alexander has me so unnerved. I talked with Leonard this afternoon, but he's such a jackass. I know he's the best attorney in the city, but I find it hard to even speak with him on the phone without wanting to choke him."

"He has that effect on a lot of people."

"Is there any word yet on Alexander?"

"Nobody's heard a thing. But there are a lot of people looking for him. I'm sure he'll turn up soon."

"I hope you're right. I also hope you don't think I'm callous being at an auction while Alexander is missing. My late husband and I would come here every year to buy and sell cars. I know it makes him happy that I keep the tradition alive. Hey, what do you think about that one? I've been waiting for it to come up."

I looked at the stage where they had driven out a small silver car. The announcer said it was a

1953 Ford Vega Roadster, a one-of-a-kind prototype. The bidding started at fifty thousand dollars and quickly went up from there.

"It's cute," I said.

"I think so, too," Muffy said. She waved over a young woman wearing a blue suit who was holding a bright yellow square of cloth. Her badge proclaimed her as "Amy".

Muffy nodded to Amy, who waved her yellow cloth and shouted at the auctioneer. The auctioneer pointed at Muffy, talked for a minute, and then pointed at someone else.

"Did you get it?" I asked.

"No, I'm being outbid. What have you found out about Alexander so far?"

"It appears he's been selling things to dealers around town. I don't know what he's selling, but they seem to get him some good money. Unfortunately, they also may have brought on this trouble. Not all of the people he's been dealing with are legitimate."

"Leonard alluded to that, but he was vague about the details. He frustrated me into losing my temper and cursing at him. He can be such a jerk."

I noticed the bidding was now at three hundred thousand dollars. Muffy nodded to Amy, who waved her yellow cloth again and shouted at the auctioneer. The auctioneer pointed at her, talked for a minute, and again pointed at someone else.

"Leonard confirmed Alexander has a girlfriend. What do you know about her?"

"I've talked to her a couple of times. Her name's Danica and she's alright. She seems to care about Alex. From what I can tell, he feels the same way about her. She's as worried as you are."

"Please be honest with me," Muffy said. "Do you think Alexander had anything to do with the dead man they found in his apartment?"

"According to the police, the man was killed somewhere else and brought to Alex's apartment. Most killers don't commit murder elsewhere and then drag the bodies back to their home. I also can't see Alex tearing up his place like that. I think it's more likely that he happened to walk in on whoever was ransacking the apartment. My theory is that they grabbed him and took him somewhere."

The bidding was now at three hundred and fifty thousand dollars. Muffy once more nodded at Amy, who waved the cloth again. The auctioneer pointed to Muffy, talked briefly, and then pointed to someone else.

"The police apparently think the same thing,"

Muffy said. "A man is monitoring both the house phone and my cell phone. From what the police say, they can trace the call almost instantaneously if somebody contacts me. They say most kidnappers use email because it's harder to trace. Of course, I don't have a computer or use email, so it will be hard for them to use that in my case."

"It would be my guess they're looking for information from Alex. I'd be surprised if they called in a ransom request."

"I think so, too," Muffy said. "If they wanted money, they would have stolen property from his apartment. If what you say is true about Alexander selling things, he's probably in serious trouble with these people."

"I'm afraid that's probably true."

The auctioneer had moved the bidding to three hundred and eighty thousand dollars and asked for three hundred and eighty-five. He held his gavel over his head.

He shouted, "Going once!" Then, "Going twice!"

I heard Muffy mutter, *"Oh, what the hell,"* under her breath. She nodded to Amy, who shouted and waved again. The auctioneer pointed at Muffy and shouted, "Three hundred eighty-five thousand!"

He then tried to move the bidding up to three hundred and ninety thousand, but there weren't any takers.

He shouted, "Going once!" Then, "Going twice!" He gave a fair warning and brought his gavel down, shouting, "Sold!"

There was scattered applause, and a man in the row behind us patted Muffy on the shoulder. Amy bent over to shake Muffy's hand, but Muffy stood up and hugged her. A man in a blue suit hustled over to Muffy. He held a clipboard with several papers on it.

I got up to leave. Muffy looked at me.

"I know you're doing your best. Call me directly if you find out anything so I don't have to speak to that idiot Leonard."

I told her I would.

~~~~

I made my way back to my car and drove home. It was getting late, and I was beat. In the back of a drawer, I found an old T-shirt of Reno's, one I had borrowed from him when we were dating.

I hadn't worn it for months, but putting it on gave me a warm feeling. I crawled into bed and was asleep within seconds.

~~~~

I woke up to the sun streaming into my bedroom window. Looking at the clock, I realized it was almost eight-thirty.

I'd run out of leads and wasn't sure where to go next to find Alex. I put on a pot of coffee and spent an hour reviewing my notes, but that didn't give me any brilliant new ideas.

Taking a long shower helped perk me up but didn't improve my mood. I put on a comfortable outfit, but that didn't help either. I decided it was time for some comfort food.

I wanted to pig out on barbeque. I needed a pulled pork sandwich with a side of beans and cornbread. I didn't care about calories or trans-fats.

I grabbed my keys and headed out the door. My go-to place was Honey Bear's on Van Buren Street, down by the airport. Sort of a long drive, but today it seemed worth it.

I walked out to my car and had the key in the door when I heard a deep male voice behind me.

"Miss Black, please do not make any sudden moves. It would be a shame to have to shoot you."

Oh crap.

I took my key out of the lock and turned. The

man with the gun was tall and dark, with broad shoulders and a thin face. His dark hair was cut short, and his face was clean-shaven except for a full black mustache. Only his eyes showed he was cruel and wouldn't hesitate to hurt me. The look in his eyes showed he might even enjoy it.

It was only then I noticed the gun in his hand. It was a cheap chrome-plated semi-automatic, a twenty-five or thirty-two caliber. It almost looked like a toy in his hand.

"Miss Black, you will please come with us." He spoke with an educated British accent with deep undertones of some other accent I didn't know.

"Sorry," I said, holding my hands up and backing away. "You've got the wrong girl. My name's Susan and I'm on my way back to the cathedral. Father O'Brien is saying mass in half an hour, and he'll be worried if I'm not there to help light the candles."

I had taken half a dozen backward steps toward the building when I bumped into something solid. I felt a hand grab a fistful of my hair and pull up hard, bringing tears to my eyes.

"Look," the voice behind me said with the same strange accent. "This American slut doesn't want to talk with us. Shall we teach her manners by forcing her to pleasure us upstairs in her very own bed?"

"Perhaps later, my brother," the first man said. "Before that, I will talk to her. If her answers displease me, you may use her however you wish."

The guy behind me must have liked this answer because he chuckled, even as his grip on my hair tightened. He took my purse from where it was hanging on my shoulder and tossed it to the guy with the gun.

Holding my bag in one hand, he used his gun to wave me over to a white Chrysler. The car was parked behind a yellow rental truck on the far side of the lot, out of sight of my apartment.

He opened the rear door and followed me in, the gun never wavering. The other man got into the driver's seat. Only then did I get a good look at him.

He didn't appear as tall as the man next to me and was about ten years younger, maybe around twenty-four or twenty-five. His face was square with a full black mustache and the same cruel eyes.

He must have seen me glancing at him in the mirror because he turned to look at me. He broke out in a nasty little grimace and chuckled.

He then grabbed his crotch and gave himself a squeeze. My stomach knotted up as the implications of the conversation, along with his crude gesture, started to sink in.

"To make things simpler for you," the first man said. "You may call me Mr. Smith. My brother, you may call Mr. Jones. I suggest you use the next few minutes to decide if you want to live."

The car took off, and we headed south. I was hoping these guys would get careless. Each time we slowed for a stop sign or a red light, I glanced sideways at Smith and the gun he pointed at me. The doors weren't locked, so I knew I could make a run for it.

If "Mr. Smith" became distracted or took the gun off me, I'd go for it. Of course, my plan rested on the assumption they wouldn't shoot me as I ran down a crowded city street on a Saturday morning. I suppose that's a lot to bet your life on.

Unfortunately, each time I glanced over, Smith locked his gaze onto mine and pointed the gun squarely at my chest. I was forced to remain still and go along for the ride.

Damn.

We drove down into South Scottsdale's manufacturing and warehouse district, just below

Curry Road. The driver turned down one side street, then another, and yet another.

The road we ended up on, which was more dirt than pavement, dead-ended at a group of shabby one and two-story block buildings. As close as I could tell, we were just north of the Salt River.

"Mr. Jones" pulled into a dirt-and-gravel parking lot next to one of the larger buildings. I looked at the parking lot through the car's window.

It was a depressing sight, full of rusted machinery, broken cinder blocks, and trash. A high chain-link fence topped with rusted barbed wire surrounded the entire lot.

Jones got out and opened my door. Smith waved his gun as an invitation for me to get out. The three of us entered the building, going into what had been the office and reception area. It was empty now; nothing but garbage and broken plastic chairs remained.

With Jones leading and Smith following, we went through a battered wooden door. Past the door was a short hallway that opened into a large room.

The space appeared to be the manufacturing area for the former business. It was apparent that, at one time, this had been a commercial printing shop.

The place smelled like a cross between a meth lab and a hot day in a public restroom. Broken glass crunched under our shoes as we walked.

A weak light came in from two dirty skylights. The light revealed splotches of bright colors on the otherwise bare concrete floor. A partially disassembled printing press sat in the corner of the room next to a broken-out window.

Tall shelves against the wall contained dozens of battered cans of ink. Bright reds, yellows, and blues had dripped over the sides of the cans and seemed out of place when compared with the dead feeling of the rest of the room.

Against the far wall was a large iron bed frame with a torn and filthy mattress sitting on top of it. Next to the bed were two battered wooden chairs.

On the floor around the bed were several empty beer bottles and half a dozen used syringes. Smith waved the gun, indicating he wanted me on the bed.

"No!" I said, stopping in my tracks.

I probably should have kept my mouth shut, but these guys were starting to piss me off.

"Look, you jerks," I said, turning to the men. "I've gone along with your bullshit games, but

I've had enough. If you want to talk to me, fine. If you want to make up stupid names for yourselves, that's fine too. But put the guns away and cut the crap."

Alright, so I don't usually talk like that. But jeez, enough was enough.

"My brother," Smith said. "Perhaps you are correct. This whore has no manners. Please teach her some."

Jones came toward me, but as he did, I snapped into a defensive position from my recent self-defense training with Gina. I spun around with a high, hard, roundhouse kick.

She would have been so proud of me. The kick was well-timed, and I caught him with the sole of my shoe, square in the face, below his right eye. The blow made a loud wet *slapping* sound.

I was about to follow up with a snap kick to his knee when a hand grabbed the back of my hair and pulled me upwards. I was off balance and swung my arms wildly. Without warning, I felt a rough *thump* as Smith's fist hit the side of my head.

Hot pain radiated outward while white spots flashed and danced before me. Stunned, I staggered sideways.

My eyes cleared enough to see Jones come at me, his cheek already reddening and starting to swell. A trickle of blood escaped his nose. Looking at his smashed face made me feel proud.

Jones raised his fist and walked toward me. I prepared myself to take another blow when Smith barked out: "No! Wait! I need her undamaged. Later."

Jones hesitated, took another menacing step toward me, and then stopped. He stared at me with a look of pure hatred.

He lowered his fist and smiled. Blood was now running down his face, and covered his teeth in a red grimace. The smile sent a shiver of fear through me.

Through blurry eyes, I saw Smith pull a pair of handcuffs from his jacket pocket. He took my arm, dragged me to the bed, and forced me to sit on it.

He fastened one cuff onto my left wrist and the other to the head of the bed frame. This left me enough slack to sit on the side of the bed.

Smith arranged one of the wooden chairs so it faced me. Lights were still dancing in front of my eyes, but Jones had moved his chair to the foot of the bed and was still staring evilly at me. He'd found a dirty rag somewhere and held it to his bleeding nose.

Cool, maybe I broke it.

I then saw the hatred in his eyes had been replaced with something worse. He was still grinning, but now his eyes had a sick look of lust and anticipation.

"Now then," Smith said. "You will tell me where my property is."

"What property?" I asked.

"Do not play games with me! My brother wants you to give untruthful answers so he may use you for pleasure, but I do not. I know it is true the pig Alexander Sternwood has my property. I want to know where they are. Where did he hide them?"

Okay, so Alex had something belonging to a couple of pissed-off guys. And it was more than one something. With that information, a few things fell into place, but still not enough for me to figure out what was happening.

The problem was I had no idea what they were talking about. Alex had been selling things, but I didn't know what they could be. My only chance was to tell them what I already knew.

"He sold them," I said. My head was still throbbing, making it hard to think clearly. "He's been selling them all week. He sold some at a place called Meyer's Jewelry and then at the Tropical Paradise. That was three days ago."

"That is false!" Smith shouted. "Without help, he could not sell all of them. Without Reinhardt, that would be impossible."

"I saw him," I said. "He met Reinhardt at the Tropical Paradise. They went into the back room of the art gallery there and didn't come out for ten or fifteen minutes. After he left, two big guys in a black Lincoln began following Alex. They've been following him ever since."

"You lie!" Smith screamed. "You cannot have heard the name of Albert Reinhardt until I said it just now. You have no idea who I'm talking about, do you?"

"It's true," I protested. "I did see Alex make a sale to Reinhardt."

"Lying whore!" Smith's face turned red as his anger mounted.

He stood up and threw his chair against the wall, where it shattered with a loud crash. His chest heaved as he began to pace back and forth.

He walked toward me and brought his arm up to backhand me but, for some reason, didn't. He then resumed pacing in front of the bed.

After about thirty seconds, he stopped, seeming to make up his mind about something. He walked over to a metal cabinet next to the broken printing press, opened the door, and pulled out a knife.

It was almost a foot long and had a thin pointed tip. There were ink spots of various colors all along the blade and handle.

Smith stared at the knife momentarily, then turned and looked at me. His eyes were open wide with excitement. His lips were parted in a cruel smile.

He walked over to where I was shackled to the bed. Bending down, he took the knife and lightly held it against my nose. He had his face less than three inches from mine. I felt his hot, foul breath against my face as he spoke.

"Listen carefully, bitch," he said. "Your life depends on your next answer. If you do not speak truly, my brother will harshly use you for his enjoyment, and I will cut you. I have not yet decided in which order these things will occur. Although it is most likely Reinhardt would have called me if he possessed my property, I must know for sure. If you have truly seen Alexander Sternwood with Albert Reinhardt, then you will be able to describe to me what he looks like, no?"

For a moment, I panicked. My head throbbed, and my mind was blank. I couldn't remember what Reinhardt looked like.

Come on, Laura. You saw him three days ago. What did he look like?

"Answer me!" Smith screamed. As I watched, he took the knife and slashed it across the top of the mattress. A deep cut opened in the padding, less than three inches from where I sat.

Little black spots danced in front of my eyes as I stared down at the cut in the mattress, horrified by the knowledge that the knife could just as easily slice open my leg.

Smith now pressed the knife against my stomach. I shuddered and took a deep breath.

"He's a little shorter than you and thin. He's about sixty years old and athletic like he runs a lot. He has short blond hair, a gray beard, and a mustache. And he had bloodshot watery eyes like he had allergies or was on drugs or something."

Smith's eyes opened wide. He started yelling to Jones in some language I didn't understand. Jones stood up, waved his arms, and yelled back. This went on for a full three minutes. They looked like a married couple having a spat.

It stopped as quickly as it started. Jones turned

and stomped out of the room. Smith looked at me for a moment, then spoke.

"We will now visit the Iceman, Albert Reinhardt. If what you say is true and he has my merchandise, then Reinhardt will answer to me, and you will live. We may even release you after you amuse us and my brother pays you back for what you did to him. If what you said is false, I will come back and deeply slit your belly. I will then watch with joy as you bleed to death before me."

Smith then stalked out of the room. I heard the front door of the office open and close. After a minute, the engine of the Chrysler turned over, then grew faint as the car pulled out of the lot.

Crap.

I sat on the edge of the bed while my whole body began to shake. At times like this, I thought I should work in a beauty salon or maybe at the library. I'd be good at that stuff. Nobody at the library threatens to gut you like a fish if you tell them they owe a three-dollar fine for an overdue book.

~~~~

It took me almost five minutes before I could think again. When my heart slowed to a fast trot, I looked down at the handcuff locked to my wrist.

Out of desperation, I yanked hard to see if I could pull my hand out. I was rewarded with a bolt of pain as the cuff bit into my wrist.

It reminded me of a Stephen King novel I'd once read. It was about a woman who was also handcuffed to a bed.

As I recalled, she had to slice off part of her thumb with a piece of broken glass before she could slip the cuff off. I hoped I could get myself free without having to resort to that.

By lifting the mattress, I could see the other end of the cuff was securely attached to the bed frame. I swung my legs around and stood up. I wrestled off the mattress and took a good look at the frame.

Disappointment hit me as I saw the frame was a solid piece of welded iron. It didn't have an opening, a gap, or any way to simply unbolt it. The bed frame was too big and heavy to drag out of the building.

Okay, let's go to plan B.

The problem was I didn't have a plan B. I didn't know how long they would be gone. If they decided I knew too much, they might come back and finish me off before finding Reinhardt. Thinking about that made my heart kick back into high gear again.

I looked around the room. Maybe I could pry the cuff off the bed if I could find a metal bar. The bar would have to be thin enough to get between the cuff and the frame but strong enough not to bend when I put my weight behind it.

I pulled the bed across the concrete floor toward the old printing press. As soon as the heavy bed started moving, it made a deafening screeching sound.

Ignoring the noise, I scanned the broken machinery, hoping to find some sort of metal rod. I spotted one piece that might work, but it was securely bolted to the body of the press.

I then tugged the bed to the metal cabinet Smith had gotten the knife from. I opened the cabinet door and looked in.

There were old ink cans and some wooden sticks, but nothing useful. In frustration, I turned and screamed:

"Damn it! Give me a freaking break!"

As I yelled, I glanced over to a stack of shelves on the far wall. My purse sat on the uppermost shelf, next to several old ink cans.

I stopped breathing. My mind was racing. Jones had taken my purse and tossed it to Smith. Had Smith gone through it? I couldn't remember.

Why had he put it there? Was there anything still in it I could use?

Well, only one way to find out.

Once again, I pulled the bed across the concrete with a *screech*. Sweat was running into my eyes, and I was nearly exhausted by the time I had crossed the twenty yards to the shelf.

I reached up to get the purse but was two feet short. I grabbed the bed with my cuffed hand and lifted it, but I still couldn't get it high enough to catch the purse strap.

I looked around for anything that could help. On the floor, twenty feet to my left, I spotted a wooden paint-stirring stick. I tugged the bed over to the stick, picked it up, and then dragged the bed back to the shelf.

Holding the paint stick, I stretched my arm to its limit. I pulled the bed several inches off the floor using only the handcuff chained to my hand.

The cuff dug into my wrist, and the pain was intense. I took a deep breath and held it.

With one last jab, I hooked my purse strap with the stick. I gave the strap a yank, and it tumbled off the shelf. I caught it one-handed before it hit the floor.

Panting and drenched with sweat, I sat down

hard on the edge of the bed frame, clutching my purse to my chest. With my whole body shaking, I opened my bag and peered in.

When I saw what was inside, I began to giggle. The giggles rose until they became full-blown laughter. I laughed so hard I couldn't breathe, tears rolling down my face. So okay, maybe I was a little hysterical.

Gradually, I relaxed, tears still streaming down my face. Inside the purse were my pistol and my cell phone.

I pulled out the Glock and felt the weight of it in my hand. I carefully aimed at the chain stretched tight between the cuffs.

I angled the pistol so I wouldn't shoot my hand or the bed. After all of this, I didn't want the bullet ricocheting back and hitting me. With a deafening *Boom!* I yanked my arm up. I was free.

With a handcuff still attached to my wrist, I got up and crossed the room to the door leading out to the offices. I opened the door a crack, then eased it open, the Glock following my every movement. Nobody was in sight.

I peered out of one of the grimy windows to see if anyone was waiting for me in the dirt parking lot. Of course, the gunshot would have alerted them to my escape if anybody had been there.

Well, I thought, *it's tough luck to anybody who gets in my way right now. I'm in a real bitchzilla kind of mood.*

~~~~

I walked outside, first to the parking lot and then to the street. I half-walked, half-ran a block to the west, then a block to the south. I crossed the road and went over an embankment.

This put me on the north bank of the Salt River. I walked half a mile west, following the river along a city maintenance path, until I came to the Scottsdale Road Bridge.

I was about to climb the embankment up to the road when I noticed I was still holding the Glock. Knowing this wouldn't do, I slipped it back into my purse.

I climbed the slope to Scottsdale Road and began walking north. I unlocked my phone and called Sophie. She answered on the second ring.

"Sophie," I said. "You're not going to believe the shitty day I'm having."

"Again?"

"Yes, again."

"Where are you?"

"In South Scottsdale, about five miles south of the office. Can you come get me?"

"Yeah, but it's Saturday. You'll owe me."

"I always owe you. Okay, I'll meet you at…"

My voice trailed off as I looked around. Okay, so where was I? Then I saw it, less than half a mile up the road.

"Sophie, I'll meet you at Jeannie's Cabaret. And, um, would you bring a handcuff key?"

~~~~

I walked into the club and collapsed on a seat at the bar. For some reason, the handcuff and chain dangling from my wrist weren't getting a lot of attention. I suppose the people here were used to seeing things like that.

I'd been in the club about five minutes when I got a call from Suzie Lu. She said one of her graduate students had cracked the password, and she had my file open. She'd be home all afternoon, and I could stop by and pick it up any time. I told her I'd be there in an hour or so.

~~~~

I was still working hard on a second Chivas at the bar when I saw Sophie walk in. She took three steps into the club and then stopped.

She opened her mouth and stared at the stage.

A blonde and a brunette had come out a few minutes earlier and were dancing on the main stage next to the brass pole.

After briefly looking at the women on the stage, Sophie's eyes slowly went from table to table and then from man to man. I saw her eyes linger on a couple of younger guys next to the main stage.

As the song ended, Sophie turned and walked over to where I sat at the bar. As she sat down, I saw her face had the pink glow she always gets when she starts thinking about men.

"This is the most amazing place," Sophie said. "There are fifty men in here who are ripe for the plucking. Those naked women did all the work of getting them hot and ready. All I need to do is to pick one out."

"Haven't you ever been in a strip club before?" I asked.

"First time ever, I swear," Sophie said. "I knew they stripped, but I never thought about what else happens in strip clubs. Now that I'm in a room full of horny men, it's got me all horny too. I think I have to find a man to use hard and nasty. Maybe I'll find one who likes a good spanking. You know, I can already feel the pressure building. I gotta relieve the pressure soon, or the results won't be pretty."

"Well, go pick out a man," I said. "But give me the handcuff key and drop me off at my apartment first?"

Chapter Ten

Sophie dropped me off at my apartment building and then took off to find a man. I first looked around to make sure the two creeps who'd grabbed me earlier weren't anywhere nearby.

I then took the stairs, two at a time, to the second floor. I walked down the hall and knocked on Suzie Lu's apartment door. After a moment, it opened, and Suzie let me in.

Today she wore a short red silk robe, black fishnet stockings, and red spike-heel boots. I walked in and looked around, but I didn't see any naked men chained to the wall.

Suzie led me to a desk in the corner of the living room. She had three computer monitors lined up in a row on the desk, looking like something in a science fiction movie.

Suzie took the disk out of her purse and handed it to me. "Here's your original. I didn't know if you wanted it back or not. I emailed you the unlocked version. It turns out the encryption software they used is an old Department of Defense program. It's been out for a while, and a lot of people use it. I had one of my grad students download the codebreaker program from an encryption group bulletin board."

Suzie turned to her computer and pulled up my file. As we waited for it to open, I asked her a question that'd been bugging me since the day before.

"Um, did that guy pay you a hundred dollars an hour yesterday just so you'd smack his ass with a paddle?"

"Well, sure, but it's not only the spanking the guys pay for. Most of my subs want the complete fantasy. I do the 'Cruel Teacher and the Bad Student', the 'Naughty Nurse and the Helpless Patient', the 'Sadistic Prison Guard and the Shackled Inmate', almost anything."

"I had no idea men even wanted that sort of thing."

"You'd be surprised. It sometimes involves some serious role-playing, but I don't mind. The guys appreciate having someone who understands their needs. Besides, I make more from being Mistress McNasty than I do from being a tenured university professor. Ironic, isn't it?"

"Don't you worry that the university will find

out about it and get upset?" I asked.

"Not really. The chairman of the Board of Regents has a weekly appointment with me. He goes for the 'Stern Mother and the Naughty Boy' fantasy. That one's very popular." She leaned over and said in a confidential tone, "Personally, I think he was weaned a little too early." Then she shrugged her shoulders as if to say, *what are you going to do?*

As Suzie talked, I noticed a small digital timer sitting on her desk. It was shaped like a chicken and was counting down to zero.

Three seconds, two, one, zero.

At zero, the timer started to cluck. It was as if the chicken had just laid an especially large egg. Suzie reached over with her slender fingers and lightly touched the reset button. The timer went back to fifteen minutes and started counting down again.

"You'll have to excuse me for a moment," Suzie said. Her voice was so quiet she was almost whispering.

She walked over to the bedroom door, slipped off her robe, and hung it on a peg on the wall. Underneath the robe, she wore a black lace and red satin Merry Widow bustier, complete with a black G-string and red garters.

The breast cups of the corset looked like two big red pointy ice cream cones. Suzie had transformed herself into Asian Dominatrix Madonna.

A large sliding bolt was used as the lock on the bedroom door. With some effort, Suzie slid the bolt to unlock the door. It slid open with a loud metallic *Snap!*

"I got the loudest bolt I could find," Suzie turned and said with a grin. "The guys are usually blindfolded, and I like them to know I'm coming in. Waiting for the sound of the door to be unbolted really drives them crazy."

She went in and closed the door.

Curiosity overcame my better judgment. I got up and stood next to the bedroom door. I couldn't hear anything inside but muffled talking. The room must be pretty well soundproofed. Annoyed, I pressed my ear to the door.

"You filthy pervert," I heard Suzie say in a soft but menacing voice. "You've been touching yourself again while I've been gone, *haven't you?*" There was the muffled sound of a strenuous protest. He must have been gagged.

"How dare you lie to me!" Suzie shouted. I'll show you what happens to naughty little boys who touch themselves without permission and then lie to their Mommy!"

There was a *whoosh*, followed by the loud *slap* of leather smacking against bare flesh. This was followed by a muffled moan.

"That was for touching yourself," Suzie said. "This is for lying to Mommy."

Whoosh-*Slap!*

Whoosh-*Slap!*

Whoosh-*Slap!*

With each stroke, his moans became louder and more urgent until they became one long, muffled cry begging for mercy. This went on for two or three long minutes. The man's screams trailed into a series of sobs and moans.

I heard footsteps approaching and backed away from the door. Suzie came out and slid the bolt home.

On another peg on the wall was a small red towel. Suzie took the towel and dabbed the sweat from her neck and forehead. She then hung the towel back on the peg and put her robe on.

"I absolutely love that guy," she said, slightly out of breath but still with that infectious smile. "He takes one hell of a hard spanking and then complains I was too soft. It's the belt for him and plenty of it."

"You're saying he *likes* it?"

"He's one of my best clients. He has a three-hour appointment, same time every week." She bent closer and whispered to me confidentially: "His wife thinks he's golfing."

"But that's three hundred dollars!"

"Well, he pays more than the man you met downstairs, plus he usually tosses in a tip on top of that. He's so sweet. I always try to think of new punishments to surprise him." Again, she broke out with a smile.

Jeez, and I sometimes think I'm the one with the issues.

~~~~

We returned to Suzie's computer to see what was in the file. What had popped up on the screen was a spreadsheet. It contained a dozen columns of numbers and letters, each with a heading in a language I assumed was Russian.

I scrolled down through page after page of numbers. Each page was the same as the last but with different numbers. The spreadsheet ended at line two hundred and eighty-seven.

"Do you have any idea what these numbers and letters mean?" I asked.

"Not a clue."

"I don't suppose you read Russian?"

"Not a word."

Great, another dead end.

Suzie sat at the computer, digging into the file, looking for hidden macros or anything else that might be in it. Finally, she gave up.

"The file is just as it appears," she said softly. "A simple spreadsheet with twelve columns and almost three hundred rows of numbers and letters. The only words on the sheet appear to be Russian, but I'm no expert. You could try translating with Google. That usually works pretty well."

She hit a button, and ten pages printed out from her printer. I folded the papers and put them in my purse. I'd need to find someone who could read Russian to let me know what I was looking at, or maybe I'd try the Google thing.

The chicken started clucking again, and Suzie stood up. "Sorry, I can't keep the councilman waiting."

"Thanks for all your help. I hope everything goes alright in there," I said, nodding to the door.

"Him? Don't worry. He's putty in my hands."

~~~~

Keeping my eyes open for the homicidal brothers, I returned to my apartment and tried to think. If the file on the disk was in Russian, what did it have to do with Boris and Ivan, the two Russians who'd tried to kidnap me? What did Smith and Jones know about the Iceman, Albert Reinhardt?

I decided to call Reno to see if he could help me put together the connection.

"Hey," I said when he answered. "Are you still keeping track of Reinhardt?

"Yes, and I'm back on the team shadowing him. The captain's getting nervous. Reinhardt never stays in Arizona this long. He'll either make the buy soon or pack up and go home. He's still up at the Scottsdale Princess. But so far, all he's done today is shoot a round of scratch golf."

"I might have some information on him."

"It figures. I'm scheduled to go back on shift at the Princess tonight at seven-thirty. There's a bistro there with an outside patio. It's on the lower level next to the pool. I'll meet you there at five fifteen."

I looked at the clock, and it was almost three-thirty. I'd have to leave my apartment by four-thirty to make it to the Princess on time.

How did Reno expect me to get ready in an hour?

~~~~

After a quick shower, I spent several minutes doing a passable job on the hair and the make-up. I put on a shiny purple top and a black skirt I save for special nights on the town.

I showed a respectable amount of cleavage between the low-cut top and my push-up bra. I took a final look at myself in the mirror and was out the door.

~~~~

Reno was waiting for me at an outside table overlooking the main pool. He stood up when he saw me and his old smile was back.

Although I'd told myself I wouldn't give him any goofy smiles or go the slightest bit schoolgirl on him, I also broke out into a big smile. I couldn't help myself. Once I saw him, I didn't care if I looked goofy or not.

The waiter came over, and we each ordered a coffee.

"Have you found Alexander Sternwood yet?" Reno asked, still smiling.

"No, there hasn't been anything. His girlfriend's beyond worried, his grandmother's still calling the mayor, and Lenny's in a near panic."

"Just your typical day at the law office?"

"Don't joke about it. I'm worried about him too."

Reno glanced down at my wrist. It had several deep scrapes and had already started to bruise.

"I wasn't joking," he said. "This is actually pretty calm for you."

"Did you forget about the dead guy I found in Alex's apartment?"

"Nope. I'm surprised you've only found one body so far."

"You're such a jerk. Have they found out anything about the dead guy?"

"Only that we still don't know who he is. Some of his clothing had Russian tags, for what that's worth. He didn't have any ID, and without his hands, he didn't have any fingerprints. Nobody matching his description has been reported missing. And, his dental records and DNA don't match anything in the database."

"So, he's still just the dead guy?"

"Yup," Reno said. "He's still just the dead guy."

"Did you find anything in Alex's apartment?"

"Not a thing. No drugs, nothing that had been

stolen. They broke and smashed everything but didn't seem to take anything obvious. You said you had news about Albert Reinhardt?"

"I was with two men, supposedly brothers, today," I said. "They were foreign with accents I couldn't place. Middle Eastern or Asian, maybe. They were convinced Alex had some things that belonged to them and that Reinhardt would want to buy these things. They were upset they couldn't locate Alex or their merchandise."

"Any idea what the 'somethings' could be?"

"Not a clue, but whatever they are, they're probably responsible for Alex's disappearance."

"Can his girlfriend help? Maybe she knows what Alex was fencing?"

"I don't think so. I get the feeling she's in the dark about all of this."

"She may know more than she thinks she knows. Talk to her. You might get more information than if a badge interviews her again."

"Do you think Reinhardt could have anything to do with Alex's disappearance?" I asked.

"It's possible," Reno conceded, "but I still don't see more than a minor connection between Alexander and Reinhardt. The other day, we saw your man possibly fencing something with

Reinhardt at the Tropical Paradise. But it's not the kind of exchange Reinhardt's usually involved in. There's a structure to his buys. It's never in a public location. There are always bodyguards, and usually multiple groups involved."

Reno took a sip of his coffee. "You said Alex was out on parole and working as a car salesman? Any dealings with Reinhardt would be out of his league. I don't even see how Alex could be a middleman on a sale like that. It doesn't make sense. Who were these brothers you were with?"

"Jealous?"

"No, but they must somehow fit in with this."

"All I know is they called themselves Smith and Jones. Smith had an English accent with something foreign mixed in. They were operating out of an abandoned printing shop south of Curry Street. It didn't look like they'd set up an office there or anything. I think it was just a place they'd found and were temporarily using."

"Let me know where it is, and we'll check it out. Do you know anything else about them?"

"They were driving a white Chrysler. It looked like a rental."

"Did you get the license?"

"Sorry, I was sorta preoccupied at the time."

Reno arched one eyebrow. "That's not much to go on, but I'll hand the information over to our squad leader and the detective handling Alexander's case. Maybe they can put something together."

~~~~

We sipped coffee for another twenty minutes, watching the sun drop below the horizon. There were several clouds in the western sky, and they had turned a bright yellow.

"It looks like a nice sunset tonight," Reno said. "Let's go for a walk. I know a good spot."

He stood up and tossed a ten on the table. We walked off the patio, around the pool, and onto a sidewalk running down to the golf course.

About fifty yards from the hotel building, a side path branched off from the main sidewalk. This path led to a secluded bench facing west. It was empty, and Reno walked me to it.

Although Reno didn't sit close to me, he was right about the sunset. It was beautiful. We watched as the clouds turned a brilliant orange and then to a dull cherry red.

We talked a little at first, then watched the darkening sky for almost ten minutes without speaking.

As it got darker, small lights along the path turned on, as did thousands in the trees throughout the resort.

"I love the lights here," I said. "It gives everything such a soft glow."

"Yeah, you always looked better in the dark."

"I can't believe you said that. You're such a jerk."

Reno looked at me. "I've missed you."

My heart jumped in my chest. Once again, I broke out with a big smile.

Damn him.

"Oh yeah? So now you miss me? What do you want to do about it?" I asked and leaned over to him. "You got any ideas? Like maybe you want to kiss me?"

"Listen, I don't need you to give me any ideas. I'll kiss you when I feel like it."

I hope you feel like it soon.

Reno must have read my thoughts. He leaned over and kissed me. It was the lightest of kisses. Our lips barely touched, but I felt the kiss down to the tips of my fingers. It was like a starter's pistol firing to wake my entire body.

He kissed me again. His mouth was slightly

parted, and I felt his tongue brush against my lips. If the first kiss had been a pistol shot, this one was a cannon blast.

My heart sped up, and I felt my face get hot. His hands slid around my waist and pulled my body to his. I reached up and grabbed his face, holding it against mine.

I found my body responding to each new kiss. It was getting hard to breathe, and I was again starting to tingle all over.

As we kissed, he lightly ran his hand up and down the inside of my thigh. The feeling was maddening, and I knew I couldn't stand it any longer. I pulled away, gave him my sweetest smile, and looked into his eyes.

"I want you, Reno."

"I know I'm going to regret this, but I want you too," Reno said, giving me another soft kiss.

"You won't regret this," I said, kissing him back.

"Oh, I probably will," Reno moaned.

Yes! The time has come.

"Do you want to go to my place or yours?" I heard myself ask.

"I can't. I have to be back up here in an hour," Reno said. "That's hardly enough time to drive down to my place and come back. Your place is even farther."

My heart sank.

It's always something.

"My car in the parking lot?" I asked.

Looking at him, I saw he was smiling and giving me *that* look.

"You want it bad, huh? Why don't we get a room here?" he said. "We could get a good start now." He leaned over and softly kissed me. "And then, after I'm done with my shift, we could stay up and watch the sunrise from the balcony in the room. They say room service here serves a great breakfast."

I flashed back to my dream about Reno and me together, here at the Princess.

"You aren't wearing your red silk boxers, by any chance, are you?" I asked.

He smiled but didn't say anything.

Oh, God!

My heart pounded harder. I could feel my body tighten at the thought that Reno and I would soon be together. I leaned over to kiss him again.

My cell phone rang.

There was an uncomfortable moment while we

both pretended it wasn't ringing. I ignored the phone, and it switched to voice mail after half a minute.

We stood up. Reno put his arm around my waist. I snuggled against him as we walked toward the main lobby and the reception desk.

My phone rang again. I ignored it again. Reno looked at me.

"It's going to keep ringing. You should either answer it and get rid of them or just turn it off."

I pulled the phone out of my bag to shut it off. As I was about to hit the power-off button, I saw it was Danica.

"Hold on one second," I said as I opened the phone. "Danica might have some word on Alex."

"Danica?" I asked. "What's going on?"

From the phone came the unmistakable sound of a woman in the depths of hysteria.

"Danica? What's wrong?"

She wasn't speaking words, merely making loud moaning sounds.

"Danica?"

Now there was sobbing and crying mixed in with the moaning.

"Danica? Where are you?"

"*I'm . . . at . . . home*," came the answer between deep sobs.

"Don't move," I said. "I'll be there in twenty minutes."

Crap.

I disconnected the phone and looked up at Reno. I expected him to be pissed.

"Go," he said. "It sounds like she needs you. If it's anything big, call me right away. I'll have a patrol car there in five minutes."

"But, our night?" I asked.

"There'll be another night."

"Yes, there will be." I hugged him, then turned and ran out to my car.

~~~~

I sped down Scottsdale Road to Danica's house. I had crazy thoughts of Alex lying dead in Danica's living room. I pulled into her driveway and knew something was very wrong.

Danica was sitting on the front edge of her porch with her legs hanging over the side. I got out of my car and walked up to her. She had a look on her face I'd seen before, the dazed and vacant stare of a woman who's been traumatized.

"Danica?" I asked. "Are you alright? What

happened?"

She looked up at me. Her face was wet from tears. "My house, go in and see what someone did to my house. It's terrible."

I eased open the front door and slipped in. The house was trashed, just as Alex's apartment had been, but on a much larger scale.

Chairs were gutted and overturned. Pictures were ripped off the walls and flung onto the floor. Books were scattered everywhere. Someone had been looking for something and didn't care about being restrained.

I reached into my bag and pulled out my pistol. I'd learned my lesson from the last time. Whoever trashed the house could still be there.

I went from the living room to the kitchen, to the garage, and then to the master bedroom. Each room was as bad as the last. Satisfied the house was now empty, I went outside, where Danica was still staring into space.

"How long have you been here?" I asked.

"About half an hour. I got home and found the house this way. I didn't know if I should call the police. I had your card, so I called you."

"Well, I doubt this was a random act," I said. "Is anything missing?"

"That's the strange thing," Danica said, "I don't think anything is. All of my jewelry is in a pile in the bedroom. The paintings are on the floor, but they're still here. Some are worth over ten thousand dollars. The TV and stereo are broken, but they didn't take them. Nothing seems to be missing."

"You'd better call the police. It's likely it somehow ties in with whatever's happened to Alex. Besides, the insurance company will need a police report to start the paperwork."

~~~~

The police came, took pictures, and dusted for prints. Danica filled out a statement and some forms. An hour and a half after the police arrived, they packed up and left.

The police didn't see a direct tie-in to Alex's disappearance. Since nothing seemed to be missing, they didn't see it as anything other than kids or perhaps an angry former boyfriend.

I still thought it somehow had to be linked to Alex. But why would someone ransack her house now? It's been my experience that the timing of these things isn't random.

What had they been looking for? Why didn't they do it yesterday or the day before? Why not tomorrow, for that matter? I still didn't know enough to come up with any sensible answers.

As I reviewed the facts in my head, I looked at Danica. She was staring at the mess in her living room, absent-mindedly petting her cat, which fortunately had escaped unharmed.

"Are you going to be okay?" I asked.

"I don't want to stay here tonight," she said. "My mom lives over in Sun City West. I don't work tomorrow. I think I'll stay the rest of the weekend with her. Maybe I'll be ready to start cleaning up the mess by Monday."

I followed her into the bedroom. She pulled out suitcases from her closet until she found an undamaged one, then laid it open on the bed. She walked around the room, picking random pieces of clothing from the closet and floor, then folded them into the suitcase.

Danica was starting to calm down, and I thought she'd be alright. As she scooped her jewelry back into a box, I told her to call me if she needed to talk. I also said I'd call her if I got any new information on Alex.

~~~~

I drove back to my apartment and climbed the stairs to my floor. I heard noises down the hallway, so I eased the pistol out of my purse.

I carefully rounded the corner and saw Grandma Peckham standing in front of her door. She was holding two large bags of groceries and trying to balance them with one hand while pushing the key into the lock with the other. I stashed the gun and took both bags, allowing her to use her key to open the door.

"Thanks," she said. "I hate to set the bags down. It hurts too much to bend over and pick them up again."

We walked into her apartment, and I set the bags on the counter.

"Thanks, again. Would you like a Diet Pepsi?"

"That sounds great," I said. "It's been a long day."

"I could sneak in a shot of Appleton. That'll help take the edge off."

"No, I'm okay. It's just been sort of a crappy day."

"Really? What happened? You were being careful, weren't you?"

I sighed and confessed. "Two guys grabbed me this morning and handcuffed me to a bed. They apparently were brothers."

Grandma looked down at my wrist, where the bruise had turned bright purple. "Oh? Brothers?"

Grandma asked, a slight smile on her lips. "You know, I once had a boyfriend who had this brother. This was before I met Grandpa Peckham, of course. I was going to college in Cambridge then, and these boys were a couple of years older than me. One night we were all at my place having cocktails, and before I knew it, all three of us were in bed. I'd never done such a thing before, but, land sakes alive, they were tigers between the sheets. They made me sore in places I didn't even think could get sore."

Eeeewww, that's an image I won't be able to get out of my head.

Grandma sighed, then sat there for a moment, staring into space with a grin on her face. She shook her head as if to clear away a happy memory.

"If you don't mind my prying?" Grandma asked. "How old were they? These brothers of yours."

"One was in his mid-twenties, the other in his mid-thirties."

"*Oh mercy!*" she said, fanning herself. "And they handcuffed you to a bed?"

"Well, yes," I protested, "but it wasn't anything like that."

"Not that I'm saying there's anything wrong with being handcuffed to a bed by two men," Grandma said. "After all, at my age, I don't know what's considered kinky or normal anymore."

"Do you think it's changed a lot since you were young?" I asked.

"Well, in my day, having a man use his tongue on a woman *down there,*" she whispered and pointed, "was considered kinky. You could even get arrested in some parts of the country for doing that. But I read in *Cosmo* last month that sex can't be considered successful nowadays unless the man first makes the woman orgasm at least three times by doing that. Well," she sighed, "if that's the case, I guess neither of us has been too successful lately."

She rested her fingertips on my arm and leaned close to me. "With the thin walls in this building," she said, "I think we'd both know if the other was having any success."

~~~~~

I returned to my apartment, but after what had happened at Danica's, I didn't feel like sitting home alone. Plus, the thought that Smith and Jones might come back for a second try was weighing on my mind.

Sophie had called earlier and said she was still

on the hunt for a man. She and Gina would be going over to Maya Day and Nightclub, a great place across the street from Nexxus.

Maybe that would be the thing to take my mind off the assignment. Who knows? Perhaps later on tonight, I'd be able to hook up with Reno after all.

I spent a few minutes in front of the mirror, refreshing my make-up and fluffing up my hair. My wrist had a broad purple bruise around it, but there wasn't much I could do about that.

I took the elevator down to the atrium, then walked out to the parking lot. The night was warm, and there wasn't even a trace of a breeze.

A black Cadillac pulled up next to me as I unlocked my Honda. The car stopped and two guys climbed out.

One was merely big, while the other was huge. The big one was in his late twenties, while the huge one was in his late forties or early fifties. Neither one was smiling.

Shit. Not again!

I dug in my purse until I found the Baby Glock. I pulled it out but realized I didn't have a round in the chamber.

"Miss Black, Tony DiCenzo would like to

have a word with you," the merely big one said, unfazed by the gun pointed at him.

My heart sped up to about one-forty, and I felt sweat break out on my forehead.

"Tough Tony DiCenzo wants to talk to me?" I said, trying to sound calm. "You're serious? Why would he want to talk to me? I've never met the man before in my life."

"I have no idea why he wants to talk to you," the huge one said, "but you can be damn sure it's important. Otherwise, why would he send us out to get you? However, we aren't here to make you do anything against your will. You don't have to come with us, but it's been my experience that it isn't wise to upset Mr. DiCenzo."

I couldn't come up with an argument against that. Besides, I told myself, the DiCenzos were somehow involved with this. Maybe I'd learn something.

Chapter Eleven

I climbed into the back of the Caddy. The huge guy closed my door and then got into the front passenger seat. The merely big guy settled into the driver's seat and started the motor.

I felt around on the seat. "Hey, wait a minute," I said. "There aren't any seat belts back here. How do you expect me to ride in a car without seatbelts?"

"Not to worry," the huge one said. "Milo is a very good driver."

"I don't care how good of a driver Milo is. You can't expect me to get in a car with two guys I don't know from Jack and ride around with no seatbelt. Are you nuts?"

The huge one looked at me like I was a slug. "So that you don't feel uncomfortable not knowing who we are, I'm Johnny Scarpazzi, and that's Milo."

Milo turned his head around from the front

seat and smiled at me. His smile revealed a bright gold tooth.

"The parts that buckle the seat belts are just wedged under the seat," Milo said. "None of the guys we normally drive around want to be seen wearing them. It's bad for their image. After a while, the latches slip into the crack and fall behind the seat. If you reach in, you can probably pull one out."

I reached down into the crack and fished out the latch. I put on the belt and felt better when it clicked. I noticed both Johnny and Milo were fumbling around, putting their seat belts on too.

What is it with men?

~~~~

Once the seatbelt thing was resolved, Milo put the Cadillac in gear, and we drove in silence. After about ten minutes, we pulled up in front of the Carmine Hotel.

The Carmine was built about twenty years before my apartment building but had been maintained a lot better. It now served the upscale business clientele who traveled to the downtown Scottsdale area.

We walked around to the side of the building and descended a wide, deep stairwell. Johnny went down first. I followed while Milo brought up the rear. A flashing red and blue neon sign proclaiming *Junior Baker's Blues Club, Music Nightly,* bathed us in its glow as we descended.

At the bottom of the stairwell, Johnny pulled open a large red wooden door, allowing the sound of music and laughter to pour out. Entering the dim club, we passed the doorman, the cashier, and the coat check girl.

The club wasn't large, but it was packed. Maybe thirty tables and a small dance floor were in front of a low stage. The high tin ceiling was painted flat black, and a half-dozen ceiling fans blew around the warm air.

The walls to the sides and behind the stage were covered with thick red curtains. Along the far wall was a bar with two dozen people leaning against it or sitting on stools.

Playing on the stage was a quartet of older black men. I recognized Junior Baker as the man sitting in the middle of the group playing electric guitar.

Baker had been playing the Blues his entire life and was a Scottsdale music legend. The band was playing an Arizona version of Chicago Blues. It had a fast beat with a pounding bass line.

The dance floor was packed. Everyone was

laughing and smiling, having a great time. If I hadn't been with the two goons, I would have liked to have stayed and enjoyed myself.

We walked to the back of the club, where three steps led up to a small room. As we approached, a large guy held up his hand to stop us.

He patted me down and searched my bag. He took out my Glock and put it in his coat pocket.

"You'll get it back when you leave," he said.

Stepping into the room, I realized it had a great view through a large cutout in the wall. The room was elevated enough to look over the heads of the people sitting at the tables and see onto the stage. The music was clear but at a softer volume than in the room outside.

Several small tables sat in the front of the room, while a couch sat at the back with end tables on either side. A dozen candles in red glass were scattered on the tables. These and a small lamp in the corner provided the only light in the room.

I recognized Maximilian at one of the tables. Seeing him again made my pulse rise another notch, but in a way that had nothing to do with fear.

Sitting alone at a table in the back corner of

the room, I noticed a tall, graceful-looking woman. She had long black hair and piercing blue eyes.

I would have described her as beautiful, but her stare sent a tingle of fear down my spine as she assessed me. Hers were the eyes of a jungle predator sizing up her prey.

And then I recognized the man standing between the two tables. He was Tough Tony DiCenzo.

~~~~

I walked over to DiCenzo. Physically, he was only slightly taller than me, but he was built like a bull.

He had the tanned skin of a man living year-round in the desert. His face was round and pockmarked, with a bulbous nose and piercing dark eyes. His black and gray hair was short and slicked straight back off his forehead.

I knew from news reports that he was in his late fifties. I also knew, by reputation, that he didn't take a lot of crap from anybody.

"So, you're Laura Black," he said. He offered his hand as he looked me up and down. "I've heard some good things about you. Welcome to my club. So, what do ya think about it?"

His voice had a Brooklyn accent mixed in with the raspy overtones of a two-pack-a-day habit. "You and me have business to discuss, but first, what'll you have to drink?"

"Scotch," I said. "Whatever you have handy, one ice cube."

"I got a twenty-one-year-old Glenlivet single malt. Best scotch in the club. You oughta try it. In fact, I think I'll have one myself."

He motioned to Milo, who relayed the drink order to a waitress walking by the alcove. DiCenzo then moved over to the couch and sat. He motioned me to a chair.

"Well, Mr. DiCenzo," I said. "This is your club? It's nice."

"I'm glad you like it, and call me Tony. Do you know, I bought this hotel almost twenty years ago? Back then, this room was just part of the hotel basement and was used by Scottsdale General Hospital for document storage. Where the stage is now was nothin' but a pile of dusty boxes going nearly up to the ceiling."

He paused and looked around as if remembering what the basement had looked like back then. "Twenty years ago, Junior Baker's records had stopped selling, and he was flat broke. As it so happened, I met him and found out he wasn't such a bad guy."

"On a hunch," Tony said, "I opened this club and let him run it. Now, he's a household name all over the world, and his record sales have never been stronger. This club has turned a profit every year for the last eighteen years. See, that's what can happen if you find someone you believe in and give 'em an opportunity."

The waitress came into the alcove carrying the tray of drinks. She set them on the end table next to the couch.

I picked up my glass and swallowed a mouthful in a gulp. Hey, at this point, I needed it. Hot pleasure spread from my throat outward. I looked up to see DiCenzo watching me.

"Damn," I said, smacking my lips together. "That's amazing."

DiCenzo picked up his glass and leaned back on the couch, a slight smile on his face. We sat silently for a few minutes, DiCenzo enjoying the music, me sipping the scotch and trying not to shake.

"Now then," DiCenzo said, leaning forward again. "To why we are here tonight. What do you know about diamonds?"

"Um, they're a girl's best friend?"

"Oh, they're much more than that. Let me give you some background on the situation I find myself in, or perhaps I should say, the situation *we* find ourselves in. Through the years, I've found that the more information a person has, the better decisions they're able to make. And I want you to make some good decisions over the next few days, Laura Black."

Something about how he phrased it made the hair on the back of my neck stand up.

"Now then," he said. "Some weeks ago, I was approached by a representative of an organization outta Russia. Seems they'd acquired a large number of high-quality diamonds. As luck would have it, they'd found a buyer in a group called the Consortium. This is an organization made up of various factions from the Middle East and Southeast Asia. They asked for my help, so they could make the sale."

"Why would they want you to get involved?" I interrupted. "It seems like it would be a straightforward deal. Wouldn't having you involved only increase their risk?"

"Yeah, you'd think that," DiCenzo said, apparently not minding my interruption. "But the sad truth is these things never go smoothly. You put a dozen stressed-out guys in a room with guns, money, and a briefcase full of jewels? Christ, something always goes wrong. Feelings get hurt, somebody says the wrong thing, or God forbid, somebody tries to change the terms of the deal just as the money is exchanged. The results are never pretty."

Tony took a sip of the scotch and continued. "The two Consortium brothers, who are currently calling themselves Smith and Jones, have somewhat of a reputation for violence, as you may have noticed. That tends to put people on edge. Also, there was the question of which country to do the exchange. Turns out there's a general dislike of Russians in the Consortium. Too much bad blood over the years. The Russians didn't feel none too safe going on Consortium territory. On the other hand, the Consortium refuses to travel to Russia because of some recent government interference in this sort of transaction. They worry about being arrested and getting tossed into some Russian prison."

"So, how do you fit in?" I asked. I was so thankful my voice was still steady. On the inside, my guts were starting to knot up.

"I'm the broker, the middle-man, the referee, you might say. I provide a neutral location for the sale. I arranged for an independent expert to verify the merchandise's quality and the method used to pay for it. What's more, I offer non-aligned security for all parties. You might say I make sure nothing goes wrong. I receive a percentage of the sales price in exchange for those services."

"But something went wrong?" I asked.

"You're damn right, something went wrong!" DiCenzo yelled, slamming his hand down on the table. Everybody in the alcove turned to look at him.

"The goddamn Russians had no more than checked into my hotel before they lost the fuckin' bag with the diamonds. That simple fuck of a Russian courier got distracted when some girl flashed her tits at him. Then some little jack-off switched the bag and walked out of my hotel with the diamonds."

Tony paused and regained his composure. I could tell by the look on his face that he didn't like to show his anger.

"It took us two days of questioning people and reviewing the security tapes until we found out what happened," he calmly said. "Then, even after we found out how it was done, we still didn't know who did it. We'd never seen the guy before and had no idea who he was."

He took another sip of his scotch and shook

his head. "Now, I've been doing this sorta thing for years, and believe me when I say security was solid. Nobody other than my top guys knew the merchandise was coming into Scottsdale. It shoulda been impossible for anyone to get at the diamonds, but it happened anyway. I've lost sleep over this one, and let me tell you, Laura Black, I *never* lose sleep over business."

"But other than losing your commission, how can this go badly for you? No one could blame you for it."

"No, that's not how it works," DiCenzo said, shaking his head. "The bag switch happened in my territory and my hotel. I'm responsible for security on this. That makes it my fault. If I don't get the diamonds back and make sure the sale takes place smoothly, I look like a world-class asshole. And believe me, I won't be known as a world-class asshole."

"Did you find out who switched the bag?" I asked. "I saw the hotel security video. You couldn't make out any details of the man who made the switch. I suspect you know my partner, Gina Rondinelli, has been looking for whoever took the bag. So far, she's come up with zip."

"That's true, I do know. And you're right. The tapes don't show shit. We might never have known who'd done it if the prick had just taken the diamonds and laid low. But he got greedy. In the end, they always get greedy. In the bag was a pouch containing three diamonds, samples, you might call them. We put the word out on the street to keep a lookout for them. They're easy to spot because they're big, three to five carats, blue-white in color, and internally flawless, rather rare."

"What did you find out?" I asked.

"It turns out the first diamond was sold to a pawn shop in downtown Scottsdale a week ago Wednesday. The jerk sold it for half of what he could have got from a proper fence. The pawnshop owner gave us a call to let us know he had one of the diamonds. We still didn't know the guy's name because he used a bogus ID, but the pawnshop owner let us have the video file from his security camera. Much better resolution than the tape from the hotel lobby. But, except for showing his picture around, we were forced to wait. Not to worry, though. I knew if he sold one diamond, he'd sell the other two. People are stupid that way."

DiCenzo paused and held up his now empty glass. Milo took off to get two more.

A bag with diamonds? Alex?

"A few days later, my old friend Jimmy Meyer called to tell us a guy matching the photo had just sold him the second diamond. Jimmy also told me he'd set him up with Ingrid at the Tropical Paradise to sell the third. Ingrid was going to handle the buy, but I also called in the Iceman to verify the diamonds were the ones we was looking for."

Milo came back in with fresh drinks. I was grateful for the scotch. It was the only thing keeping me from running out of the building, screaming at the top of my lungs.

"At this point, we only wanted to find out who the guy was and where he lived," DiCenzo continued. "After the sale at the Tropical Paradise, we had additional pictures of him. We got his license plate from the security cameras in the parking lot. From that, we discovered his identity."

"So, who was it?" I asked, although I already knew the answer.

"I thought you would have guessed by now," DiCenzo said. "It's your buddy, Alexander Sternwood."

Well, I saw that coming.

"How could he have been so stupid?" I said aloud.

DiCenzo made a small grunt of disgust and continued. "So, Sternwood makes the sale to Ingrid. Then, what do you know? When we reviewed the Tropical Paradise security tapes, we found someone was following him. That someone was you."

Shit, I should have seen that coming too.

"From the cameras in the parking lot, we also got your license plate. From that, we discovered who you were and that you worked for that shyster Lenny Shapiro. So now you can see how you're beginning to fit in."

Yeah, what the hell did I walk into?

"I sent Max over to Lenny's to do two things. The first was to find out what you knew about Sternwood and the diamonds. The second was to press you into helping us look for the bag. Sometimes people get lucky, and maybe you'd come across it without knowing what it was. As it turns out, you were approaching Sternwood from the angle of keeping an eye on him for his grandmother. For us, that was perfect. You had a legitimate reason to follow his every move. I've had a team following you to see where you went and who you've talked to."

Okay, so hearing this pissed me off. I knew I should have kept my mouth shut, but hey, that's just me.

"You've had guys following me? Did they happen to notice I almost got shot by the Russians and was kidnapped by Smith and Jones? If I'm so freaking important to you, why'd you let them almost kill me?"

As I was yelling, I glanced over to see Max with a slight smile on his face. Milo had crept over to where we were sitting, presumably to get between Tony and me in case I got out of hand. Tony absent-mindedly waved Milo away.

"Laura," DiCenzo said. "No need to get your panties in a twist. We were aware of your confrontation with the Russians. As a matter of fact, it was Max here who fired the shots that got you outta that one. Maybe he shouldn't have done it. We're not supposed to be taking sides in the recovery of the diamonds, but it seemed to have worked out for the best."

I looked over at Max, who was still smiling and holding up his glass in a salute. It was a sweet gesture, and seeing his eyes on me gave me a warm feeling. It was a nice distraction.

"We also saw Smith and Jones take you," Tony said. "But, we didn't know at the time if you were working with or against them. By the time we found out they were trying to pump

272

information outta you, you'd already helped yourself escape."

DiCenzo reached over, picked up my hand, and examined the bruise on my wrist. "We didn't interfere because we weren't needed. Actually, you handled yourself pretty good in there. It made me think you were somebody I could do business with."

Well, that's great. I almost get killed just to impress the freakin' Godfather.

"Tony," I said. "If you knew Alex stole the diamonds, why didn't you pick him up and question him until you found out where they were? I suppose that's what I would have done."

"Yeah, that mighta worked," DiCenzo said. "But what if he had a partner who was holding the diamonds and would bolt if Alex didn't call-in every half hour? We might never have found them. We figured he'd lead us right to the diamonds if we followed him. No need for a heavy hand.

"You probably already know this," I said. "But Alex disappeared two days ago. They also found a dead guy in his apartment, minus his hands. Do you know what's going on?"

"Matter of fact, I do," DiCenzo said. "You know Alexander's gone missing, but what you may not know is the Russians have him."

"Boris and Ivan?"

DiCenzo smiled. "That's not their names, but yeah, those two."

"Is he alright?"

"At the moment, he's doin' okay."

"What about the dead guy?"

"After the diamond courier lost the bag, Moscow sent orders to get rid of him. This was not unexpected. You can't lose that much merchandise and expect to come out in one piece. After taking care of the courier, the two Russians left the body in Alex's apartment. That was after they had chopped off the hands. I heard they sent them FedEx to Moscow as proof of the job."

Tony sipped his drink and shook his head, as if the thought of mailing hands across the world was the most ridiculous thing he'd ever heard of.

"After placing the body in the apartment, they performed that messy search. We, of course, already knew the apartment was clean because we'd already searched it. Unfortunately for Alex, he came home while they were still there. The Russians had been keeping an eye out for him, just like us, in hopes he would lead them to the diamonds. They saw Alex's appearance as a golden opportunity to learn what he did with the diamonds directly."

"Why'd they put the dead guy in the apartment?" I asked. "It doesn't make sense."

"Leaving the courier there was stupid. All that did was pull the police into it. The Russians were going to use the courier to send a message to Alex -- 'Come up with the merchandise, or else.' Of course, since they snatched him as soon as he came home, the message was probably lost on him. From what I hear, he's confessed to giving the bag to someone else."

"Tony, there were two guys following Alex around on Tuesday and Wednesday. They were involved in a smash-up on the highway Wednesday morning. The car was registered to Arizona Security Enterprises. Were those two guys working for you?"

DiCenzo looked at me, a spark of surprise in his eyes.

"So, you knew about those two? Yeah, they're mine. Damn shame about them losing Alex. We didn't pick him up again until he came back to his apartment later that night when he was grabbed by the Russians."

I took another sip of my scotch and gathered my thoughts.

"Okay," I said. "I'm confused. You said Alex had already sold all of the diamonds in the bag. What's left to look for?"

"Like I said, the three diamonds in the pouch were only samples," DiCenzo said. "Hidden in the bottom of the bag are more diamonds."

"How many more?"

"A lot more."

"Tony, that doesn't help me much. I'll need to know what I'm looking for."

DiCenzo looked at me for a moment; he then hardened his eyes. The sight of Tough Tony DiCenzo staring at me like that was beyond creepy.

"Alright," he said, "you're looking for almost three hundred diamonds. Altogether, they weigh a little over half a pound. They're all big, three to five carats, perfect color, and most are internally flawless."

"Half a pound?"

"Yeah," he said. "Half a pound. So now you know why everyone's so stirred up."

DiCenzo paused to take a drink. "Laura Black," he said, his voice softer now. "Since we're working together on this one, let me ask you something. The past few weeks, the city's been uneasy, but maybe not so much that you'd hear about it. Something fundamental has shifted, but I can't put my finger on it."

"Like what?" I asked.

"When something's about to happen, something big, I mean, you tend to get warning signs. Sometimes they're subtle, but I've had warning bells going off in my head for a couple of months now."

"What have you felt?"

"Nothing on the surface, you understand, but on the loading docks, the warehouses, and in the back rooms, people are uneasy. My guys tell me a lot of the independent illegals have disappeared. I don't think they actually went anywhere, but they're keeping off the street. The heads of the gangs in south Phoenix have dropped outta sight. From what my sources tell me, even the cops have felt it. Since you get around during the course of your daily activities, I was thinking perhaps you might have felt something amiss."

"Not a thing, but I've been busy the last few weeks with an assignment, and then this new case with Alex came up."

"At first, I thought this Alexander Sternwood thing might have something to do with it, but now I'm not so sure. Nevertheless, keep your ears open and let me or Max know if you see something that doesn't feel right. Can you do that?"

I was about to tell Tony the whole situation didn't feel right when Johnny came over and whispered something to him, waving his arm toward a door along the back wall. The whispering and arm-waving continued for almost a minute.

DiCenzo spoke a few sentences to Johnny. Johnny nodded his head and left the room through the back door. Three men then appeared, and DiCenzo waved them in.

Two goons walked a third man over to where DiCenzo was sitting. Everyone in the alcove turned to see what was happening. As soon as the third man entered the room, he started talking.

"Tony, I want you to know I'm so sorry about what happened. I was out of my mind. I just went a little nuts that day. I'll pay for everything, and I swear to you it'll never happen again."

"You'll have to excuse this interruption," DiCenzo said to me. "I have to take care of some unfinished business. This piece of shit standing here is Sonny Boy Muzzi. He used to work for me, bringing merchandise up from Mexico. He's been hiding in his sister's basement for a week, but she ratted him out to us this afternoon. Seems she didn't want any part of hiding his sorry ass any longer."

Although DiCenzo was talking to me, he kept his voice loud enough so everyone in our little room could hear him speak, even over the music played on stage.

"A few months ago, Sonny Boy took it into his head to start banging the wife of the manager of the Headhunter Lounge at the Tropical Paradise. She also works there as a cocktail waitress."

DiCenzo looked at Sonny. "And in case you didn't know, that's one of my bars, in one of my hotels."

DiCenzo paused and took a sip of his scotch. "It got to the point where he was nailing her two, three times a week. He even started renting rooms at the Tropical Paradise so they could meet on her dinner break. The manager of the lounge caught wind of it and started missing work. He'd wander through the hotel, listening at doors, trying to catch her in the act. It was starting to affect his performance at my lounge. Not to mention it was starting to creep out the hotel guests. I mean, here's this guy walking up and down the halls, pounding on room doors whenever he hears someone inside having sex."

DiCenzo motioned Milo for two more drinks.

"To help straighten things out, I sent a couple a guys over to have a little chat with Sonny. No violence, you understand, just a friendly conversation. Personally, I think it's a little unseemly that the wife of one of my guys is disrespecting him like that. In my heart, I couldn't let it go on. Things like this always lead to trouble."

Tony paused, as if gathering strength to control his emotions.

"So, after we had our little chat with Sonny here, what does this piece of shit do? He goes over to the Tropical Paradise, walks into the Headhunter, and smashes up the whole goddamned lounge. He smacked around the girl tending the bar when she tried to stop him. He even used a chair like a baseball bat to break the lights that hung over the tables. Then just to top it off, he throws the chair over the top of the bar. It wiped out a dozen bottles of my best booze, all top-shelf stuff. By the time hotel security got there, Sonny had bolted. You know the rest. So, now that I have him, I've gotta figure out what to do with him."

Sonny started up again. "Tony, look, I've learned my lesson. I'll pay for everything and leave the state. I'll never bother you or your business again, ever. I swear."

DiCenzo turned to look at him. He spoke in a low menacing tone. "What the hell do I look like to you? Do I look like someone you can fuck with? Do I look like someone whose bar you can smash up and then just walk away?" DiCenzo dope-slapped him across the top of his head. "Well, do I?"

Sonny shook his head back and forth like a bobblehead doll. DiCenzo looked over at me. "So, Laura Black, help me out. If you were me, what would you do with this piece-of-shit scumbag?"

Jeez, how do I get myself into these situations? I'm giving a gangster advice on delivering mob justice to a wayward henchman? Okay, stay calm. Just think like a mobster.

I took a long sip of my fresh scotch and put on my best gangster face. I looked over at Sonny Boy Muzzi. He wasn't acting much like a tough guy today. His head was hanging down, and he looked like he was about to cry.

"Hey, having an affair is a two-way street," I said, adding as much bravado to my voice as I could without having it shake. "He didn't make her do nothin' she didn't want to do. So, I'd give him a pass on that one. Maybe your lounge manager is lousy in the sack. Who knows? But tearing up your lounge, that's completely different. He smashed the lamps? Slapped around a bartender? Threw a chair over the bar and wiped out the good booze? Hell Tony, if I was you, I suppose I'd shoot him."

Shoot him? Crap. Why did I say that? I didn't mean to. It just slipped out.

DiCenzo looked at me for a moment and then nodded his head. "Shoot him? Okay, we'll shoot him."

Sonny Boy's head shot up, his entire body shaking. Terror filled his moist red eyes. "No, please, Tony, no. I'm so sorry. Don't do this, and I'll make it up to you. I swear on my children. Please don't do this!"

DiCenzo dismissed him with a slight backward wave of his hand. "Get this piece of shit outta here." The two goons began to drag Sonny back out.

Oh Jeez! Did I just hand that guy a death sentence? Crap! Okay, stay calm. How the hell can I fix this?

"Hey," I said. "Hold it a minute."

Everyone stopped and turned to look at me. DiCenzo's drink was in his hand, stopped halfway to his lips. He was staring at me, opened-mouthed.

"Um, in thinking about it, we probably

shouldn't shoot him. Hell, if we shot somebody every time they smashed up a bar, there wouldn't be many of us left. Come on, haven't we all smashed up a bar once or twice before? I mean, it's a *bar*. They're sorta made to get smashed up."

There was a general murmur of assent. Everyone in the room nodded their heads, and there was some laughter from two goons at the table near the door. Even DiCenzo nodded his head, and a shadow of a smile appeared, probably remembering the last bar he'd smashed. This went on for a few seconds, then DiCenzo spoke: "Now, you're not suggesting we just let him go, are you?"

"Um, *nooo*," I said. "You'll need to teach him a lesson, of course. People can't go around feeling like they can smash up one of your bars without suffering some sort of consequences."

DiCenzo grinned again. "Okay then, if we're *all* in agreement." He looked at Johnny and the two guys holding Sonny Muzzi. "Take him out and do what we'd talked about earlier."

With Sonny muttering tearful thanks, the two goons walked him through the back door. I looked over at DiCenzo, who was sipping his scotch and watching Junior Baker and the band.

"Um, Tony, you weren't really going to have

him shot?" I asked. "Were you?"

"Well, personally, I thought shooting him was a little severe. But since you're my guest tonight, I thought I'd cut you some slack. But, if the truth be told, his fate was decided before we even brought him here."

DiCenzo let out a small chuckle. "But from the look on Sonny's face, he thought we'd go through with it. That's what's important."

DiCenzo took a sip of his scotch and then waved his hand. "Besides, word of this will get out, and people will be less eager to mess with my interests. Besides, as an interesting turn of events, Sonny Boy now owes you a favor. You saved his life. You never know when that could come in handy."

He owes me a favor? Yeah, or else he'll shoot me for handing him a death sentence.

"What's going to happen to him?"

"Oh, they'll just rough him up a little, then break a couple of fingers."

"Rough him up and break a couple of fingers?" I asked, my voice rising.

"Don't worry about it," DiCenzo said with a dismissive wave. "That guy acted like an asshole, and he knows he's getting off damn lucky."

DiCenzo lit a cigarette and leaned back on the couch. Five minutes later, the band finished their set and headed backstage. DiCenzo turned to me.

"Now then, back to our business. I got a hunch about you, just like I had a hunch about Junior Baker. I think you got what it takes to be somebody. So, I'll make it simple. I need you to find the diamonds and bring them to me. I'll broker the sale, and everything will be aces. You'll even get a cut for helping me out."

"What if I can't find the bag?" I asked.

"Then, we've all got a problem," DiCenzo said. "And trust me, Laura Black, you don't want to be in the middle of one of my problems."

"Fine," I said. "But if I'm on your side, either call off your watchdogs or at least tell them to help me out the next time I get in a jam. And make sure Smith and Jones don't come anywhere near me. I've been looking over my shoulder ever since I got away from them."

"Fair enough, Laura Black. You'll have nothing to worry about from them. Okay, enough business for one night. I'll have Max give you a ride home. He's a nice guy. You should get to know him."

Max stood and walked over to where I was sitting. I stood up and followed him out of the room. After I collected my gun from the goon at the bottom of the stairs, we wound our way through the club and went outside.

Chapter Twelve

A black Mercedes roadster was waiting by the curb. An attendant opened the passenger door, and I got in.

As I sat, a man came out of the hotel and motioned to Max. The two men stood together and talked to each other for several minutes.

The feelings I got when sitting in the Mercedes were similar to sitting in Danica's Porsche. But while the Porsche was all about raw power and speed, the Mercedes was more about elegance and sophistication. Sitting in the big leather seat made me feel safe, and the knot in my stomach started to unwind.

As I started to breathe normally again, the events of the last hour played through my mind.

What was I thinking? Agreeing to work with a mob boss?

Without warning, hot tears began to run down my face. I couldn't stop them and didn't even want to try. They were helping to wash away the memory of what just happened.

The door opened, and the interior lights came on. Max got in, and I could see him looking at me.

When faced with a crying woman, most men handle it badly. I was expecting him to attempt some words of reassurance or maybe even offer me a hug. Instead, he gave me a slight nod and closed the door. For some reason, that simple nod of understanding made me feel better than if he'd tried to comfort me.

He put the car in gear, and we became enveloped in the hum of the engine and the glow of the dashboard lights. After a full minute of silence, he spoke.

"You did pretty well in there with Tony. He brought you in because of your abilities, but now he respects you. If you want to know the truth, I think you charmed him."

"I charmed Tough Tony DiCenzo? How can you know that?"

"I've been with him for years. Most people either fawn all over him or try to act tough. You treated him with respect but also as a friend. He values that more than anything. Of course, this diamond business is serious. It's about the worst thing that's happened in the last couple of years.

Charming or not, we're all in serious trouble if this doesn't work out."

I let that last sink in for a minute.

"Who was the woman at the corner table?" I asked. "The scary one in the black leather."

"That's Gabriella."

"What does she do?"

"She's mainly for emergencies."

"Emergencies?"

"I don't think you want to know."

We rode in silence for another minute. My mind was racing in a dozen different directions at once.

"What was Tony talking about when he said something's wrong in the city? It seemed to bother him as much as the missing diamonds."

"Well, that's the big question lately. Something's going on, and it seems to be pretty important, but we don't know what it is. It's a big mystery, and in our business, nobody wants a mystery."

"Tell me about it."

"At this point, there isn't a lot to tell. A couple of people have gone missing. A few payments haven't been made. Some shipments never arrived, and the worst part is we don't know who's behind it all."

"No idea?"

"Just a possible name -- Valentino. Ever heard of him?"

"No, but everything that's happened tonight has been new to me. If I do hear anything, I'll let you know."

"Tony would appreciate that. Is there anything else you'd like to ask?"

"Tony said you were the one who shot up the Russians' car when they were about to grab me. Thanks for doing that. It pulled me out of a tight spot."

He gave a short bark of a laugh. "No problem. It's lucky for you I was there. Those Russians aren't nice guys."

"Some things about the shooting still bother me."

"Like what?"

"Why were you there in the first place? Do you normally follow women around and shoot at people who bother them?"

"After Alex took out our two guys, I thought I'd fill in for a while. No one knew where Alex was, so I followed you. I figured you'd run into him eventually. We hadn't yet put together that Danica Taylor was a close girlfriend, or else we could've found him sooner."

"How did you know where I was?"

"We put a tracking device on your car."

"It figures. Do you always carry around an assault rifle?"

"Not always."

"I'm a little upset you shot my car. I just got it paid off, and until last week it didn't have a scratch."

"Sorry gorgeous, it couldn't be helped. The Russians had to see that both cars were getting hit. Otherwise, they might have decided to stick around and have a war. I didn't want anybody getting killed. I only wanted them gone. Besides, from what I've seen of your car, no one will notice a bullet hole."

I took the opportunity to slug his arm. It felt like hitting a brick wall. He turned his head and smiled at me.

"Last question," he said. "We're almost there."

"Why did you kiss me the other day?"

He didn't answer right away. I could sense him thinking about it. At last, he said: "I don't know why I did that. It's out of character for me to kiss a woman I don't know. If I offended you, I'm sorry. There was just something about the way you were looking at me."

"And how was I looking at you?"

"It was like I'd opened the door to my bedroom and unexpectedly found you lying naked on my bed. It somehow felt like you were offering yourself to me. I didn't really think about it. I just did it."

Come to think of it, you weren't far off.

"Oh, um, okay."

The car glided into my parking lot. Max found a space and pulled in but left the motor running. He walked around and opened my door. I got out and faced him. I could feel a mutual attraction as we stood facing each other, our bodies only inches apart.

He pulled a card out of his shirt pocket and held it out. "Here's my cell phone number. I keep it on twenty-four hours a day, seven days a week. If you find the diamonds, or if you need me for anything else, give me a call."

As I took the card, our fingers touched. It sent a warm tingle up my arm.

"Um, are you married?" I asked.

"No, not married."

"You have a steady girlfriend?"

"No, but I've been having some naughty thoughts about a woman I met a few days ago."

"Hmm, lucky girl," I said as I felt warmth flood through me. He was standing so close I could feel the heat from his body. I was hoping he'd want to kiss me again. Who knows, maybe this time he'd even finish what he started with the first kiss? Perhaps he'd like to go up to my apartment and make a night of it?

"I hope you don't take this the wrong way," I said, even as I took half a step closer. "But, as a general rule, I don't get romantically involved with members of organized crime."

"I figured that; you seem like a nice girl. But I'm not going anywhere, and there's always a first time for everything."

Yikes!

~~~~

I went up to my apartment, checked to make sure no one was hiding anywhere, and fell into bed. Although I was asleep within minutes, it wasn't a good sleep. I tossed and turned all night.

I dreamed about Reno holding me while I pressed my face against his chest. I had dreams about when I first saw Danica and Alex at the dance club. I had dreams of Max and the kiss. Mostly, I had dreams about Tony DiCenzo and the missing bag.

In the last dream, DiCenzo appeared in my bedroom. He was standing over my bed, talking in his soft voice: *"Trust me, Laura Black, you don't want to be in the middle of one of my problems."*

I woke up with a start and looked at the clock, five forty-two. My heart was beating fast, and I knew sleep was over for the night.

I went into the kitchen and put on a pot of coffee. Marlowe came in and looked up at me, wondering why I was up so early.

I fixed us both a big breakfast. Partly because it was something to do and partly because I had a killer headache.

The headache was mainly a result of stress rather than the scotch I had drunk in the club the night before. I rarely get a hangover from the good stuff.

As we ate, I told Marlowe about Junior Baker's and my meeting with Tough Tony. Marlowe's always a great listener but not much in the way of an advisor.

After talking with Marlowe, I realized that thanks to my meeting with DiCenzo, I most likely had everything I needed to solve this puzzle. I just needed to put the pieces together.

I took a hot shower and slipped on a black T-shirt and cargo pants. I put my hair up in a ponytail and only put on enough make-up to cover the bags under my eyes. I felt like a commando going into enemy territory and wanted to look the part.

Sitting at the kitchen table, I made a list of every place that was relevant to the case. I was determined to visit each one and see if I could turn up anything new or at least find something to jog my memory.

I called Sophie and asked her to meet me at the office. She was still in bed and not happy to be woken up on a Sunday morning but said she'd meet me there in an hour.

While driving to the office, I called Gina. She was also still in bed but woke up immediately. I gave her the basics of my meeting with DiCenzo the night before.

"So, it *was* Alex who switched the bag," Gina said. "That would explain why DiCenzo wanted you to be on the assignment. His grandmother had already permitted you to snoop into Alex's private life."

"Do you think I should go to the police and let

them know the Russians have Alex?"

"Tough call," she said. "But I would say no. You don't know where they're holding him, and it seems likely he'll be safe, at least until the diamonds are found. Besides, if the police start questioning everybody about the Russians, Tony DiCenzo will know where the information came from. That's not a good position to put yourself in."

"Anything new with the bag hunt?"

"The hotel sent over security videos from every available camera angle from when the bag was switched. They're sitting on my desk if you'd like to review them, but they didn't seem to show anything new. I've almost completed the interviews with everyone working in or around the lobby during the switch, but I haven't found anything helpful. There're copies of my notes on my desk. I have two more interviews scheduled today, one at ten and one at two."

~~~~

I made it to the office and started reviewing the videos. Gina was right. They didn't show anything new. I could only find Alex on one camera angle other than the one we'd already reviewed in Lenny's office.

That camera showed him walking from the

back of the building into the main lobby. He was carrying the empty black bag and disappeared from camera view when he crossed into the main lobby to meet the Russians. I made a mental note to check which parts of the hotel he would have had to pass through to come in from that angle.

I then read Gina's notes of her interviews with the people working in or near the lobby that day. Several people remembered seeing the Russians, but nobody remembered seeing either Alex or the bag switch. Several men remembered the brunette and how she'd lost her bikini top, some going into incredible detail about the woman and the event, but again, there was nothing helpful.

Sophie came into the office holding a big cup of convenience store coffee. Her hair was a hot mess, and she only had a touch of makeup.

"This had better be important," Sophie said. "I only had about four hours of sleep before you woke me up."

"How was dancing at Maya?" I asked.

"We had a great time. Why didn't you come over? I was hoping you would. We had a cabana near the pool and everything. I even had a guy lined up for you. He was single and had money. He was disappointed you didn't show up after I told him how skinny and sexy you were. Where were you anyway?"

"Oh, I was having a crappy night."

"Again? Really? What happened this time? Somebody handcuff you to a bed again? Or did someone else take shots at you?"

"Two of DiCenzo's goons invited me to a meeting with Tough Tony. DiCenzo said Alex was the one who made the bag switch. He also said from now on, I'm personally responsible for finding the bag. If I don't, then I'm in it deep."

"You're serious? You got to meet Tough Tony DiCenzo? What's he like? Is he as creepy in person as he sounds over the phone? Did he shoot anybody while you were there? From what I hear, he orders people dead all the time."

How do I explain I gave out the death sentences last night?

"Nope, nobody killed, but I still didn't have a lot of fun. But now I need to find the bag, and I need your help."

"You need me to ride along with you again? Should I bring my gun?"

"Bring it if you want, but you shouldn't need a gun. I need someone to help me look around for things I might have missed. I've looked through the videos and read Gina's notes, but they don't help a lot. We're going to have to check out a few places."

"Okay, you've got me until four o'clock. My cousin's getting married tonight, and the family will disown me if I don't show up. You should come too. It'll be fun. They've hired the band *Dog Farts* for the reception."

"Thanks, but Alex and this gym bag thing will likely keep me busy full-time."

"I figured. Speaking of those videos, you should've seen the guy who brought them over. His name's Milo, and he's gorgeous. I like my men big and solid. It's too bad he didn't know how much I like to be hugged and kissed, like when that guy walked up and kissed you."

"I've met Milo," I said. "Next time I see him, I'll let him know about your needs."

~~~~

We went to Alex's apartment first. Crime scene tape was still on the door, but nobody was watching, plus Danica had given me a key.

We slipped in and started searching. Although some of the clutter had been rearranged, the place was still a mess.

Somebody had cleaned up the kitchen, throwing away the perishable food that had been tossed on the floor. I guess the police thought rotting peas and french fries wouldn't help the investigation.

Sophie searched in the kitchen and the living room. I searched the bathroom and the bedroom. I found nothing useful in the bathroom, but the bedroom looked more promising.

In the corner of the room was a desk. I remembered it as having a computer, along with several stacks of papers. The laptop was gone, presumably still in the crime lab, but the papers were still there.

I sat down and started on the first pile. It seemed to consist mainly of old bills. Unfortunately, as I went through the stacks, I didn't find anything helpful.

I'd just finished the last stack when Sophie came into the bedroom holding a small key.

"I found this in a drawer in the kitchen," she said. "Looks like a mailbox key."

While Sophie searched the living room, I went down and used the key in Alex's mailbox. There were two flyers from Walmart, a catalog from Land's End, and a couple of pre-approved offers for credit cards. There was also a letter from *Catalina's*, a high-end jewelry store in downtown Scottsdale.

I took the letter and went back up to the apartment. Opening it, I saw it contained two diamond appraisals dated four days before Alex disappeared.

The first stated the object being appraised was a 4.21-carat diamond. There were a lot of numbers and letters describing the diamond, but my eyes went to the bottom of the page. The appraised value was listed as $33,500 per carat for a total value of $141,000.

The second was an appraisal for another diamond. This one was valued at $36,700 per carat for a total value of $157,000.

I took the appraisals and put them in my purse. Sophie didn't find anything in the living room except for a handful of hundred-dollar bills, which had been hidden in the pages of an old Bible.

I wondered how the people who ransacked the apartment could have missed it. Maybe they weren't looking for money.

"You know, it's a damn shame we don't know if Alex is dead or not," Sophie said. "If he were dead, he wouldn't need this money. As it is, I have to put it back. If I took money from his Bible and he was still alive, I'd probably burn in Hell. Maybe even *La Llorona* would come for me."

"Who's *La Llorona*?" I asked.

"*La Llorona* is the weeping woman of the river. A long time ago, she drowned her children."

"Why'd she do that?" I asked.

"In order to keep a man. I guess he hated kids. But then she killed herself out of grief over what she did to her children. Her spirit still roams lakes and rivers, looking for her kids. Now she's so old and blind, she can't tell if you're one of her children or not. If she finds you, she just grabs you and pulls you under the water."

"Nice story."

"It's mainly a way to keep kids away from rivers, but I've always been scared to death that someday she'd come looking for me."

"Then you're probably right to leave the money there," I said.

~~~~

The next stop on our list was Scottsdale Audi. Sophie stayed in the showroom looking at the new cars while I went in and found William Martin. Even though it was Sunday morning, he seemed energetic and happy to see me.

"On the Tuesday before he quit, was Alex at the Scottsdale Blue Palms?"

"I don't know," he said. "But I can find out in two seconds."

He turned to his computer and typed for several minutes on the keyboard. At last, he looked up.

"Yes, that Tuesday, Alex delivered a new Audi TT Roadster to a client staying at the Blue Palms. Is it important?"

"I don't know. I'm just checking out a story I heard. I'll let you know if I come up with anything."

I stood up to leave. He again gave me the thumb and forefinger gunslinger's salute.

~~~~

Next, we drove over to the Tropical Paradise. Ingrid wasn't working at the art gallery. Instead, a pushy older man kept telling us he could arrange financing on any piece in the gallery. We left without making a purchase and without finding out anything new.

~~~~

From the Tropical Paradise, we stopped at the Scottsdale Blue Palms and the scene of the bag switch. Sophie and I walked around the main lobby, then into the back hall. The video from the hotel security camera showed that Alex had come into the main lobby from this semi-hidden back part of the hotel.

As we explored, we found nothing in the back lobby but a few shops and a rear entrance. Sophie decided to look around in a shop that sold high-end shoes and purses. I went out to see what was beyond the back hallway.

I opened the door and went out into the warm Arizona sunshine. I followed the path from the back lobby and saw it wound down to a parking lot and the main pool area. I assumed Alex had come up this way to make a quieter entrance into the lobby.

I turned and climbed back up the path to the rear entrance. Sophie had moved to a souvenir shop. She was holding up a paperweight of a dead scorpion encased in clear plastic.

"Isn't this the nastiest thing you've ever seen in your whole life?" Sophie asked. "I can't believe the things they sell to tourists. I hate scorpions. Looking at it makes me want to throw it on the floor and stomp on it."

"So, go ahead. Buy it and stomp on it."

"Nah," she said, holding the paperweight up and looking at it from the side. "You know what I'm gonna do instead? I'm gonna buy it. But then I think I'll keep it on my desk. It'll be sorta like having the world's ugliest pet. The best thing about this kind of pet is that I'll never have to feed it, or walk it, or pick up its crap from the carpet. Then, if I ever do get tired of it, I'll take it out and stomp on it. Maybe I'll even run it over with my car."

~~~~

Meyer's Jewelry was our next stop. Jimmy Meyer was there, still looking like the world's oldest hoodlum. We browsed the store for several minutes without finding any clues.

Sophie bought a lovely silver and turquoise ankle bracelet. She stopped outside the store and added it to the collection on her ankle.

It was getting late in the afternoon. I dropped Sophie off at the office in time to go to the wedding. She flipped me off when I told her to catch the bouquet.

~~~~

I called Max, and my heart did double time when he answered. I asked him if the bag had been found.

"There hasn't been any word on it," he said.

"What if the Russians or the brothers find it first? Won't they just take the diamonds and leave the country?"

"The Russians are the sellers. If they find the bag, they'll call and tell us they have the diamonds. Then the sale would take place, and everybody's happy. If the brothers find it first, they might try to sandbag us for a day or two. They'd then most likely insist they'd been insulted and try to leave the country with the diamonds. We've taken safeguards against that possibility."

"So, what do you think? Does anyone have the bag yet?"

"I don't think so. I talked to both groups about an hour ago. I didn't detect anything like that. They're all the same ill-tempered jerks they've always been. Both groups are still demanding we find the diamonds and conduct the exchange. We have men shadowing both groups. Other than the fact that the Russians are still holding Alex, nothing of note is happening."

"Any word on how Alex is doing?"

"None at all. The Russians are playing this pretty close. But it wouldn't make sense for them to kill or even seriously harm him. Every move they make is directed by Moscow, and they don't kill or maim without reason. He should be okay if there's still a chance to get the diamonds back."

I said goodbye to Max and disconnected the phone.

~~~~

I drove through the now-darkened streets of Scottsdale, ending up in front of Dos Gringos. I felt more than a little hungry and knew a three-pack of street tacos would hit the spot.

I went to a booth and ordered the tacos and a Corona. Strangely, the sound of people laughing and the music playing in the restaurant helped me think.

In about ten minutes, the waitress delivered my dinner and another beer. As I slowly munched the tacos, I started at the beginning, piecing together what I knew.

The Russians brought the bag containing the diamonds into the country a week ago Tuesday. Alex delivered a car to the Blue Palms that same morning. While there, he stole the bag from the Russians.

I'd confirmed Alex was leading his usual life until he was asked by his boss to drive the car to the resort. Until he went to the Blue Palms, Alex didn't seem to be involved with any of it.

After he stole the bag, Alex most likely took it back to his apartment. He'd probably looked into the bag on the way.

This could account for where I found the CD, under the seat next to the passenger door. If Alex had just seen the pouch with the three diamonds, he wouldn't have noticed if a disk had fallen out.

Alex had two of the diamonds appraised, but he didn't wait for the official reports once he was told they were real. He fenced the first diamond at a pawn shop in downtown Scottsdale.

He got a pile of dough, quit his job, and then went crazy spending the money. A few days later, while I followed him, he fenced the second diamond at Meyer's Jewelry and the third at the Tropical Paradise.

Jimmy Meyer alerted Tony DiCenzo that he'd bought one of the missing diamonds. Ingrid Shanker, the pinched-faced art dealer, called DiCenzo and told him Alex was in the gallery fencing the third diamond with the Iceman, Albert Reinhardt. At that point, DiCenzo's men began trailing him.

Since Alex was fencing the diamonds, DiCenzo's guys naturally assumed Alex was the one who had the bag and was acting alone, but they couldn't know for sure. If they were wrong and they grabbed Alex, his partner would bolt, diamonds and all, never to be seen again.

Instead, they followed Alex for a couple of days to see if he would lead them to the bag and the rest of the diamonds. They'd already searched his apartment and knew the diamonds weren't there.

DiCenzo discovered my involvement through the hotel security videos at the Tropical Paradise. He then used Lenny to hire Gina and me to help him independently search for the missing bag.

DiCenzo probably told the Russians and the Consortium brothers he would have me assigned to the case. Tony didn't realize how quickly the Russians and the brothers would become impatient and that both groups would try to kidnap me to find out what I knew.

The Russians then tried a more direct approach. They trashed Alex's apartment. When they didn't find what they were looking for, they kidnapped Alex hoping to torture him to find out what he knew.

The brothers were also frustrated the diamonds hadn't been found. Since the Russians already had Alex, they decided I would be the next best hope of finding what they wanted.

Unfortunately, for them, I was able to escape. I knew they would've come after me again if DiCenzo hadn't warned them off. So now there was nothing for them to do but wait. At least, I hoped they would wait.

Danica's house was trashed the day after the Russians kidnapped Alex. Under torture, Alex must have spilled the beans that Danica was his girlfriend and where she lived. The Russians must have thought her house would be a likely place for him to hide the diamonds.

I also assumed the reason my apartment hadn't been trashed was that DiCenzo's men had already gone through it and had told everyone it was clean. Maybe I needed to install another deadbolt.

So where was the bag? If Alex thought the gym bag was empty, there was a real possibility he'd thrown it away. A shudder went down my spine at the thought of that.

No, if Alex had simply thrown the bag away, he would have confessed that to the Russians. They would have then tortured him until they were convinced he was telling the truth. Everyone would've stopped looking for the bag, or at least they'd be looking for it in the Maricopa County landfill. Since that hadn't happened, it must still be around somewhere. The question was, where?

~~~~

After dinner, I got back in my car and drove around Scottsdale. This helps me think, and sometimes I'll go past something that will jog my memory.

I shoved an old Katy Perry CD into the player and turned the sound up. The light, bouncy music helped me concentrate.

I cruised around the clubs in Old Town Scottsdale. I canvassed the neighborhood around Alex's apartment. I drove around Gainey Ranch. I even headed back up to the north Scottsdale golf resorts.

After almost two hours of driving, I had to admit I had nothing. I drove back home to Marlowe and went to bed.

~~~~

I spent another sleepless night and got up in a bleary-eyed depression. A hot shower helped clear my head.

I pulled on a pair of jeans and my favorite red knit top, swiped on some make-up, and again did the ponytail thing with my hair.

I got in my car and headed to work. Even though nothing was going on at the office, I didn't want to sit at home waiting for another idea to pop into my head.

~~~~

I walked into the front part of the office. Gina was nowhere to be seen, but Sophie had just arrived. I could tell this because she was still reading the Surfline Southern California Surf report on her tablet.

I'd seen her do this a hundred times. She'd been a California surfer chick in her youth, and old habits die hard. She heard me coming in from the back offices and looked up.

"They must be having a storm in the Pacific today," she said. "Laguna has overhead waves this morning. I'd love to be back there. It would give me a chance to wear my purple wet suit. I haven't worn it in years."

I plopped down on the chair beside Sophie's desk.

"Wow," she said, "you look terrible. No luck finding the bag last night?"

"Nope," I said, "And I'm out of ideas. I don't know where to go next. How was the wedding?"

"It was great. I met a cute electrical engineer. He works at the Intel plant in Chandler."

"Did Gina come up with anything yet?"

"She has an interview today with a man who knows the woman in the lobby who lost her bikini top. Gina hopes to get a line on whoever paid her to flash her boobs. Apparently, bikini woman works at Jeannie's, so Alex probably knew her, and it was most likely him."

"We've assumed it was Alex, but if it wasn't, we'll have something new to go on. I'm out of leads. I have no idea where the freakin' bag is."

After that, we both sat in silence. Sophie had stopped looking at her tablet. Instead, she stared into space, chewing on her lower lip, apparently deep in thought. I was about to ask her about it.

"There's one thing I don't get," Sophie slowly said. "We don't think Alex had anything to do with this until he showed up at the Blue Palms that day to deliver the car, right?"

"True," I said. "Before that, he seemed to be leading a normal life."

"Okay, that makes sense. But, if that's true, Alex didn't know he would steal the Russian's bag until he saw it that morning. Maybe he went to the front desk to ask about the person he was delivering the car to? Maybe he saw the little guy holding the bag tightly to his chest? Maybe he could tell it was valuable? Maybe he somehow talked bikini-girl into losing her top to create a distraction? I get all that. What I don't get is where did he get the bag he used to make the switch? Odds are pretty low he happened to be carrying around the exact same color and type of gym bag."

It was like somebody turned on a light in my head. It was so obvious. Where *did* Alex get the bag? A bag that was so identical, the Russians didn't know it was switched until they opened it?

I'd assumed he'd had some time to plan this out, but Sophie was right. This was most likely a spontaneous event for Alex. He had to get a bag from somewhere in the hotel. If I could find out where Alex got it, maybe I'd have a clue for finding the one that was switched.

We didn't see any gym bags in the hotel when we were there the day before, but we also hadn't been looking for one. Maybe I should look again.

~~~~

I drove up Scottsdale Road to the Blue Palms. I walked into the lobby for the second time and looked around.

Several shops were in the front and back lobbies, but none sold gym bags. One shop carried luggage, but the smallest piece was much larger than Alex's bag on the videotape.

I asked the woman behind the counter if they sold gym bags or anything small enough to resemble one. She said no but suggested I try the souvenir shop.

The souvenir shop sold backpacks and beach bags but no gym bags. I walked around the area and looked for a locker room or a weight room without luck.

Dejected, I walked over to a comfortable couch and sat. Where could Alex have found a gym bag at a moment's notice? At most, he would have had five or ten minutes before the Russians and the bag disappeared forever. Not to mention he also had to convince a woman to flash herself in public.

I let my eyes wander around the back lobby. I ended up glancing at a shop I'd seen before. Again, it was like somebody turned on a lightbulb in my head.

When Gina and I first saw the security video, Lenny said the small black bag was a gym bag. I hadn't questioned it. Gina hadn't either. It sort of looked like one, and we assumed Lenny knew what he was talking about.

But with the poor quality of the video, it could have been any type of bag. All of the guys had assumed it was a gym bag. Mobsters are tough guys, after all, and tough guys carry black gym bags.

I got up and walked into the shop. Thirty seconds later, I knew where Alex had gotten his bag. I also knew what he did with the bag after he had taken the three diamonds out of it.

Chapter Thirteen

I sped down Scottsdale Road and raced into Danica's subdivision. I pulled into her neighborhood and drove to her house.

When Danica answered the door, she looked better than she had Saturday night, but I could tell she still hadn't gotten a lot of sleep. She was wearing only a hint of make-up, and her hair was bunched in a loose knot on top of her head. It was the closest I'd ever seen Danica to being messy.

"Hey," I said, letting myself in. "How's the clean-up going?"

"Oh, it's going alright. There's just so much damage. It's going to take a few days to go through everything. The police came over again this morning and were here for almost an hour. They left a few minutes ago. I think they're now trying to see if this has anything to do with Alex."

We walked through the destruction of the living room and into the kitchen. Danica pulled an open bottle of white wine from the refrigerator.

She poured out a full glass and handed it to me. She then refilled hers, which had been almost empty. Danica held her glass up and looked at it.

"For some reason, they decided not to break my wine glasses. I thought I should celebrate by using them a lot today."

I held up my glass, and she tapped it with hers. It made a pleasant ringing sound.

"The other night, you thought nothing was taken," I said, taking a sip of the wine. "Have you discovered anything missing yet?"

"I've spent all morning sorting through the mess. The insurance company wants me to make a list of everything that's missing or damaged. I've gone through the entire house, and I haven't found anything missing. Damaged, yes. Destroyed, yes. Missing, no."

"What about your purse?" I asked. "The big black shoulder bag you've been carrying around all week."

She looked at me like I was slightly short of insane. "I don't know. I put it in the closet a couple of days ago. I'll go see if it's still there."

We got up and went into the living room. She walked into her bedroom, only to return a moment later. I knew the answer by the look on her face. I felt my heart sink.

Two chairs in the room were still more or less intact. I sat in one and waved for Danica to sit in the other.

"Tell me about the bag," I said. "When did you get it?"

"There's not much to tell," she said. "It's a Ferrucci Spy bag. I got it last week, on Tuesday, I think."

"I saw you at Nexxus last Monday. You had it there, so you must have bought it before then."

Danica blushed two shades of red.

"Danica," I said. "What is it? Tell me what's wrong."

"If I tell you something, you've got to promise never to tell anybody. I'd never do anything to hurt Alex."

"Okay," I said, mentally crossing my fingers. "I promise. Now, what is it?"

"Well, the Saturday before he disappeared, Alex and I had dinner at Different Pointe of View. It was so wonderful. That restaurant has one of the nicest views in the city. I could tell Alex was excited about something. He can't ever hold a secret. After dinner, he gave me a shoulder bag. He even tied a red bow to the strap. Seeing the look on his face as he gave it to me made me so happy. He hasn't been able to afford many presents, so this was a big deal for him. It was a Ferrucci, a Spy bag, like the one they took from my closet."

Danica leaned over and whispered, "But that one wasn't a real Ferrucci. It was a knockoff, like they sell over the border in Rocky Point or Nogales."

"Did Alex say where he got it?"

"He was a little vague about that initially, but he eventually said he found it."

"He said he found it?"

"He said he found it in the trash at the back of the Scottsdale Blue Palms."

"In the *trash*?"

"I know, but he said the rich women staying there are always tossing away things like that. He said that for some women, spending two thousand dollars for a purse isn't any more of a big deal than me paying two hundred dollars for a pair of shoes. When they get tired of their purses, they just toss them. I know I've sometimes done the same thing with shoes when I'm tired of them."

Man, I'd really like to take a crack at her closet.

"But since the bag was a fake, I thought maybe the woman was too embarrassed to keep it."

"Did he say what he was doing up at the Blue Palms? That's quite a ways from where he lives or worked."

"He was delivering a sports car to a woman staying at the resort. He said he was driving the car around to the back and saw the purse sitting on top of a pile of boxes in a dumpster."

"Was there anything in the bag when he found it?" I asked.

"I don't know. When he gave it to me, it was empty. I even checked the pocket."

"Tell me more about it. You said it was a knock-off? Are you sure? How do you know it wasn't real?"

Danica sat there, giving me a look.

"Hey," I said. "Don't give me that look. I need to know. I wouldn't know a real Ferrucci from a fake Ferrucci if it hit me in the head."

Danica looked down at my bag, eighteen dollars at Bargain Barn. This brought a sad smile to her face.

"Okay," she said. "Well, the exterior fabric and hardware were alright. Maybe those parts were even real Ferrucci. But there were several parts of the bag nowhere near Ferrucci standards."

"Like what?" I asked.

"Well, first of all, it felt wrong. Real Ferrucci's are light and have a very smooth and balanced feeling. They sort of *swing* as you walk with them. This bag felt too heavy and wasn't balanced at all, like maybe the straps were stitched in the wrong position. And there was a cheap leather insert sewn into the bottom. The quality of the leather and the stitching were nowhere near the quality of the rest of the bag. You could also tell it was a fake Ferrucci because they used a cheap interior fabric; that's always a dead giveaway."

"I take it you didn't tell Alex it wasn't real?" I asked.

Her eyes softened. "Oh no, I didn't have the heart. You should have seen him. He was so proud of it. I didn't care that he'd given me a bag he pulled out of the trash or wherever he got it. It was sweet he thought of me. He thought he had found a real Ferrucci, a two-thousand-dollar bag. It would have crushed him if he discovered it was a knock-off."

"Where is the bag now? The fake Ferrucci?"

I saw that Danica was searching her mind. I didn't want to make it worse for her, but if she'd thrown the bag away, the Russians would probably kill Alex, but not before I choked her to death first.

"Um, I'm sorry," she said. "But I really don't remember."

"Come on, Danica," I said. "Think. When was the last time you had it?"

"Well, the only time I took the bag out was when we went to Nexxus for champagne. That was two nights after Alex gave it to me. We went to celebrate Alex getting his trust fund money."

"That's when I saw you with it."

"I couldn't help noticing our waitress kept staring at it. I could tell she knew it was a knock-off. It was so embarrassing. I decided to get a real Ferrucci and get rid of the fake. Alex would want me to use the bag whenever we went out, but I couldn't be seen in public with a fake Ferrucci."

"So, you went shopping for a real one? When was this, the next day?"

"That's right. I remember I didn't know what to do with the fake. I had the bag in the car when I drove to Biltmore Fashion Park. I was thinking I had to get rid of it so Alex wouldn't find it. I stopped by work first to pick up my cowgirl costume. I needed to drop it off at the dry cleaners. A guy had thrown up on it."

Ugh, gross!

She saw the look on my face.

"It happens sometimes," she said. "Oh, now I remember. I stuck the fake in my locker at the club."

Yes!

Mentally, I pumped my fist up and down and made silent *wooo-hooo* noises. Outwardly, I did my best to remain calm.

"Okay, that's great," I said. "Now then, is it still there?"

"I don't know. Christy saw me put it in the locker. She dances at the club too. I've known her since I started there. She said it was a hot-looking purse. I told her it was a fake, but she said it looked real enough to her."

"Did she take it?"

"Well, not then. But I said she could have it if she wanted it. She told me I was sweet and she'd pick it up later. I think she knows my locker combination, so unless she forgot, she might have it by now."

I felt my heart sink again. It looked like I had found DiCenzo's missing bag of diamonds, and now it was most likely gone again.

Why does my life suck so much?

Danica was watching me. She could see something was wrong.

"What is it?" she asked. "Why is a fake Ferrucci so important? There isn't anything in it, and it can't be worth more than about fifty dollars."

I decided to level with her, more or less.

"Anthony DiCenzo is looking for that bag. He was sorta responsible for keeping it safe, and then it disappeared. I had a meeting with him, and he asked me to help him get the bag back. He's not the kind of guy you refuse."

Danica's eyes got so big I was surprised they didn't fall out of her head. Her breathing sped up, and her face flushed a light crimson.

"You mean the bag I loved, the bag I was embarrassed by, and then the bag I gave away? That was Tony DiCenzo's bag? Tough Tony? The mobster?"

Her voice came out in a loud but squeaky shout. *"Oh, my God!* You've got to get it back to him! Nobody messes with Tough Tony, and I mean nobody. People who mess with Tough Tony have a habit of disappearing. You had a meeting with him? Oh my God, Alex. Do you think Tough

Tony took Alex?"

"When I talked with DiCenzo, he said his people didn't have Alex, but I get the feeling we'll need to get the bag back to DiCenzo before Alex is released."

Danica stood up and began pacing back and forth, not knowing what to do.

"Look," I said. "This should be easy. Is your friend Christy working today?"

She shook her head back and forth. "No, Monday's her day off."

"Why don't you call her and see if she has the bag."

"I can't. She doesn't use cell phones anymore, she's lost like four of them, but I know where she lives."

"Great," I said. "Why don't you go over to her house and see if she has it. I'll go to Jeannie's and see if the bag's still in the locker."

She looked at me and nodded. So far, so good. "Call me if you get it. If I get it first, I'll call you. Before you go, call the manager over at Jeannie's. Let him know I'm coming to get something out of your locker. Is there a lock on it?"

"Yeah, you need to keep things locked up there. The combination is thirty-six, twenty-four, thirty-four." She paused and blushed again. "My measurements."

I just looked at her.

"What?" she asked. "I wanted a combination I could remember."

~~~~

I almost flew the eight miles down Scottsdale Road to the club. I pulled into Jeannie's lot, parked in the first spot I saw, and ran to the door. The bouncers knew me by now and let me in without a word.

I made my way backstage and found the door to the dressing room. An unfamiliar bouncer stood at the entrance, looking unhappy that I was there. My explanation that I had permission to get a purse out of Danica's locker didn't impress him.

I talked to him for five long minutes before he ultimately called the manager to see what to do about me. Fortunately, Danica had put a call through to him, and I was allowed in.

The dressing room was larger than I expected. Four make-up chairs were on either side of the room, each in front of a well-lighted mirror. Several mirrors were covered with photos of kids, men, and pets.

I counted six women in the room. Nobody

seemed to care I was there. I guess they supposed if the bouncer let me in, I must belong there.

I went to a woman who was seated in a make-up chair. She'd just finished with her mascara and was now outlining her lips with a dark crayon.

"Excuse me," I said.

"Oh, hi," she said. "I'm Cherry. Is this your first day? Go and grab an empty locker. The costume racks are two doors down the hall, on the right. Go and pick out whatever you think will fit. I'll help with your make-up if you'd like."

I was getting frustrated. I only wanted to get to the damned locker.

"Thanks, but I'm looking for Danica's locker. She sent me in to get something out of it."

"Too bad," the woman said, looking me over. "A lot of the guys like skinny girls. You'd make some good tips. Danica's locker is the one on the far right, but I think it has a lock on it."

"That's okay," I said. "I've got the combination."

With my heart pounding, I went to the locker. It had a cheap dial lock with a stainless-steel body and a black dial. It was the kind of lock we had back in high school gym class.

I looked at the lock and realized I'd forgotten

how to open them. Was it left-right-left or right-left-right? After the first number, did the dial have to go around once to the second number, or twice? It took me three tries until I heard the soft metallic snap, and the lock pulled open.

Danica's locker was stuffed to the bursting point. I started pulling out things at random.

There was a sequined red, white, and blue outfit with a matching bikini top and thong bottom. The outfit was held together with Velcro. For quick tear-away action, I assumed.

I took the outfit from the locker and tossed it on a chair. Next was a blue silk harem-girl costume with the same Velcro fasteners. This outfit joined the first on the chair.

Next, I pulled out the red and white leather cowgirl outfit. I looked but didn't see any throw-up stains on it. That went on the chair too.

At the bottom of the locker was a pair of red cowboy boots, probably for the cowgirl costume. I pulled out the boots, then I saw it.

Underneath the boots was a black bag. I pulled it out. There was the double "F" on the clasp signifying the bag was indeed a Ferrucci, real or fake.

I was so excited I almost squealed. I closed my

eyes and held the bag to my chest, waiting for my heart to slow.

I allowed a tiny thought of optimism to creep into my head. *Perhaps things would work out okay? Perhaps Tony DiCenzo wouldn't have me hunted down? Maybe I could still get Alex back alive?*

Naaah, it was too much to hope for. I decided to stick to finding out what was in the bag and hope everyone came out in one piece.

I was dying of curiosity about what was in the bag, but I didn't know who might be watching. I took the bag by its straps and swung it back and forth.

Danica was right. It did feel too heavy, and it did seem out of balance. I've never owned a Ferrucci, but I was so pleased I could feel that for myself.

I looked inside the bag and saw it was empty. I also saw the leather piece sewn to the bottom, although, to me, it looked like it belonged there. I felt the sides and bottom of the bag, but I didn't feel anything lumpy or out of place.

I wanted to rip the bag in half to see if anything was inside, but I decided the dressing room of a strip club probably wasn't the best place.

There, I thought, that was a good decision. Tony DiCenzo would have been proud of me.

My heart was still pounding, and I felt like throwing up as I carefully returned the clothes to the locker and walked back out to my car. I thought the office would be a good place to meet up with Danica and find out if anything was in the bag.

I pulled out my phone and called her, but she didn't answer. I supposed she was still busy looking for Christy, wherever she lived. I left a message to meet at the office and gave her the address.

~~~~

I drove into downtown Scottsdale and pulled into my parking space behind the office. I looked around to see if I'd been tailed.

I didn't see anyone. Of course, that didn't mean anything. These guys had been following me for days, and I never knew.

I unlocked the back security door and went in. After pulling the door shut, I felt relieved when I heard the heavy lock snap into place. Sophie was up front, typing at her computer. Gina was nowhere to be seen.

"Sophie," I said. "Where's Gina?"

"She's still out doing the last interview. I thought she'd be back by now."

Great, of all the times for her to be gone.

I held the bag up. Sophie looked at it, and her eyes grew wide.

"Is that what I think it is?"

"You're not going to believe how I got it, and you're gonna poop out kittens when you see what's inside. We've got to open it up. Is Lenny here?"

"Nope, he's out greasing palms at the courthouse. He won't be back for another hour or two."

"Good, that works. Give Gina a call and have her get back here as soon as she can. I'll lock the doors. We can use Lenny's office."

~~~~

Two minutes later, we were both sitting at Lenny's desk. I'd used a letter opener to rip open the seam holding the leather insert to the bottom of the bag. It was sewn in better than I'd originally thought, and it took a while to pull it apart.

"So, are you going to tell me what's supposed to be in there?" Sophie asked, sticking her head halfway in the bag.

"Hey," I said, "move your head. What's in this bag is maybe nothing, but what's in this bag is maybe something that'll save my butt."

With one last yank, the leather pulled free. I reached in and jerked on a cloth-wrapped bundle glued to the bag's bottom. With a ripping sound, the bundle tore free.

I held it up to look at it. It was about six or seven inches wide, a foot long, and an inch thick.

Surprisingly, it was flexible and supple. I supposed this helped hide the fact it was sewn into the bottom of the purse. A stiff bundle would have given it away.

I took a pair of scissors and cut the cloth away to reveal a large piece of opaque blue gel, sorta like a big gel shoe cushion. I felt around on a corner of the gel and found a hard lump.

I pushed on the backside of the lump, and something popped out the front. It fell on Lenny's desk with a gentle *clink*.

Sophie and I just sat there, stunned. We both stared at it for a full ten seconds. Sophie then reached down and gave it a light flick with her finger. It rolled a few inches across the desk and then came to a stop.

"Um, is that a diamond?" she asked.

"Sure looks like one," I replied.

"It's a big one."

"It sure is."

"I don't think I've ever seen one sparkle quite like that."

"Me either."

"Think there are more diamonds in that big hunk of blue goo you're holding?" she asked.

"Yup."

"Any idea how many more?"

"Oh, two hundred and fifty, maybe three hundred."

"You're shitting me?"

"Nope."

"Um, you wouldn't mind telling me a little bit more about this, would you?"

"Sure," I said, popping out another diamond from the strip of blue gel. It, too, fell onto the desk with a *clink*.

"These diamonds belong to members of the Russian Mafia, who have kidnapped and are torturing Alex Sternwood to get them back."

Clink.

"These are the same Russians who tried to

kidnap me out by Saguaro Lake."

Clink.

"The Russians brought the diamonds to Scottsdale to sell them to two brothers from a group called the Consortium."

Clink.

"These are the same two who kidnapped and threatened to kill me."

Clink.

"Alex stole the bag from the Russians in the lobby of the Scottsdale Blue Palms. Well, to be technical, he switched it with an identical bag he'd just bought or stolen from the hotel dress shop."

Clink.

"Inside the bag, Alex found three diamonds and a computer disk. Alex didn't know the bag contained anything else, so he gave it to Danica as a present."

Clink.

"Danica thought the bag was a fake Ferrucci and was too embarrassed to be seen in public with it. So, she bought another bag, a 'real' Ferrucci. She put this one in her locker at Jeannie's Cabaret, where it's been sitting since last week."

Clink.

"The Russians found out from DiCenzo that Alex had the bag. They ransacked his apartment, looking for it. Under orders, they killed the diamond courier, cut off his hands, and left him in Alex's apartment. They did this as a warning to everybody that they were serious about getting the bag back."

Clink.

"Unfortunately, Alex walked in on them, and they took the opportunity to kidnap him."

Clink.

"Alex must have told the Russians he gave the bag to Danica. They searched her house on Saturday and took the Ferrucci she had just bought. I imagine they got pretty upset when they found out there was nothing in it."

Clink.

"Tough Tony DiCenzo, the mobster, is brokering the sale of the diamonds between the Russians and the Consortium. He asked me to help him find the bag and get the diamonds back before more people get killed, or worse, before everybody gets upset and goes home."

Clink.

"Oh, um, okay," Sophie said. "Thanks for

clearing that up."

We sat in silence as I pushed out diamonds, one by one, *clink, clink, clink,* from the blue gel. The diamonds were starting to form a pretty little pile.

As I pushed, Sophie picked up one of the diamonds and rolled it between her fingers. "How big do you think these are?"

"According to DiCenzo, they're all three to five carats, and most are internally flawless."

"Not bad. Did he happen to mention what color grade they are?"

"Must have slipped his mind."

I sat there for almost fifteen minutes, popping out diamonds. My fingers were starting to get sore. Sophie had gotten her tablet and was looking up something on the Internet.

With a final push, the last diamond popped out and landed on the glittery pile.

"Any idea of how much is there, altogether?" Sophie asked.

"Oh, about half a pound," I said.

"Oh really? Half a pound, huh?" Sophie asked and started punching numbers into the calculator on Lenny's desk. After a moment, she stopped.

"Okay," she said, taking a deep breath. "Half a pound of diamonds is roughly two hundred and thirty grams. I looked it up, and there are five carats to a gram, so there are a little over eleven hundred carats there."

"Did you say *eleven-hundred* carats?"

"Yes, shut up. According to the Internet, a diamond that's in the three to five-carat range, is internally flawless, has an ideal cut, and a good color is worth about $33,000 a carat. It's about what the appraisals we found at Alex's said yesterday. This means your pretty little pile there is worth about, um, *thirty-seven million dollars!*"

Thirty-seven million dollars?

Damn!

We both sat there for a minute. My brain had temporarily gone numb. Sophie was pushing the pile of diamonds around on the desk with the tips of her long fingernails. I watched as the diamonds sparkled.

"What's going on? *And what the hell's on Lenny's desk?*" a loud voice behind us demanded.

We both turned to see Gina standing in the doorway.

"Hey, Gina, good news!" Sophie said, holding up the ripped and battered Ferrucci by one strap.

"Laura found your missing bag."

"Right at this moment," Gina said. "I wasn't talking about *the bag*. I was talking more about these."

Gina went to the desk and picked up a handful of diamonds, letting them fall through her fingers. They tumbled back on the desk to again form a shimmering mound.

"Um, they're diamonds," I said.

"Yeah, big sparkly ones," Sophie added.

"So why is there a pile of big sparkly diamonds on Lenny's desk?"

"We didn't think we should have them on Sophie's desk," I said. People could see them from the street."

"Yeah," Sophie added. "You know, you can't be too careful when you have thirty-seven million dollars' worth of diamonds sitting out on a desk."

Gina pulled up a chair, and we again sat in silence for a couple of minutes, contemplating the diamonds. We all started to run our fingers through the pile. I picked up a few diamonds and let them fall back on the mound. Sophie finally broke the silence.

"So, Laura, what are you gonna do with all these big sparkly diamonds?"

Okay, good question. It was the same question I'd been asking myself. So, what was I going to do with the diamonds? I should have said I was taking them to DiCenzo, but I didn't.

Instead, my fingers were still dancing over the shining mound. My mind was thinking about what I could do with thirty-seven million dollars.

What would I do first? An around-the-world cruise? A red Ferrari? Buy shoes that weren't on the clearance rack?

Damn, the possibilities were endless.

I shut my eyes and shook my head to clear it.

Okay, back to reality.

"Oh, I need to get them back to DiCenzo," I heard myself saying. "A lot of people are likely to get hurt if I don't, including me."

"You know," Gina said. "In theory, we could disappear into Mexico with that pile of rocks. We could each live like a Persian Princess."

"Yeah," said Sophie. "I have a cousin near Guadalajara who's been known to sell things like this from time to time. He could help us out. I always thought I should've been born rich. This would help make up for it."

"Oh, I know, and it's so tempting," I said, "but I can't. I don't want to spend my life on the run, no matter how much money I get out of it."

"Maybe we could each take just one then?" Sophie asked. "They'd never miss a couple of little ones."

"It would be the same as taking the whole lot," I said. "I'd never be sure who knew I did it or who might want to get even someday. If I'm going to do this, it's with a clean conscience."

"You know," Sophie pouted, "sometimes I really hate that conscience of yours."

Chapter Fourteen

I grabbed the phone from Lenny's desk and called Max. He answered on the first ring.

"Max, I have the diamonds. What do you want me to do with them?"

"Lock the doors and stay put. Milo and I will be down in ten minutes."

"You already know where I am?"

"Of course."

"Then you already knew I had the diamonds?"

"Not exactly knew, but yeah, we suspected. Tony got a call about twenty minutes ago from the Consortium brothers, Smith and Jones. They've got your friend, Danica."

"*Oh my god!* Danica? Is she alright?"

"She's okay, for the moment anyway. They picked her up just after she visited a friend of hers who also works at the club."

My voice dropped to a whisper. "That would

be Christy," I said, becoming very afraid for Danica. "She thought Christy might have the bag, but it was still in her locker at the club."

"After the brothers kidnapped your friend, they apparently slapped her around some. They then threatened her with worse violence unless she talked. She told them all she knew about the bag in her locker and that you were on your way to get it. The brothers are convinced you've recovered the diamonds. They're demanding the exchange take place at three o'clock. That's a little over an hour from now."

"Okay, what next?"

"Tony agreed, on the condition you've actually been able to locate the diamonds. I've called Reinhardt and the Russians and told them to stand by. I also told the Russians to make sure they bring Alexander Sternwood with them. The exchange will take place at a secure location in north Scottsdale, by the resorts. Hold on a second..."

On the phone, I heard the muffled sound of Max telling DiCenzo it was me on the phone and that I had the diamonds. I then heard DiCenzo giving orders to several men, one after another. After a pause, Tony took the phone from Max.

"Laura Black, this is Tony DiCenzo.

Maximilian tells me you've found the diamonds. Is this true?"

"Yes, I've got them right here. Milo and Max are coming to get them."

"Yeah, it's a good idea not to have you or the diamonds unprotected from here on out. You're at your place of employment, I hear. That's good. You'll be safe there until they arrive. Then we'll all head to the exchange."

"Tony, are you still having me followed?"

"I've got two of my best guys on you. They're very discreet, but per our agreement, they've been told to give you a hand if you need one. They're parked down the street, keeping an eye on things."

"Tony," I said, starting to get upset. "If you knew I already had found the bag, why didn't you just come get the diamonds?"

"That's not how I operate. You're on my team. I knew if you had the diamonds, you'd let me know."

"Yes, but how could you be sure? What if I just found the diamonds and took off?"

There was a pause at the other end of the phone.

"You seem like a nice girl, Laura Black. Let's not even joke about that, okay?"

Yikes!

"One last thing," DiCenzo said. Is there anybody with you but your two coworkers, Miss Rondinelli and Miss Rodriguez?"

"No, it's just the three of us. How did you know?"

"How I know is not important. If you will, put me on the speakerphone."

I hit the button, so Gina and Sophie could also hear DiCenzo. Sophie crossed herself.

"I have some information about your friend Danica. The brothers are keeping her in the same abandoned print shop where they took you a few days ago. I assume you remember the one I'm talking about?"

"I remember that place all too well," I said.

"The brothers will be leaving there shortly to come here for the exchange. From the way they talked, they'll be keeping Danica around for a celebration party afterward. To be honest, it didn't sound none too pretty for your friend."

Oh my God.

"Normally, I wouldn't interfere in something that wasn't none of my business," Tony continued. "But since you helped me recover the diamonds, I feel I owe you. Besides, those two fuckin' guys give me the creeps."

"Tony," I yelled at the phone. "You don't know what they're going to do to her. We've got to get her out of there!"

"Oh, I gotta pretty good idea what they're gonna do to her, but no, Laura Black, I need you up here with me. Besides, I can't be directly involved. I'm officially neutral in all of this, but perhaps one of your friends would be willing to help her?"

"Mr. DiCenzo," Gina said. "I'll get her. After what they almost did to Laura, I wouldn't want them to have another chance to do that to somebody else."

"That's Miss Rondinelli speaking, isn't it?" DiCenzo said. "I've heard good things about you over the years. Please, call me Tony. Maybe you and I can do business together someday."

"Sure, Tony," Gina said diplomatically. "Maybe we can."

"Okay, Laura Black," DiCenzo said. "You've done real good so far, but don't let your knees get weak. Milo and Max will be there to get you in a few minutes. We still got a shitload of stuff to do, and trust me, this is gonna be an interesting day." With that, DiCenzo hung up the phone.

~~~~

I went into the bathroom and found a metal bandage box in the first aid kit. I dumped out the bandages and walked back into Lenny's office.

Sophie helped me scoop the diamonds into the box. Then I pushed the container into the front pocket of my jeans. There was a bulge in my pants, and the box barely fit, but I was unlikely to lose them.

Sophie and I walked back to the cubicles and found Gina getting into her combat gear. She'd fastened on a bulletproof vest and was in the process of strapping on a Velcro web belt, complete with her Beretta, stun gun, and collapsible billy club. Watching Gina gear up, I started to realize what I'd gotten myself into.

"Sophie," I quietly said. "You gotta come with me."

"Me?" Sophie squeaked. "Oh no, no way! Tony DiCenzo didn't say nothin' about bringing me. Take Gina. She'd be way better than me. Those two brothers are nasty, not to mention those Russians who tried to shoot you. I don't want to be anywhere near any of them. Look at Gina here. She lives for this. Take her instead."

"Gina's going to get Danica, and I can't wait for her to return. Please, Sophie, I need you. I can't do this alone. Besides, if you don't go, you'll be cranky for weeks because you missed everything. Remember the last time?"

Sophie nodded her head and then gave an exasperated sigh.

Gina opened a drawer in her desk and pulled out a chrome-plated thirty-two caliber semi-automatic pistol. "You'll do great, but would you like to take this?" I saw Sophie look at Gina, then at the gun.

"Well, alright, I'll go," she said. "I'll use my own gun, not that little pea-shooter. But, Laura, I swear, if I get shot, I'll be *so* pissed at you."

We followed Sophie out to her desk, where she opened her bottom drawer and took out her bag. She reached in and pulled out a Smith & Wesson .357 magnum.

"*Damn,* that's a Dirty Harry gun!" Gina said. "Where'd you get that?"

"It's my brother's. There was some trouble back home last week. I'm holding it for him until things settle down."

"Well," Gina said. "That should do the job."

Outside we saw a black BMW sedan pull up. Milo was driving. Max got out and stood next to the car.

A black Town Car, no doubt from Arizona Security Enterprises, pulled out from where it had been parked halfway down the block and slid into place behind the BMW.

"Well, girls," I said. "It's showtime."

~~~~

We drove in silence toward the resorts of north Scottsdale. Sophie sat up front with Milo. I was in the back with Max. As if my heart wasn't already beating hard enough from outright fear, sitting next to him had kicked it up a couple more steps.

Besides questioning me with a raised eyebrow, Max didn't object to Sophie coming with us. For her part, Sophie seemed to be handling the situation as well as could be expected.

She'd pressed herself against Milo, but in her case, it wasn't because of her libido. She had the fingers of her left hand embedded in Milo's thigh, and I could tell how frightened she was.

Damn, I really hate this part of the job.

We drove north until we came into the heart of the golf district. Instead of pulling into a resort, we turned down a side street, then another, and yet another. We ended up on a narrow dirt road that wound through a desolate desert area near the back of a golf course.

After half a mile, the road ended in a dirt parking lot in front of a large blue metal building. The parking lot was at least an acre in size and was surrounded by dozens of half-dead fan palms and stunted orange trees.

Several pieces of golf course maintenance equipment were parked in the dirt lot, all in various states of repair. The large metal building looked like the garage and workshop for the bigger pieces of equipment.

Max collected our guns and put them in the glove compartment. He smiled as Sophie handed over the magnum. Sophie and I looked at each other and shrugged.

We got out of the car and walked toward the building. Sophie grabbed my hand and held it in a death grip. She was so scared I could hear her teeth chattering.

Standing in front of the large open doorway was Tough Tony DiCenzo. Flanking him on either side were two beefy guys, each dressed in a blue sport coat, each holding an assault rifle.

Although DiCenzo was dressed casually in slacks and a golf shirt, the look on his face was far from casual. The look on his face was all business.

DiCenzo stood like a bull in the center of the

doorway, his eyes intent and narrowed. He glanced toward Sophie, then to Max.

I saw Max give a barely perceptible nod. At this signal, Tony's face softened slightly. We reached the doorway, and Tony held out his hand to Sophie.

"I'm Tony DiCenzo," he said. "I take it you're Sophia Rodriguez?"

Sophie put out a shaky hand. She opened her mouth and let out a small squeak we all took for a *yes*.

"The others will be here shortly," Tony said to all of us. "Come on, let's go back to the office and have a seat."

We followed DiCenzo inside. The interior of the building was a large open room with an oil-stained concrete floor. It smelled of gasoline and freshly-cut grass. A half-assembled tractor sat off to the left side.

The entire right side of the building consisted of a single enclosed office. This is where we headed. The two goons with the guns stayed at the main door.

We'd almost reached the office when we heard the sound of an approaching car. DiCenzo told us to go to the office and wait. He then went to welcome the newcomers.

The office's interior consisted of a beat-up couch, some metal chairs, a wooden conference table, and a couple of green Formica-topped desks. Last year's calendar was nailed to the wall and featured a bikini-clad brunette straddling a muffler. Against the back wall stood a row of mismatched metal filing cabinets.

From the fresh scratch marks on the floor, I could see both the furniture and filing cabinets had been moved around recently. Windows were looking both into the interior of the building and to the outside yard. The air in the office smelled of oil and cigarettes.

In the back corner of the room was a portable bar, along with four black bar stools. It looked so out of place I assumed it was brought here just for our meeting.

Behind the bar was the woman I'd seen at Junior Baker's, two nights before. Max had said her name was Gabriella. He'd also told me she was used mainly for emergencies.

She was dressed in black leather pants and a red leather shirt. Her top was open to expose an eyeful of cleavage. Her long black hair was pulled back into a ponytail. She was as beautiful and dangerous-looking as I remembered seeing her

Saturday night in the club.

Ingrid Shanker, the pinched-faced woman from the art gallery in the Tropical Paradise, was sitting at the wooden conference table near the side of the room. She was typing on the keyboard of a notebook computer.

The table was partially covered with a large piece of black velvet. The cloth was positioned so it sat in a shaft of sunlight shining in from the window. Next to the computer was an expensive-looking digital scale.

~~~~

We heard the opening and closing of car doors and the muffled sound of Tough Tony talking to two men. After a moment, DiCenzo came into the office. Following him were Boris and Ivan, the two Russians. Held between them was Alex Sternwood. He looked terrible.

His hands were cuffed behind him, and he struggled to keep up with the Russians. His face was a mass of angry red and purple bruises. His nose was bent to one side. Both of his eyes were blackened, and one of them was swollen shut.

The Russians stopped and flung him to the floor in front of Sophie and me. Alex tried to get up but then collapsed. I would've assumed he was dead if it weren't for his moaning.

I started to take a step forward, but DiCenzo held up a hand to stop me. He spoke to the Russians in a firm but courteous voice:

"Thank you for bringing this man. I consider it a personal favor to me. Do you have any conditions for his release?"

Boris stepped forward. "Do you have possession of the diamonds?"

"I do," DiCenzo said.

"Then you may have this one. We have extracted all needed information and have taught him it is a mistake to steal from us. I had wished to eliminate him, but we are under strictest orders not to do so. He is very fortunate that he got off so lucky."

Ivan took a step towards where Alex was lying. He pulled a handcuff key out of his pocket and casually flicked it away. The key bounced off Alex's back and landed on the floor with a ringing sound.

Alex made another attempt to push himself up. Again, he collapsed, this time falling on his side. He lay there with his eyes wide open. He was panting, but at least the moaning had stopped.

Even though I was horrified at what'd happened to Alex, I was also touched by what

DiCenzo had said. I'd told Tony I had the diamonds but never showed them to him. DiCenzo was risking his reputation, and possibly even his life, on me being honest with him.

In a way, he was very sweet, but it was more than that. Somehow, I'd become a trusted part of a powerful team. Granted, it was a team of gangsters, but it still made me feel like I'd accomplished something good.

DiCenzo walked over to where Alex was lying and bent down to quietly talk to him. "The Russians may be done with you, but I'm not. You've cost me time, you've cost me resources, and you almost fucked up my reputation. I'm not through with you yet, and that's a fact."

DiCenzo stood up and turned towards Sophie. "In the meantime, Ms. Rodriguez, would you please go with Mr. Sternwood? It would be best if he has someone kind and understanding near him for the next few hours. Milo will take you both to a clinic where they'll fix him up and not ask a lot of questions."

I saw Max talking to himself, then I noticed he was now wearing an earpiece. Sophie and I went over to see about Alex. I picked up the key and gave it to Sophie, who unlocked the handcuffs.

Thirty seconds later, Milo pulled into the

building and parked a black SUV in front of the office. Two goons appeared out of nowhere, scooped up Alex, and laid him on the back seat.

Sophie got in on the seat next to Alex. Milo backed out of the building and took off.

The sound of Milo's car was fading down the road when we heard another vehicle come into the yard. DiCenzo didn't even have time to walk out of the office before there was the skidding of tires and the slamming of car doors.

There was loud shouting in that weird foreign language. I'd never figured out what it was, but I hated hearing it. My stomach tightened to the point I thought I would throw up.

Hearing their voices brought back all of the horrible details of a few days before. Hate and rage welled up inside of me.

I thought about grabbing a gun and shooting them both as they entered the room. Okay, maybe it wasn't the way to solve anything, but it still sounded like a good idea.

Smith and Jones strolled in, looking smug as ever. Each had on a brown leather bomber jacket and gold-rimmed sunglasses. Jones's nose was swollen, and he had two black eyes.

The brothers loudly complained that DiCenzo

should have personally driven them from their hotel. They were offended that representatives of the Consortium were being treated so disrespectfully.

DiCenzo gave them a clenched teeth apology, and the brothers seemed temporarily mollified. Jones then saw me standing against the wall. Our eyes made contact, and he flew into another rage.

"What is this one doing here?" he shouted. "We will not conduct business with this whore in the building."

I know I should have kept quiet, but I was pissed. "What have you jerks done to Danica? Where is she?"

"We haven't done anything to her, yet," Smith said, amusement now in his voice. "There hasn't been enough time to do more than teach her a few manners."

His smile was small, sick, and evil. "Although, my brother has told her in some detail what he will do to her when we return. I'm afraid he's in the mood to abuse an American harridan after what you did to his face."

"If you two assholes hurt her, I'll hunt you down like dogs. I'll shoot you in places that won't kill you, but you'll wish like hell it had."

"Still your tongue, bitch," Jones shouted. "Why do you anger over that one? She is only a filthy American whore, an unclean slut who dances naked for money. She will be with a true man for the first time in her life. If she pleases me, then she will live. If she does not, I will cut her for the joy of watching her bleed."

I took a step forward. I really needed to hit someone. Max took hold of my arm, stopping me before I could get closer. I tried to shake loose of his grip, but it was no use.

Tony stepped between the brothers and me. "People, there ain't no reason to act like this. I don't give a damn if you like each other or not. We're here for business, not to go off on each other."

DiCenzo turned to the brothers. "Gentlemen, this woman is here at my invitation and under my protection. I expect you to treat her with some courtesy."

"Miss Black," he then said, turning to me. "What these men do with your friend ain't none of my business. Any problem you have with them needs to be taken up after our business is finished."

DiCenzo then took a step back and smiled. It was a friendly smile. "Now, as a favor to me and to help things go smoothly, would everybody keep their emotions in check for the next couple of hours? After that, I don't give a fuck what you do to each other."

DiCenzo looked at me. I nodded my head, indicating I would comply with his request. He then looked over to the brothers.

Smith waved his hand impatiently. "Let us proceed," he said in a disgusted tone. "That one is not important enough to waste further breath on."

Still wanting to hit someone, I walked to the window and looked at the dirt parking lot. A black SUV pulled into the lot and came to a stop. A driver got out and opened the rear door.

I watched as Albert Reinhardt, the Iceman, stepped out. He carried a stainless-steel briefcase, the kind popular with drug dealers and concert promoters.

The driver got back into the SUV, and it pulled away. Reinhardt walked into the office, and Tony introduced him to the group.

Boris pulled out a yellow CD case and handed it to Tony. "On this disk is a list of every diamond that will be exchanged," Boris said. "You will see this list exactly matches the information that has already been provided to you."

Tony handed the disk to Ingrid, who put it in an optical reader attached to her computer. After a moment, a spreadsheet opened on the screen.

I only glanced at it, but it was enough to see it was the same spreadsheet I'd seen in Suzie Lu's apartment two days ago. I felt the room go still as everyone turned to look at me.

"Alright, Laura Black," Tony said. "It's time for the diamonds."

I reached into the front pocket of my jeans and pulled on the bandage box. I tried three times but couldn't pull the box out of my tight pants. It was wedged in, and I couldn't grasp the slippery metal sides.

Panic began to set in as I looked up to see everyone in the room staring at me. Smith and Jones were making sounds of frustrated disgust.

I had an uncomfortable vision of having to unzip my pants to get the box out. Finally, with a sense of desperation, I gave a hard yank, and the box pulled free.

I walked to the table and slowly poured the half-pound of diamonds into a pile in the middle of the black velvet. Sunlight from the window shone down on the mound, shooting thousands of bright rainbows throughout the room. It was like standing next to the world's most brilliant disco ball.

Gabriella let out a gasp. I also heard a collective sigh from the men in the room.

DiCenzo walked to the table and bent over the pile. "These things have been causing me nothing but trouble for weeks, but Jesus, they're fuckin' beautiful."

Reinhardt pulled out a chair next to the table. He opened his briefcase and took out a case containing jeweler's tools and a small box.

He set the box on the table next to the scale and opened it. Inside was a row of seven or eight diamonds. The diamond on the left was a brilliant clear white. Looking down the row, each diamond was a little more yellow. The diamond on the far right was a golden honey color.

Under the watchful eyes of the brothers and the Russians, Reinhardt took out a pair of tweezers and picked up a diamond from the top of the pile.

He pulled out a small jeweler's loupe and inspected the diamond for about twenty seconds. He brought out a small light that cast a purple glow and held it against the diamond as he continued his inspection.

He then held it close to his mouth and breathed

on it momentarily before looking at it underneath his loupe again. He next compared the diamond in his tweezers with the diamonds in his box, moving it back and forth over the row of diamonds before putting it on the scale and weighing it.

He spoke to Ingrid, who then typed some numbers into her computer. She gave a nod and pointed to the spreadsheet. At this, Reinhardt brightened.

"The first stone I have examined is a true diamond," Reinhardt said. "It exactly matches a diamond on the list, number two hundred and forty-seven."

With this announcement, the tension in the room noticeably dropped. Reinhardt placed the diamond on a piece of blue paper lying on the desk in front of Ingrid.

She folded the paper into a rectangular packet, about three inches wide by two inches tall. She wrote some information on the paper before putting it in a long zippered carrying case.

Reinhardt and Ingrid repeated the operation with the next diamond. Ingrid checked off another diamond from the list, and now the leather case contained two blue packets.

Tony walked over to Max and me and said,

"This will take about two hours. Ice is the best there is, but there are almost three hundred diamonds to look at. This is where tempers begin to flare. People don't like to stand around doing nothing. Makes them feel too exposed."

Tony nodded to Gabriella, who started dropping ice cubes into a row of glasses she had lined up on the bar. The sound of the ice seemed to lighten the mood a bit.

The brothers approached the bar and demanded Jack Daniel's American Whiskey. The Russians stayed at the table, not taking their eyes off the diamonds.

Tony went to the bar and began talking to the brothers. It sounded like they were discussing golf swings.

Max also went to the bar and talked briefly with Tony and the Consortium brothers. He returned to where I was standing, holding a drink.

"I thought you might need this," he said, handing me the glass.

It was a scotch with a single ice cube floating in it. A tingle of electricity shot up my arm as our fingers brushed against each other.

"Scotch with one ice cube?" I asked him.

"Surprised I remembered?"

"No, I bet you have a *very* good memory."

"I've been remembering lots of things about you lately."

"Really? Maybe we should get together sometime and see what's been on your mind."

"Maybe we should," said Max. He then walked back over to where Tony was standing.

Jeez, what's wrong with me? I'm at a Criminals-R-Us convention and flirting with one of the hoodlums.

I watched him walk away and noticed how good he looked in a suit. For a moment, I forgot about being in a room full of diamonds, guns, and dangerous people. It was a nice distraction.

As Reinhardt and Ingrid continued with the inspections, I noticed there was never a point that either Max or Gabriella wasn't within three or four feet of Tony.

I also noticed whichever one was nearest Tony, they stood so they were looking past DiCenzo and at the people standing in the room. They acted as his bodyguards but transitioned so smoothly that I doubt anyone else noticed.

~~~~

After what seemed like forever, Reinhardt finished examining the last diamond. By this time, the brothers had each downed six or seven whiskies and were starting to get a little loud.

Reinhardt spoke to Ingrid, who typed the information into the spreadsheet. There was another brief conference between Reinhardt and Ingrid, after which the Iceman stood up.

"Mr. DiCenzo and gentlemen, every diamond on the inventory sheet has been accounted for and is as represented. There are two hundred and eighty-three diamonds with a total weight of one thousand one hundred and sixty-three carats. The remaining three diamonds on the list have previously been accounted for."

Damn, I'm glad I didn't pinch one.

DiCenzo turned his head to me and gave a nod. Max, who was seated behind Tough Tony, raised his hands and silently clapped for me. The smile on his face was beautiful.

Ingrid put the last of the blue packets in the leather case and zipped it up. Reinhardt took the case and placed it in his steel briefcase. Acting with the utmost care, he locked the briefcase and set it on the table in the middle of the black velvet.

With this final task completed, he gathered his tools and tucked the scale under his arm. Ingrid turned off her computer and put it in a padded case.

They said their goodbyes to DiCenzo, the brothers, and the Russians. They both walked out of the office, and a moment later, I heard cars starting up in the parking lot.

Smith pulled out a cell phone and made a call. When the phone was answered, he spoke five or six rapid sentences. He then passed the phone to Jones, who also said half a dozen quick sentences into the phone.

DiCenzo walked over to where Max and I were standing. "The exchange will be in the form of an electronic funds transfer. Much safer than carrying cash and won't leave an incriminating paper trail if done correctly. It will simply be one business legitimately transferring money to another. Happens millions of times a day."

Boris pulled his cell phone out. He dialed a number and spoke into the phone for thirty seconds in a low murmur. There was a pause as Boris passed the information to Ivan.

Ivan took the phone and listened intently for almost a minute. Ivan spoke one sentence and returned the phone to Boris, who listened for a full minute.

Without disconnecting the phone, Boris placed it on the table. From their postures, I knew something was wrong. Boris and Ivan talked to each other in rapid-fire Russian and then seemed to come to a mutual agreement.

Ivan separated from Boris in a way that made me think of a two-man military team preparing to go into combat. Boris spoke to DiCenzo in a loud voice that was meant to carry, not only to all of us in the room but to those on the phone as well.

"Mr. DiCenzo, there is a problem here. The electronic transfer was for two-million dollars less than we had agreed to. Please explain the meaning of this."

Smith spoke up. "That's for your incompetence in losing the diamonds. It's our fee for making us hunt like dogs to get them back. You're lucky to get as much as you did. Take our money and be at peace."

Boris pulled a semi-automatic pistol from a shoulder holster and leveled it at Smith's head. "I must inform you that we are under strictest orders to not permit you to leave until Moscow is wired the additional two million dollars."

Jones pulled a pistol from behind the small of his back and pointed it at Boris' chest. "Take the diamonds," Jones quietly said to Smith, who walked over and picked up the briefcase. Ivan pulled his piece and brought it to bear on Jones.

Gabriella brought out an Uzi from behind the bar and leveled it at the two brothers. A smile of pleasure lit up her face.

Max was next to Tony in an instant, pistol drawn. Smith had also pulled a piece and was pointing it at Ivan. It had quickly become a stalemate, a Mexican standoff.

Tony and Max looked at each other. I saw volumes of information pass between them, although neither spoke. Tony then looked at the ground and shook his head. I heard him mutter, "I don't fuckin' believe it."

Max lifted his hand to the microphone in his earpiece and quietly talked into it for about twenty seconds. He then gave Tony a slight nod. Tony seemed to relax slightly.

"Boys," Tony said. "This don't help nobody. The price was agreed on weeks ago, and the merchandise has been delivered as promised. So, Mr. Smith, either wire Moscow the rest of the money or this deal don't go down at all. I've got a dozen men in and around this building. You ain't gonna get even one diamond out of here unless this deal goes down smoothly."

"Oh, but you are wrong, son of a pig. We *can* take them. We will now be allowed to walk out with the diamonds, or everyone here will die."

Jones then unzipped and opened his jacket. He was wearing a vest packed with enough explosives to blow the building apart three times over.

"Jesus Christ!" Tony moaned, more in exasperation than from fear.

I dove behind a desk and looked around to see if there was a way out. So, okay, guns I could sorta tolerate. Bombs were definitely a no-go.

Gabriella stood there looking to Tony and Max for instructions. From the look of joy on her face, I could tell she was hoping for a shootout.

It's funny, but as I looked closer, I saw her look was more than just joy. She was breathing in short gasps, and her face had taken on a light pink glow, the same look Sophie gets whenever she's about to get lucky with a man. It was a look of desire, quickly building to ecstasy.

Wow! Go figure that one out.

Tough Tony DiCenzo stood there, unmoving. His eyes had narrowed, and he looked pissed. Max talked quietly into his earpiece. His gun was still in the other.

The brothers started yelling in their weird language, and the Russians started yelling in Russian. Neither side was doing a lot to calm the situation.

On the back wall of the office, underneath the window, a panel approximately three feet wide by four feet high swung open, creating a small doorway to the outside. Johnny Scarpazzi's face appeared in the opening, signaling DiCenzo to come through.

With the grace of a cat, Gabriella moved from behind the bar and positioned herself next to this new door. Max pushed DiCenzo in her direction.

Max acted as Tony's bodyguard while Gabriella covered their escape. He then looked over and motioned for me to follow.

We formed a line. DiCenzo was in the lead. Max was in the middle, acting as a sentry. I was at the end, hoping they would both go faster. The yelling was getting louder, and I didn't think it would be much longer until somebody started shooting.

DiCenzo made it to the door. I saw several pairs of hands waiting to pull him to safety. Suddenly, a voice cried out. It was Smith.

"American! You will not escape. If I am to die today, so shall you!" With that, Smith spun around and fired at DiCenzo.

As soon as Smith turned, Max was in the air,

diving in front of Tony. The bullet from Smith's gun hit Max squarely in the chest.

The impact of the slug knocked him into Gabriella, who was sighting the Uzi at Smith. The arm holding her Uzi was knocked upward.

There was a loud *buuuuurp* as a dozen bullets sprayed the ceiling. As she pulled the trigger, I saw her lips had opened into a moan of ecstasy.

Arms reached in and pulled Max through the opening. Gabriella was on her back. She was trying to get up, but the impact of Max's body had knocked her senseless. I saw her shaking her head to help clear her vision.

Smith aimed at Tony's head. DiCenzo turned and stood facing the man. He didn't try to run. I guess he's not the type to back down, even in death.

I was crouched against the back wall, next to the window. Jones was still in a standoff with the two Russians. Their eyes were all locked onto each other. Everyone was waiting for the other to flinch.

Seeing that DiCenzo wasn't running, Smith smiled, savoring the moment. I saw his finger tighten on the trigger, and without thinking, I ran and lunged at Smith's gun.

I hit him against the side of his arm just as he fired. He was solidly built, and I merely bounced off, but it was enough for his shot to go wild. The bullet struck the wall slightly to the left of where DiCenzo stood defiantly.

At the sound of the shot, Jones glanced over at Smith. It was only for a moment, but that was enough. Boris and Ivan each fired simultaneously.

I didn't see where Jones was hit, but I saw him start to go down. That was good enough for me.

Gabriella had made it to her knees and brought the Uzi to bear on Smith, who had turned back to fire at the Russians. Then everybody started shooting.

A hand grabbed me by the shoulder, and DiCenzo tossed me across the room toward the escape door. I landed hard and felt my lungs empty with an *oof*. Several pairs of hands yanked me through the door.

I stood up and turned. As if in a slow-motion dream, I saw DiCenzo being pulled out of the doorway. Gabriella was next, still firing her Uzi into the building, even as she was dragged out. Goons surrounded us, and we all limped toward a waiting line of cars.

I heard more shots being fired from inside the building. It seemed like Boris, Ivan, Smith, and

Jones would finish each other off after all. Johnny Scarpazzi was waving his arms and shouting that we had to get out on the back road.

I looked ahead and saw Max being helped into the back seat of a car. His eyes were dazed but open and very much alive.

I looked but didn't see any blood. In my slow-motion time frame, that sight both surprised and pleased me. I wanted to go to the car and find an explanation for why he was still alive, but my legs weren't responding.

I stumbled four or five steps away from the building when a blinding flash and a tremendous explosion occurred. Something that felt like a big warm hand shoved me hard. I flew forward ten feet and landed on my face, pieces of the building landing all around me.

I pushed myself up and tried to step toward the car when something smashed against my head. Bright lights danced in front of my eyes as I went down to my knees, feeling the pain of the impact.

The bright spots turned to black spots. Then the blackness grew until the daylight faded and was gone.

The pain faded.

Then there was nothing.

Chapter Fifteen

When I came to, I was in a semi-private room of a very modern hospital, and I had a bitch-kitty of a headache. Laying in the bed next to mine was Max.

He was bare-chested except for the tape wrapped around his ribs. He looked surprisingly good for someone who'd taken a bullet to the chest. He was awake and smiled when he saw me checking him out.

"I thought you'd be dead," I mumbled. I found it hard to focus my thoughts, and my words were coming out with difficulty.

"Hope I didn't disappoint you."

"No, I'm happy to see you're alive. What happened? I saw you get shot."

"Bullet-proof vest."

"Oh, I didn't think tough guys like you were into things like that."

"After today, I may never take it off."

I looked out the window and saw the orange glow of a sunset or maybe a sunrise. It was hard to tell which it was.

"How long have I been out?"

"It's been about fourteen hours, but you haven't been unconscious the whole time. You woke up a couple of times last night."

"Huh, I don't remember that."

"They've wheeled you in and out of the room several times. You've had X-Rays, CAT scans, MRIs, and I don't know what else. So far, they've been letting you sleep it off, and no one's in a panic over you. I take it as a good sign."

"That still doesn't explain what happened to me."

"You got hit with a shoe. I saw it happen. The explosion must've shot it pretty high in the air. When it fell, it landed on your head."

"Still, a shoe shouldn't have knocked me out."

"Well, um, there was still a foot and part of a leg in it. I think it was Smith's."

Uuggh.

Black spots danced in front of my eyes, and I fell back on the pillow, letting the darkness take me away from that horrible image.

~~~~

When I woke up again, the room was much brighter. I was guessing it was around mid-day.

Max was still there, sadly now wearing a shirt and reading a book on a Kindle. Somehow, I was disappointed to see he was fully dressed. I kind of liked it the other way.

"Welcome back," he said. "How do you feel?"

I thought about it for a moment. The headache was gone, and I wasn't feeling fuzzy anymore. "Better," I said. "I actually feel better."

"Good," he said. "When we get out of here, you and I have some unfinished business."

"Hey, it's not my fault the building blew up. They started shooting at each other. You can't expect bullets and bombs to live in harmony. Sooner or later, something's going to explode."

"I'm not talking about the building. I'm talking about the kiss we shared at Lenny's office the other day. You owe me at least one more after everything we've been through. Although this time, I'll kiss you without your friends watching. I hate short kisses."

That sounds yummy.

I looked down at myself and realized I had nothing on but a flimsy hospital gown. I tried not to think about who had undressed me and who had put me into the gown.

"Um, do you know where my clothes are?"

"There's a big plastic hospital bag on the chair," Max said. "I would assume they're in there."

I slowly got out of bed, acutely aware that my ass was exposed by the back of the gown. I saw the grin on Max's face as he appreciated my predicament. I grabbed the bag and shuffled sideways to the bathroom to get dressed, Max's soft laughter following me.

~~~~

Five minutes later, Tony DiCenzo came into the room. Milo and Sophie followed him. She was carrying a bouquet of flowers. My heart was still pumping double time from my conversation with Max.

"Hey, Laura, these are for you," Sophie said, laying the flowers on the table by my bed. "I thought you'd never wake up. We've been in here most of the night and all morning. The doctors say you check out okay. You can go home anytime you want."

"Tony," I asked. "Is everything alright?"

"It's been a long night for all of us.

Everybody's been very busy. Milo, would you mind escorting Miss Rodriguez back to her place of employment so she can pick up her car? Max and I need to talk with Miss Black for a few minutes longer."

Milo acknowledged the order and turned to leave.

"Looks like I'll be seeing you *later*," Sophie said.

From the look on her face and the tone of her voice, I doubted she would let Milo stop at just taking her back to her car. I hoped Milo had a good strong heart.

When we were alone, DiCenzo pulled up a chair and positioned it between Max's bed and mine.

"We've had us quite a time yesterday and last night," he said. "I thought those guys were going to conduct business with some honor. Maybe I shoulda known better, but I've dealt with them before, and everything went okay. Of course, if somebody goes into it intending to stir things up, there isn't much you can do about it."

"Did everybody get away okay?" I asked.

"Everybody but Reinhardt. We knew the cops had been trailing him, so we set up a diversion to free him up. After that, he drove his car to within a few miles of the buy. One of my guys then shuttled him back and forth. I thought that would do the trick."

"What happened?"

"Unfortunately, the cops weren't fooled for as long as we'd hoped. One stopped Ice after he had gotten back to his car and had driven about a mile. Ice didn't have anything incriminating on him when he was stopped, of course. The cop questioned him and searched his car. They even brought in a K9 unit to help find evidence. When the car came up clean, the cop let him go."

"I'm surprised they released him."

"They might later try to tie him in with the explosion and the bodies, but I doubt it. When the cop stopped Reinhardt, he was a good five miles away from the building that blew. They might not even make the connection at all. But, in the end, they'll have nothing."

"But won't the police make a connection with the guys in the building and you? They must have come into the country using passports. They stayed in your hotel. Doesn't that leave a trail?"

"Fortunately, none of them were traveling under their real names. The police won't have a clue who they were. We show them as checking out the day Alex disappeared. How could any of this be our fault?"

"What about your building?" I asked. "Buildings don't blow up by themselves."

"We had a team in the building before the fire department arrived. They scattered enough money and drugs around to give the cops something interesting to think about. I don't think we'll have any problems there. They know the resort belongs to me, but other than that, there is nothing to tie our guys to it. It'll likely go down as a random drug deal that went bad."

"Won't the police find the diamonds scattered in with the bodies?"

"Fortunately, my guys were able to recover most of the diamonds. The steel briefcase they were in took most of the explosion. It was burnt and ripped but still mostly intact. We'll be able to turn over all but five of the diamonds, including the three Alexander sold. The Consortium is sending over some new guys to pick 'em up. Max will lead the team in charge of the handover."

"You're still giving the diamonds to them? After what happened?"

"Sure, they paid for them. We've found out the Consortium never authorized the reduction in payment. As far as they knew, the full sum had been transferred. Smith and Jones decided to skim on the deal themselves. The loss of the bag made too perfect of an excuse for them to pass up. With the help of an accomplice in the Consortium, they diverted the two million into a private account in the Cayman Islands. Fortunately, the deal was set up so quickly they were sloppy about it, and the transaction was easily traced."

"So things are good now?"

"The Consortium has already wired the remainder of the money to Moscow. They've apologized to both the Russians and me for their irresponsible men. They even offered to buy me a new building to compensate for the one that blew up."

"Are the Russians in Moscow okay with the apology?" I asked.

"Okay enough to wire my fee. Our two Russians left their phone line open after receiving instructions. Moscow heard the whole thing. They're convinced our two dead Consortium friends were acting independently, and both paid for their stupidity with their lives."

I shook my head. Amazed at how events unfolded.

"I can't believe Smith and Jones thought the Russians would accept less than the full payment or that they could steal all those diamonds just because they had a bomb," Tony said. "If that were the case, guys would be bringing bombs whenever anybody made an exchange. They made a serious miscalculation, and it cost them."

"I'm surprised Moscow and the Consortium aren't more upset."

"It may be hard to believe, but all things considered, the deal went down pretty smoothly."

"Tony, people were killed."

"Yeah, but the brothers brought it on themselves. You can't walk into a deal like that, ready to double-cross everybody and expect to come out clean. Their superiors were more than happy to wash their hands of them. The two Russians died with honor. Moscow considers the two guys you called Boris and Ivan to be heroes. Their pictures are probably already up in a bar somewhere in Moscow."

"Seriously?"

"Dead serious. And I imagine their families will be well taken care of."

DiCenzo shifted in his seat and looked at me.

"We're almost done here, but we've got something personal to settle between us. I've never had my life saved twice in one day before.

Max and me have helped each other out more times than I care to remember. He's the only person I completely trust, and that's saying something. But you, Laura Black, that's completely different. You stuck your neck out to help me. I won't forget it. We now have a bond between us, and I owe you a favor. Whatever you ask of me, if it's in my power to do so, I will. Of course, as a friend, you can come to me anytime if something minor comes up."

Yikes! It was like talking with Don Corleone.

"Tony, is Danica alright?"

"Your co-worker, Miss Rondinelli, did a good job of getting her out of the building where they were holding her. She'd been roughed up a little and got bruised in a couple of sensitive areas, but she's otherwise alright. She came in to be checked out and ended up spending the night in the room with Alex."

"How is he doing?"

"He had a broken nose, a couple of cracked ribs, and four broken fingers. He also had a lot of bruises, but he wasn't otherwise seriously injured. They were both released this morning."

"What about the police? There was a dead guy in Alex's apartment when he was kidnapped. They're going to want to know what happened."

"Alex knows he stole a bag from three guys at the Blue Palms two weeks ago. He knows there were three diamonds in the bag. He knows he fenced the three diamonds and made a nice chunk of change. He knows the same three guys met him in his apartment four days ago, only one of them was dead. He knows they grabbed him and broke his fingers until he told them he'd given the bag to his girlfriend."

"Do you think he'll tell everything to the police?"

"I'm sure he will, but when Alex is questioned, that's all he'll know. He's smart enough to know he stole from the wrong people. He also knows what'll happen if he guesses too much about what happened."

"What are you going to do to him?"

"The toughest thing I had to do last night was to figure out what to do with that little prick. I got the diamond he sold to the Iceman at the Tropical Paradise. Still, the first two diamonds he fenced came out of my commission. Plus, he almost got me into more trouble than I knew how to get out of."

"Tony, please let Alex off the hook. You can use that as my favor. He didn't know that he was doing anything against you. He was just stupid."

"No need to use your favor on that. I've already made an arrangement. Last night I called Muffy Sternwood and let her know what happened to Alex, well, the basics of it anyway. I wanted her to know the actual truth of the matter."

"You know Muffy?"

"Her late husband and I used to do business together in the old days. She knew what a tight spot Alex was in. She reminded me she owns a prime piece of land in north Scottsdale. She also knows I've wanted to buy it for years. She's been sitting on it, even though I've offered her a good price several times. She said she'd let me have it to build a new resort on, but only on the condition we split ownership fifty-fifty."

I started laughing. "Muffy Sternwood? You and Muffy?"

"Yeah, go figure. I hate having partners, but that's how the world works."

DiCenzo stood up. "I know you're both anxious to get out of here, but walk with me for a moment, Laura Black."

I stood up, and we walked out to the hallway. At the far end of the hall were two goons. One was near the elevator, and the other was posted at the stairs.

At our end of the hall, it was just Tony and me. It was the first time I'd ever been alone with him. It was kind of a creepy feeling.

"Now that business is out of the way," DiCenzo said. "I think you should consider going out with Max. Do you know he's mentioned you a couple a times over the past few days? He's a great guy. I think the two of you would work out well."

"Thanks, Tony, but I think I'm already in a relationship. He's a Scottsdale cop."

At that, Tough Tony DiCenzo started laughing. It was an honest laugh that came from deep down.

"Well, Laura Black, I won't comment on your choice of boyfriend, but I'm truly happy for you. Of course, these things sometimes have a way of falling apart. If that day comes, then I think you should consider Max."

"I'll keep it in mind, Tony. I really will."

With that, Tony stuck his head back into the room. "Max, would you mind driving Miss Black back to Lenny's office? Her car's still there."

~~~~

Twenty minutes later, Max and I were sitting in the parking lot behind the office.

"Before you go," Max said. "Tony wanted you to have this."

He handed me a small white envelope the size of a thank-you card. There was something lumpy in the envelope, along with what felt like a card.

I fingered it, wondering what was in it. Tony had said if everything worked out, he'd give me a cut.

My first thought was the envelope was too small to hold cash. My second thought was it was probably also too small to hold a check. That is unless it had been folded two or three times.

"Do I need to open it now?"

"It can wait."

"Good, I've had all the excitement I can handle, plus the explosion ripped a hole in my favorite shirt. Tell Tony thanks for whatever it is."

"You did great yesterday," Max said. "Not many veterans could have done as well as you did your first time. If you ever consider a career change, we could probably find a place for you with us."

"Thanks, but I hope you understand I only helped out Tony because I didn't have a choice. I would never have done it if Alex's life wasn't on the line. The type of work you do isn't for me."

"I understand. It's not a lifestyle for everybody, but what about you and me? Would you like to get together sometime? Maybe see where this could lead?"

"Well, yes, but no. I'm becoming involved with a Scottsdale cop. I need to see where it's going before I can get involved with anyone else. Besides, I think I told you, as a rule, I don't get romantically involved with organized crime figures."

"True, you did. Nevertheless, I'm still not going anywhere. So, find out if you and this cop are right for each other. If you are, then I'm happy for you. If not, then give me a call."

"It's a deal," I said, holding my hand out. Instead of shaking it, he bent over and softly kissed me. His kiss was brief but had the effect of igniting every nerve in my body.

How can he do that?

Max leaned back and saw my reaction to his kiss. "Yeah, it's a deal," he said.

~~~~

I went into the office and checked in with Lenny. I gave him an edited version of finding the bag and Alexander, but Lenny wasn't interested in hearing the details.

He already knew the outcome and was thrilled things had worked out so well. He would get a massive fee from DiCenzo for finding the bag and an even bigger fee from Muffy for finding Alex. He even made a vague reference about giving Gina, Sophie, and me a bonus for the great work we'd done, like that would ever happen.

I then drove home for a shower and a change of clothes. As I drove, the events of the past few days kept replaying in my mind. I think I was looking for an explanation for everything that had happened. By the time I pulled the car into my parking lot, I'd decided I needed a scotch.

A good scotch.

~~~~

I took the elevator up and unlocked my door. As I walked in, Marlowe greeted me with a rub against my leg. I apologized for being gone for so long and opened up a can of Super Supper to make up for it.

He sucked down the entire can of food, then walked to the corner of the kitchen and threw up. Things in my apartment had returned to normal.

I stripped off my shirt and blue jeans with relief. I then took a long shower that was hot and relaxing. I felt the tensions of the day drain from my body. By the time the shower was over, I decided, in addition to a good scotch, I needed Reno.

He answered his phone on the first ring. When I discovered he would finish work at about five, I suggested we meet at Frankie Z's for drinks and conversation at seven o'clock.

"I heard Alex turned himself in," Reno said.

"He'd been kidnapped by the two men who killed the dead guy in his apartment. The two men have since disappeared. Lenny's representing him, so you know he won't let Alex say a word."

"And, knowing Lenny," Reno said, "he'll make the whole thing disappear. In two weeks, nobody will remember there was a dead guy."

"It wouldn't surprise me."

~~~~

As I drove to Frankie Z's, my body again started to warm up to the thought of seeing Reno. I recognized these feelings for what they were. Lust, certainly, but maybe something more.

It felt good to be with a man like Reno. I didn't know if he'd turn out to be the great love of my life, but he was as close as I'd gotten so far. A brief vision of Max floated across my mind, but that was a problem for another day.

I pulled into Frankie's parking lot at ten

minutes after seven, almost on time. Frankie was playing hostess again and greeted me with a warm smile.

I found Reno waiting at a corner table in the lounge. He looked up and saw me as I walked into the room. He took me in with his eyes, and a grin spread across his face.

"You cleaned up well today," he said, the grin still wide.

I took a moment to look him over. I was starting to tingle in all the usual places and felt truly happy for the first time in a very long while.

"You know," I said, "I think this may turn out to be a *very* good day after all." Reno's face flushed as he started to catch my not-so-subtle drift.

Dominic came over before Reno could say anything. We both ordered a scotch.

"I'm glad you found Alex," Reno said. "Homicide has all but cleared him already."

"What about your guy, Reinhardt? Did he ever make his buy?"

"We don't know. We lost him for about three hours yesterday. It's possible he made the deal then."

"How'd you lose him?"

"I didn't lose him. Two detectives from the day shift were watching him. Every day at two o'clock, Reinhardt has gone into a restaurant over on Shoeman Lane. He reads the paper, drinks three beers, and has a bowl of shrimp chowder."

"Okay, what happened yesterday?"

"Yesterday, he went in the front door and then went straight out the back. Our guys were parked out front and didn't notice anything for over twenty-five minutes."

"Ouch."

"Reinhardt's been using four different rental cars. All of them have a tracking device on them. When they called in to get Reinhardt's location, dispatch told them the other three cars were parked in various parts of the city. One was in north Scottsdale, in a city park near the resorts. One was parked on the street in downtown Scottsdale, near the art galleries, and one was up in a group of high-dollar houses on the south side of Camelback Mountain."

"Sounds like your guys had a dilemma," I said. "What'd they do?"

"Knowing Reinhardt's MO, they converged on the art gallery location. Unfortunately, Reinhardt's car was still parked, and there wasn't anybody in it. They canvassed the area, but they never found him."

"What about the other two cars?"

"One was reportedly on the move, coming off of Camelback Mountain. The guys converged on that one, only to find it was being driven back to the airport by a guy from the rental car agency. About two hours later, the third car, the one by the resorts, was reported to be moving. A rookie patrolman was the first to Reinhardt's location in north Scottsdale. Instead of calling it in, he decided to stop Reinhardt. The rookie then gave him the third degree on the side of the road."

"Doesn't sound like a good move," I said.

"Nope. Reinhardt consented for the officer to field-search his car. There was nothing in the vehicle, and we had nothing to hold him in Scottsdale. He flew out of the country last night. We don't know if it was because we spooked him or if he was finished with whatever business he had. We'll probably never know."

"I heard on the news that a building caught on fire near the resorts yesterday. Could he have been involved in that?"

"It was more like the building blew up," Reno said. "But it isn't likely Reinhardt was involved. The lab guys are still checking it out, but it appears to be some kind of drug deal. As far as we know, Reinhardt never handles drugs or anything that explodes."

Reno took a sip of his drink. "It *is* interesting the building that blew up is located at a resort controlled by the DiCenzos. I can't help but think there's something more to this. There've been too many DiCenzo coincidences, but I can't see any direct connections. If there were, I wish I'd spot one. I'd love to get a crack at bringing down Tough Tony."

As Reno talked, I couldn't help wondering how I kept getting myself in the middle of everything. Reno must have seen the thoughts on my face.

He looked like he was about to ask me something but let it go. Instead, he took a long sip of his scotch.

~~~~

The evening crowd started to drift in. The scotch had relaxed me, and being with Reno felt terrific. Talking and laughing with him made it feel like we hadn't just spent a year apart.

Dominic came over with the bill for the drinks. I told Reno I'd get it and dug in my purse. As I pulled out my wallet, something fell out and landed on the table.

"What's that," Reno said as he bent closer to look at it.

It was the small envelope Max had given to me from Tony. I'd put it in my purse and had forgotten about it.

I knew opening it in front of Reno was a bad idea, but my fingers had taken on a will of their own. I blame the scotch. I pushed my finger into the envelope and ripped open the flap.

Inside was a folded piece of blue paper. My heart started to race as I unfolded it. Something bright fell out and landed on the table with a *clink*.

Crap!

It sparkled like fire even in the dim lights of the lounge. I picked it up and looked at it.

"Damn," I said.

In the back of my mind, I remembered asking Tony about the diamonds. He said he was turning over all but five of them to the Consortium. I guess I knew where one of the five was.

"Wow, it looks real," Reno said.

I thought about telling him everything but quickly decided against it. I wasn't exactly sure how illegal my involvement had been. I *was* sure Tough Tony DiCenzo wouldn't be pleased if I talked about his business to a cop.

"Um," I said, "I asked Gina to get me a fake diamond last week when she was in Las Vegas. She must have put it in my purse. You're right, though. It does look real. They sure can do wonderful things in the lab these days."

Reno looked at me for a moment. It was hard to read that look.

Finally, he asked: "Can you imagine what this would be worth if it *was* real? It looks perfect, and it must weigh four or five carats. You'd be talking about having a hundred and fifty, maybe even two-hundred thousand dollars rolling between your fingers."

"Do you know what I'm thinking?" I asked. "I'm thinking this would make a beautiful pendant or maybe even a ring."

"A ring?" Reno asked. He had a twisted look on his face, as if I'd said something scary.

"Um," he said, "exactly what kind of ring did you have in mind?"

I just smiled at him.

His face flushed bright red.

"Uh, maybe we should discuss this over dinner?" he said.

I smiled at him again and said in my smoothest voice, "Dinner's a start, but maybe we should discuss this over breakfast."

Reno caught my meaning and smiled back at me. It was his old smile, the one that always made me melt.

"Alright," he said, "over breakfast."

Yes!

About the Author

Halfway through a successful career in technical writing, marketing, and sales, along with having four beautiful children, author B A Trimmer veered into fiction. Combining a love of the desert, derived from many years of living in Arizona, with an appreciation of the modern romantic detective story, the Scottsdale Series was born.

Comments and questions are always welcome.
E-mail the author at
LauraBlackScottsdale@gmail.com
Follow at www.facebook.com/ScottsdaleSeries/